# THE VISITORS

## ALSO BY GREG HOWARD

*Middle School's a Drag, You Better Werk!*

*The Whispers*

## FOR OLDER READERS

*Social Intercourse*

# THE VISITORS

## GREG HOWARD

G. P. PUTNAM'S SONS

**G. P. PUTNAM'S SONS**

An imprint of Penguin Random House LLC, New York

First published in the United States of America by G. P. Putnam's Sons,
an imprint of Penguin Random House LLC, 2022
Copyright © 2022 by Greg Howard
Excerpt from *The Whispers* copyright © 2019 by Greg Howard
Excerpt from *Middle School's a Drag, You Better Werk!* copyright © 2020 by Greg Howard

Visit us online at penguinrandomhouse.com

Library of Congress Cataloging-in-Publication Data
Names: Howard, Greg (Gregory Steven), author.
Title: The visitors / Greg Howard.
Description: New York: G. P. Putnam's Sons, [2022] |
Summary: "When a group of kids explore a deserted, haunted plantation,
they befriend a young ghost and together uncover the dark secret of his
past that led to his mysterious death"—Provided by publisher.
Identifiers: LCCN 2021041740 (print) | LCCN 2021041741 (ebook) |
ISBN 9780593111888 (hardcover) | ISBN 9780593111895 (ebook)
Subjects: CYAC: Ghosts—Fiction. | Haunted places—Fiction. |
Plantations—Fiction. | Gays—Fiction. | Bullying—Fiction. |
Forgiveness—Fiction. | South Carolina—Fiction. |
LCGFT: Novels. | Ghost stories.
Classification: LCC PZ7.1.H6877 Vi 2022 (print) |
LCC PZ7.1.H6877 (ebook) | DDC [Fic]—dc23
LC record available at https://lccn.loc.gov/2021041740
LC ebook record available at https://lccn.loc.gov/2021041741

Book manufactured in Canada

ISBN 9780593111888
1  3  5  7  9  10  8  6  4  2
FRI

Design by Suki Boynton • Text set in Janson MT Pro

*for Travis*

# THE VISITORS

*Owning our story and loving ourselves through*
*that process is the bravest thing we'll ever do.*
—BRENÉ BROWN

*Be not discouraged.*
*There is a future for you . . .*
*The resistance encountered now predicates hope.*
—FREDERICK DOUGLASS

# 1

IF YOU EVER find yourself at Hollow Pines Plantation, the first thing you'll notice is how quiet it is. No birds singing. No crickets chirping. No frogs croaking. It's like they were all scared off by something—something invisible. Invisible, but everywhere. Kind of like God, but also not like God at all.

It's not a peaceful kind of quiet either. It's more like an everything-here-is-dead kind of quiet. Every once in a while, though, we get visitors. They can make a ton of racket, and they usually end up being real sorry for it. Hollow Pines doesn't like being disturbed. Hollow Pines likes the quiet. And Hollow Pines always gets what it wants. I should know. It wanted me.

I used to be one of those noisy visitors. Back when I lived just down the road a ways, I would sometimes ride my bike to the deserted plantation. I thought it was a pretty cool place back then. It was like having my own huge secret hideout.

There's a sign at the turnoff on the highway—crooked, dingy, and rusted, like it doesn't want to be spotted too easily.

HOLLOW PINES

EST. 1718

Once you turn at the Hollow Pines sign, you'd go down a dark mile-long dirt road that snakes through a forest of soaring pine trees so tall they look like they're racing one another up to heaven. Pine trees grow like weeds around here, and that's why a lot of folks in Georgetown County work at the paper mill. My daddy, my uncle, and my granddaddy—they all worked there. Daddy probably thought I'd grow up to work there too, but I had other plans. I always wanted to be a TV news anchor, like Mr. Walter Cronkite. It's a real job. But, like Grandma sometimes said, *That's neither here nor yonder now.*

At the end of Hollow Pines Road, two crumbling stone columns at least three times as tall as I am stand guard on either side of the road, with huge old oil lanterns mounted on them. Vines choke the lanterns, and bright green moss has near about swallowed the stone columns whole. I always wondered what the gates of hell looked like until I saw what's left of the Hollow Pines Plantation gates for the first time. Not really come-on-in-and-sit-a-spell-looking so much as come-on-in-because-this-is-your-last-stop-forever-looking.

Just beyond that, you'll find Live Oak Lane—a long, straight-shot sandy driveway of sorts that runs all the way up to the manor house. It's lined with rows of massive live oaks on either side, which I reckon is how it got its name.

Spanish moss drips from the sprawling branches like fat clusters of dried-up Silly String draping the road, looking a little creepy and kind of beautiful all at the same time. I always thought *live oak* was a funny name for the trees. Aren't all trees live somethings? I mean, we don't go around saying *live magnolias* or *live maples*. But I guess in a place like Hollow Pines, it's best to call out the living things whenever you can.

After you pass through the stone columns and onto Live Oak Lane, you'll find yourself smack-dab in the middle of the old slave village. Only a handful of run-down cabins are left, their roofs dipping low as if their load is just too heavy to bear anymore. A small chapel stands in the center of the village, but for the life of me I can't think what them enslaved folks had to be praising Jesus about. But Grandma used to say, *Hope dwells in peculiar places.* And I guess she was right about that.

Even though there're only about six cabins left in the slave village, Grandma said there used to be dozens upon dozens of them lining Live Oak Lane, clear up to the manor house. She said that a long time ago, half of the rice crop in the entire United States of America came from the plantations right here in Georgetown County. Of course, America wasn't nearly as big back then as it is now, but still, that's a heck of a lot of rice.

"Why'd they put those cabins right up there in the front yard for everyone to see?" I asked Grandma one time. "Weren't they ashamed of themselves for owning real live people and making them work for no money?"

Grandma shook her head and lowered her voice. "No, they weren't ashamed none. The folks who owned all the plantations 'round here wanted their fancy guests riding up to the manor house to see how well-off they were. Black folk were treated like property back then, and the more of them a man owned, that meant the more money he had."

That's one of those things about the plantations around here that they never taught us in school.

"I'm glad people ain't slaves no more," I said to her.

Grandma huffed a little at that and spat chewing tobacco juice into an empty Campbell's soup can. "One kind of slavery goes away, and another takes its place."

I'm not sure what Grandma meant, but that's all she had to say about that.

There're all kinds of crazy ghost stories about Hollow Pines—some true and some just plain old foolishness. People say the spirits of the hundreds of men and women who were forced to work the plantation and died here roam the grounds at night, looking for lost loved ones or for a way to escape their miserable existence. That one is only partly true. I've never seen hundreds of them, but there're a few lost souls still around, like Retha Mae, Emma, and Cousin Cornelius. As ghosts go, they aren't scary at all—at least not to me. But then there's Culpepper, and that's a different thing altogether.

The story goes that one of the owners of Hollow Pines Plantation by the name of Jackson Culpepper the Third— a pure devil of a man, from what I know of him—strangled his wife, Rebecca, with his bare hands right there in her bedroom on the second floor of the manor house. Folks say she can sometimes be spotted at night, up in the far-left window. That story is *definitely* true. I've seen Miss Rebecca with my own two eyes—up close. Most of the time, she just stands there in the window of her bedroom, holding a candle with one hand and her neck with the other, staring out into the pitch-black night.

Nobody has lived up in the manor house in a whole lot of years, not since way before I came to be stuck at Hollow Pines. But that don't stop the visitors from coming. People, mostly good-for-nothin' teenagers, sneak onto the grounds now and then, looking for adventure or some mischief to get into. Cousin Cornelius scares most of them off before they get too far. He hasn't ever scared me, though. Maybe it's because I'm only twelve and not a good-for-nothin' teenager. And I never will be.

The last time I ever rode my bike from our house to Hollow Pines—I can't be sure of how long ago that was, because time is slippery here—something bad happened over at the winnowing barn. I don't remember exactly *what* happened, because I've spent about every day since then trying to forget the bad parts of the story, and I've gotten real good at the forgetting after all these years. Sometimes I wonder if the not-remembering has something to do with what's keeping me here.

All I know for sure is that a boy was hurt, and it was my fault. I don't know exactly how he was hurt or what my part in it was, though. Those memories are gone, and I say good riddance. Ever since then, I haven't been able to leave. So I try my best to carry on like the other lost souls around here, wishing for the day when we might all find a way to move on. But wishing is easy at Hollow Pines.

It's the being stuck here that's hard.

# 2

IT'S ONE OF the not-too-terribly-sad mornings at Hollow Pines, March or April maybe—I can't be sure which. An ocean-blue sky blankets the plantation from end to end, big fluffy clouds wafting by like giant gray and white sailboats out on a Saturday morning cruise. The Lowcountry sun carves sparkling diamonds out of sandy patches in the yard, and the jasmine-scented air almost makes Hollow Pines smell like a safe and peaceful place. Almost.

I know there's a breeze, because the sprawling, spidery limbs of the live oaks overhead wave bulky gobs of Spanish moss at me real slow and proper-like, like tree beauty-pageant contestants or some such. But I can't actually feel the breeze anymore. That's one of the things I hate about being stuck here. We lost souls can't feel much of anything that nature has to offer—the sugar-like sand between our toes, the thick blades of grass tickling our ankles, the afternoon sun toasting our cheeks, or the cool breezes in the fall and the warm breezes of spring, like today. I can't even feel the sticky, wet heat of South Carolina summers pooling under my arms anymore, but I don't miss that too much.

Back when I came to be stuck at Hollow Pines, none of the other lost souls explained the rules to me. I'm not sure any of them know all the rules anyway. We just figure things out as we go along. All I know is what I *can* do and what I *can't* do. I keep a running list in my head, adding to it as new discoveries are made. Things like:

*Living folks can't see me unless I want them to.*

I try not to show myself too often. I don't want to give someone a heart attack or anything.

*I can't feel the breeze on my face.*

Like I said, I hate that one.

*I can walk through doors and walls.*

That's a really cool one that television shows and movies usually get right.

*I can pick things up, move things, throw things, open and slam doors.*

That one comes in handy when I'm trying to scare off some visitors.

*I can still smell the jasmine and the honeysuckle.*

Thank the good Lord above for that.

The rules don't always make sense. Like how animals can sense my presence long before live humans can. Or how when I touch a living person, it feels amazing to me but apparently has just the opposite effect on them. Believe me, I've tried it. I thought about putting together a manual for new souls who become lost at Hollow Pines, a welcome packet of sorts. But I was the last soul to get stuck here. So far.

I stand in the middle of Live Oak Lane, halfway between the manor house and the old slave village, my bare feet being gobbled up by the fine, sugary sand that I can't feel. I watch it spread apart, making room for my sinking heels and rising between my toes like a live thing trying to swallow me whole. I don't have much need for shoes, seeing as my body isn't real anymore.

I stare down the lane to the stone entry gates—well, the stone columns, that is. There aren't any actual gates anymore. But the columns stand there just as proud as they can be all the same, mocking me and reminding me of the number one rule of Hollow Pines Plantation.

*I can't leave.*

I've tried to leave Hollow Pines more times than I can count. Tried just about everything I can think of. But nothing ever works. Some mornings I'll walk right past those stone columns, even though I know what's going to happen. No sooner do I take a step through than I'll find myself walking in the opposite direction, right back onto the plantation toward the manor house. It's the same with the woods surrounding Hollow Pines. I'll march into the tree line with hopes of finding my way out of here, but I always end up right back where I started—every single time.

I don't think I can take the disappointment of trying and failing to leave again today. So I just stand there staring at the empty space between the two columns, imagining myself strolling right on through. And wishing at the very least that we'd get some visitors soon—some nice ones this time. Not the good-for-nothin' teenager kind.

It's been so long since I've seen faces other than those of the lost souls stuck here with me—no offense to Teacherman, Miss Rebecca, Retha Mae, and the others, because I like their faces just fine. And just because Hollow Pines hates visitors doesn't mean that I do. Part of my job around here is to help scare them off, mainly for their own protection. But I'm not real good at it. Not as good as Cousin Cornelius or Miss Rebecca or Preacher, and definitely not as good as Jackson Culpepper the Third.

As ghosts go, I'm probably the worst. I don't really see the point of making someone so scared they cry or pee their pants. I've been that person before—the one crying and peeing their pants—back when I was part of the living world. Trust me, it's no fun at all.

I like following the visitors around—listening in on their conversations, imagining what their lives out in the living world are like, giving them a few fun goose-bump moments that they can giggle over and tell their friends about when they get home, without scaring them half out of their minds.

Actually, it's best that we don't get many visitors, but it's just so lonely here. So lonely that sometimes all I want to do is sit right down in the middle of Live Oak Lane and cry. But wanting to cry and remembering how are two different things. And you can't do the one without the other. Believe me, I've tried plenty.

Cousin Cornelius says the world has forgotten us. I sure hope he's wrong about that, but sometimes I wonder if *anyone* remembers me. It's been so long that I shouldn't be mad at them if they don't. I hope at least one person out there remembers me. Like my sister—if she's still alive, that is. If I could leave Hollow Pines, I would want to find her before she leaves the living world—make sure she's okay and know that she found some happiness in her life, like I never could. But I don't reckon I'll ever be able to, and the weight of that is sometimes just too heavy to bear.

With no visitors in sight, I let out a disappointed sigh and head over to the kitchen house. Since I can't eat anything—because of not having a real body and internal organs and such, plus there's no food around here anyway—I usually just sit at the table in the center of the kitchen house every morning, listening to Retha Mae and Emma chatter away while they pretend to work.

Retha Mae was the cook here at Hollow Pines a long time ago, and she's still going at it every day like someone forgot to tell her that she's dead now and doesn't have to do that anymore. Emma helps Retha Mae out and does the cleaning up after. She used to work here at Hollow Pines too, when she was part of the living world, but she and Retha Mae didn't get paid nothing for working here back then. Nothing more than heartache and trouble, that is. Over the years, I've learned that the Old South was not as glamorous and grand as I was taught in South Carolina history class. Well, maybe it was for the white folks, but certainly not for the Blacks.

One time, I asked Retha Mae and Emma why they still work so hard when they don't have to. Retha Mae thought about that a minute and then said, "I do for me now. Not for them." Like that should've explained it all to me. It didn't. Emma must have noticed that I had a not-understanding look on my face, so she added, "Idle hands is the devil's workshop." Then she nodded once, like that was all she had to say about that.

Retha Mae and Emma don't seem to mind me hanging around the kitchen house while they work as long as I stay out of their way. But Emma has been known to swat me on the behind with a spatula when I rest my elbows on the table, like I'm a little kid or something.

"Was you raised in a barn, boy?" Emma will say sharply sometimes.

Emma is forever trying to boss me around, but I think it's funny when she swats me on the behind, because I can't even feel it. Emma has a slender frame like Mama did and she's a lot younger than Retha Mae. Emma couldn't have been but a few years older than my sister, maybe around eighteen or nineteen, when she left the living world, but you'd never know it by the way she acts—which is like someone's mama.

Retha Mae, on the other hand, reminds me of my

grandma. She's a short, round woman with a lot of hard years etched into her face. She walks with a limp on her right side and carries a heavy load in her deep-set eyes. Retha Mae's a little tough to figure out. She might seem just fine one minute—humming away in her rocking chair on the porch of the kitchen house or taking a late afternoon stroll down Live Oak Lane—and then she'll be wiping tears from her eyes with the hem of her apron the next. Every now and then, I can pull her out of her gloom by saying something funny that causes a smile to tug at her tight lips until her face blossoms into the most beautiful thing you've ever seen in your life. But that cloudy film of sorrow coating her eyes never fully clears no matter how broad her smile.

"Shut that door before you let all the mosquitoes in South Carolina in here, boy," Retha Mae says when I enter the kitchen house, but not unkindly like Emma would.

I could remind her that the two windows are nothing but gaping holes in the wall, but I think better of it and ease the door closed behind me.

"Good morning, Miss Retha Mae," I say with a respectful nod.

"Oh, is it now?" she shoots back. "And what has you all cheery today?"

Her tone is teasing, so that's a good sign. Before I can think of how to respond, Emma comes in through the back door, carrying a fistful of freshly picked wildflowers in one hand and a small branch of honeysuckle in the other. She pays me no mind, not even a quick *Good morning, boy* thrown my way. Emma is not a rude person, not really. I think she just likes to keep me in my place. I don't mind so much, though. She arranges the flowers in a dusty clay pitcher and sets it on the table in the center of the room. The flowers are meant to cheer Retha Mae up and they do their best every morning. The sweet wafting fragrance begins seasoning the stale air of the kitchen house almost immediately. I catch the slightest hint of a smile softening the hard edges of Retha Mae's face when the aroma reaches her.

"Out the way, boy," Emma says, scooting by me to set the table with the handful of plates and utensils that have survived over the years.

"Good morning, Emma," I say with the biggest grin I can muster, to soften her up. "You look very nice this morning."

Emma eyes me suspiciously until a reluctant smile stretches out her face. "Morning."

Mission accomplished.

Retha Mae is going through the motions of making breakfast, like she does every day. This morning she serves up thick slices of country ham, eggs over hard, and hoecakes drizzled with honey—at least that's what Emma tells me it is, because there isn't any real food in sight. Retha Mae just likes "cooking" what she pleases after years of following the strict menus of Miss Rebecca and the manor house mistresses that came before and after her.

Being in the kitchen house when Retha Mae is cooking reminds me of sitting at the table in my grandma's kitchen while she worked. My mouth waters a little at the memory. What I wouldn't give for one more meal of Grandma's cooking—fried chicken and pork chops, yellow rice and giblet gravy, green beans, turkey, perlo, black-eyed peas, and mustard greens. Everything she made tasted like home.

I don't know exactly why Retha Mae and Emma are stuck here. They don't talk too much about their time on the plantation back when they were part of the living world. Maybe they just want to put those memories to rest forever. I can understand that.

We sit at the table, finishing breakfast in silence until a question rolls off my tongue, as questions are sometimes known to do.

"Do you think I'm stuck here because I can't remember the awful thing that happened the last time I came to Hollow Pines?"

It's a question that I've asked before. But none of the lost souls ever have any answers for me. Well, any that they're willing to share, that is. It doesn't stop me from asking, though. Retha Mae and Emma both look up at me, then share a knowing glance. Emma rolls her eyes and looks back down at her rusted tin plate, like my question is a waste of her time. Maybe it is.

Retha Mae huffs a little, shaking her head. "So, you can't remember the *one* terrible thing that happened to you here, is that right?" Her face has a hint of a hard edge at first, but then it softens a little. She reaches across the table and pats my hand. "Well, lucky you, boy. Lucky you."

And that's all Retha Mae has to say about that, so I let it go. Again.


I WALK DOWN Live Oak Lane to the slave village to visit with Cousin Cornelius, like I do every morning after breakfast. He's always sitting in the rickety old rocking chair on the front porch of his cabin, rocking back and forth and smoking his pipe out in broad daylight, like it ain't nobody's business but God's. I don't know why Cousin Cornelius is still here either. He's not a big talker, and I've learned the hard way when to just leave a lost soul be.

Emma told me one time that Cousin Cornelius used to be real important on the plantation, or as important as any enslaved person could be here, I guess. He was the foreman, which Emma said is like the assistant to the white overseer. But the way she said it, I got the feeling that there's some real bad blood between her and the white overseer—a man called Deacon Pope.

I've never asked Emma about it, because Grandma used to say that I was raised better than to get all up in somebody's private affairs. That's true, but it's also true that God made me real curious about things that aren't supposed to be my concern. My sister sometimes said that I was nosy. And, boy, was she right about that.

I find Cousin Cornelius sitting in his usual spot on the front porch of his cabin, his rocking chair positioned so he's draped in the sleepy shade of the nearest live oak sprawl. I sit on the top porch step—my usual spot—leaning against the rotted wood post and hoping the roof doesn't cave in on us. The roof looks like it's been thinking about giving up the ghost for a lot of years now but just can't make up its mind if it's worth all the effort and fuss.

"Mornin', Cousin," Cornelius says, tipping his straw hat at me with a little chuckle.

"Cousin," I say back, with a nod and a little chuckle of my own.

Cornelius goes right back to rocking in his chair, puffing away on his pipe, and not paying me too much mind. He just rocks and puffs, rocks and puffs.

The first time I met Cornelius, he called me Cousin. I thought that was kind of strange, so I asked him why he called me that. He said that everyone around these parts was kin in one way or another—Black, white, it didn't matter. Your blood was bound to have mingled somewhere down the line. Now, when I walk up to his cabin every morning, he tips his straw hat slightly and mumbles, "Mornin', Cousin." I don't mind it at all. It makes me feel like I have family here to pass the time with until I figure out a way to move on.

We sit there all quiet-like for a while, listening to the breeze coming up off the canal behind the manor house and rustling its way noisily through the giant branches hanging overhead.

I'm not sure how old Cousin Cornelius was when he left the living world, or how long he's been stuck at Hollow Pines. His hair is mostly white under his straw hat, and his dark skin is creased, dented, and dusty with the wear and tear of time. His clothes—faded denim overalls over a plain white cotton T-shirt, and work boots mud-scuffed from here to high heaven—are as old and worn as Cornelius himself. If I had to guess, I'd say Cousin Cornelius left the living world when he was around eighty years old or some such. But he never talks about his before time, or his life on the plantation, for that matter. Retha Mae says that's because as foreman he had to boss his own people around and had to do things he has a lot of regrets about. It was hard not to ask what kind of things she meant, but I remembered my manners and didn't pry.

Even though he doesn't do much of it himself, Cousin Cornelius likes it when I talk. He'll point at me with his pipe and nod when he's ready for me to tell him about current events. That's his favorite thing for me to talk about. He likes to hear what's been going on in the living world since he left it. I don't mind it either. I used to have to do current events a lot in school, and I was always pretty good at it, because Daddy and Mama let me watch the *CBS Evening News with Walter Cronkite* with them every night after supper. Daddy considered anything Walter Cronkite said on the *CBS Evening News* to be the absolute gospel truth. I think he trusted Mr. Cronkite more than he trusted the president. Or our pastor.

I only have twelve years' worth of current events

stored up in my brain and I don't remember much about the first few years of my life, but Cousin Cornelius doesn't mind if I repeat stories over and over. He especially likes the ones about Dr. Martin Luther King Jr. He got a hard, sorrowful look on his face when I told him about the year 1968, when Dr. King was shot and killed in cold blood, though. I've tried telling Retha Mae and Emma about some current events from my living years, but they act like it's all fairy tales. You should have heard them laugh when I told them about the Civil Rights Act of 1964, which gave Black folks the same rights as white folks. At least that's what it was meant to do. But Cousin Cornelius listens and doesn't interrupt me by laughing.

"President Nixon sent the troops to a place called Cambodia," I say when he points at me with his pipe this morning. "It's close to Vietnam, where my uncle David is."

*Or* was, I think to myself. *That was so long ago I'll bet Uncle David is home now.* I swallow hard. *Or dead.* I think again of my sister, praying she's still out there somewhere.

"Anyhow, some people got all riled up about it," I say, like Walter Cronkite would. Or maybe like Walter Cronkite would if he were a twelve-year-old kid from Georgetown, South Carolina. "There was a lot of trouble over it at this school in Ohio, and they called in the National Guard."

Cousin Cornelius glances over at me with one eye squinted. That's his thinking eye. He puffs and rocks, smoke drifting up out of his pipe like it ain't got nowhere in particular to be. I always thought that was a pretty good trick, since I've never seen him light his pipe with a match, not even once. I nod at him to confirm that what I'm saying is the God's honest truth, because Mr. Walter Cronkite said it right there on the television set in our living room.

Truth be told, I've been known to make up some of the current events from time to time. Once, I told Cousin Cornelius that the Beatles robbed a bank in Charleston and made off with over a thousand dollars. And this one time, I told a real good one about how a man flew to the moon and walked on it, and how there's all kinds of people living up there now, with a Hardee's and a Five & Dime and Winn-Dixie grocery stores and everything. The part about the man walking on the moon is true, but he didn't build a Hardee's or a Winn-Dixie. He just took a stroll, planted an American flag, stole some rocks, and then hightailed it out of there. I feel a little bad about making up current events sometimes, but I get tired of telling the same stories over and over again.

"The National Guard soldiers shot some of the students over at that school in Ohio," I say. "Four of them even died."

I lower my head, because I didn't make that one up either. It's a terrible story that Mr. Cronkite told us about on the *CBS Evening News* not long before I got stuck here at Hollow Pines.

After my silent prayer for the dead students in Ohio, I tell Cornelius one of my made-up stories about a robbery at Hooper's Store over on Sesame Street. That doesn't even get a grunt from the old man, so I look up at him to find that he ain't paying me no mind. He's puffing on his pipe and staring out toward the entry gates with those wrinkled gray eyes of his. I wait for him to look back at me before I continue with my news report, but he never does.

Feeling a little annoyed, I turn around to find out what could be more interesting than an armed robbery on Sesame Street. That's when I see them and scramble to my feet. A group of visitors rides past the stone columns on real fancy-looking bicycles, the sandy road whipped into a frenzy under their spinning tires. And just like that, a big old mess of dark clouds rolls in overhead, dimming the ocean-blue sky and casting a mile-long shadow over the plantation.

Like I said, Hollow Pines doesn't like visitors.

# 3

**MY HEART THUMPS** hard in my chest. *One,* because it's been so long since we've had visitors, and *two,* because these visitors seem to be around my age. There's three of them—boys, it looks like. The one out in front has shiny hair the color of November leaves and skin nearly as pale as the sand he's riding on. He's wearing jeans with ripped holes at the knees and a white undershirt, from which his long, lanky arms grow out like the spindly branches of the live oaks above. The two brown-skinned kids trailing him look like they could be brothers, the way they favor each other. They even sit on their bikes the same way— both hunched over the handlebars like they're excited about where they're going but not quite sure they ever want to get there.

A good-sized dog the color of a high-noon sun darts past the stone columns, catching up to the boy at the head of the pack. A little pang of worry settles in my gut. I'm not afraid of dogs. I love dogs. But dogs get funny around here, because they're a lot smarter than people and they can sense things that people can't—things like me.

I look over at Cousin Cornelius before the visitors get too close. "Don't scare them off just yet, okay?"

He gives me that double-squinted-eye *What're you up to?* look of his, then puffs a couple of times on his pipe. After a few more seconds, he gives me a quick nod and I relax a little. Cousin Cornelius could give the visitors a good fright if he had a mind to. I've seen him do it plenty of times. He's real good at it.

As the visitors and their worrisome golden dog approach the slave village, they slow down to a respectful pace, like they just pedaled right up into the middle of a graveyard. I guess this place *is* sort of like a graveyard, or a museum. One that should probably be burned to the ground for all the bad things that happened here.

As they roll by the chapel, it holds the visitors' attention. Even as decrepit as it is, the chapel is still kind of beautiful, with faded whitewashed walls, sharp pointy edges, and a little bell tower sitting beside it. I wonder for a second if they can hear Preacher in there. Some days you can hear him preaching up a storm and singing songs about the troubles and trials of this world. But he's quiet today.

Now that they're closer, I see that the one riding in the middle isn't a boy at all, but a girl. Her lips and cheeks blush with a store-bought shade of red. Her hair is short except for a single braid trailing the length of her neck, a small pink bow tagging the end of it. She looks a whole lot like the boy following her—they must be brother and sister.

The visitors keep moving, finally passing right in front of us, not even a couple of car-lengths away, pedaling just enough to stay upright on their bicycles. Cousin Cornelius keeps his word and they don't see us because we don't want them to. The only odd thing the visitors might see right now is a rickety old rocking chair moving slightly back and forth, because Cornelius is not about to give up his mornin' rockin' for nobody.

*That must be the wind, right?*

That's probably what they're thinking as the old man rocks. The last puff of smoke from his pipe floats in front of my face, and I shoo it away real fast. I'm not sure if the visitors saw it or not. It was just a baby puff. Cornelius is teasing them. He likes to do that to visitors.

"What's up with these clouds?" the girl says, slowing to a stop and squinting up at the sky. "That storm is supposed to stay south of us."

She pulls something out of the pocket of her navy shorts. As she stares at it, I realize it's one of those magic pocket phones that some of the visitors in recent years carry around. They're a lot smaller than the bulky lime-green phone that sat on the end table at my house, and they don't have any wires or even a finger wheel to dial the numbers with. Visitors just poke at the magic pocket phones with their thumbs and expect their calls to go through. But that kind of magic doesn't work here. I don't know if it's because of all the lost souls clogging up the airways with their suffocating sadness, or the mischief of the bad things in the shadows, or just the fact that Hollow Pines is tucked so far away in the woods.

"Can't check the weather," the girl says. "No signal."

The pale-skinned boy in front stops and glances over his shoulder at her. "Figures."

His voice is lower than mine, and it doesn't crack like mine does a lot. I'm able to get a better look at all of them now that they're closer, gawking at us without even knowing it. The brown-skinned boy and girl look so much alike that they could be twins and not just brother and sister. She wears a baggy white T-shirt with the words BORN THIS WAY printed on the front in large glittered letters. Her maybe-twin brother is thinner than she is and he wears a blue tank top and faded jean shorts. A bulky red backpack tugs on his bony shoulders.

The pale-skinned boy looks over our way—right at me, actually. I know he can't see me, so it's a little creepy the way he's looking at me so hard. But that's when I get a good look at his face. It's a nice face with eyes the color and size of walnuts and a small button nose. His large round eyes look kind, but they also look a little sad. Tired and weary. Like the boy has the weight of the world on his shoulders.

The big golden dog stops sniffing around and looks over at us, ears up. It's a beautiful dog, a golden retriever. I know because that's the kind of dog I always wanted, but Daddy wouldn't hear of it. A low growl rumbles up from the dog's throat. I hold my breath, as if that could help anything.

The pale-skinned boy walks his bike a few steps over to the dog. "What is it, Goldie?"

The boy with the red backpack has been riding in circles around the other two, but he stops and faces the cabin. I hold real still. Cousin Cornelius doesn't stop rocking, but neither of us look Goldie in the eye, because that's usually a dead giveaway to them. Most dogs don't mind us too much once they get to know us, but they're all a little skittish at first. I don't know why.

"You sure this is a good idea, T?" the backpack boy asks the pale-skinned boy.

"Yeah, Goldie doesn't seem to like it here," the girl says, nodding over at the still-agitated dog.

"*I* don't seem to like it here," her maybe-twin brother says.

The pale-skinned boy shoots them a questioning look. "You want to win the school media fair, right?"

The girl lets her head fall back with a long sigh, then looks at him again. "The extra credit we earn if we win is literally the only way I'm getting an A in social studies."

"I already have an A in social studies," her maybe-twin brother says. "But Dad said winning the media fair would look good on my college applications."

"Dad's already talking to you about college applications? You're *twelve*," the girl snaps, her face going hard.

Then she sighs, shaking her head. "Typical. He hasn't mentioned college to me."

The girl's brother doesn't look her in the eye. He just shrugs uncomfortably, eyes locked on the ground.

The pale-skinned boy they call T looks back and forth between them, I guess sensing the same tension that I do. Finally, he nods once. "Well, I need my share of the prize money to pay for journalism camp, or else I'll be stuck with Sheila for the whole summer. So, I guess that's three yeses."

*Journalism camp?* I've never heard of such. I would've loved to have gone to a summer camp like that. When I was part of the living world, I used to think about going to college one day at the University of South Carolina to study journalism, so I could learn how to be a news anchor as good as Mr. Walter Cronkite. I've never met another kid my age who was interested in that kind of stuff too.

T walks his bike forward a few feet, reaches down, and tugs on Goldie's collar, pulling her back away from the cabin. Cousin Cornelius doesn't take his eyes off the dog, not for a second. He's been leery of dogs ever since I've known him. T sits up straight on his bike seat, gazing down Live Oak Lane toward the manor house in the distance.

"Okay, then," he says. "Mateo, get out the Tascam and the headphones."

"On it," Mateo says, hopping off his bike and easing it to the ground.

He drops to his knees, slides the backpack off his shoulders, and rummages around inside. By the look and sound of it, he has just about everything under the sun in there. After a little more digging, he pulls out a gray-and-black rectangular gadget that looks like some kind of fancy walkie-talkie and a set of black headphones.

"Be careful with that stuff, little brother," the girl says. "The librarian said if we break it, we buy it."

Mateo ignores her, fiddling with some buttons on the handheld gadget before handing it all over to the boy called T.

"Just press the center button when you're ready to record," Mateo says.

"I know," T says with a little irritation in his voice.

"And remember to speak slowly," the girl adds. "When we interviewed the sheriff, you kept talking too fast."

T lets out an annoyed sigh and settles his gaze on them. "Guys, I got this."

He pulls on the headphones, plugging the end of the cord right into the side of the walkie-talkie-looking gadget. I glance over at Cousin Cornelius, but he doesn't look at me, just keeps his narrowed eyes locked on the visitors as he puffs and rocks.

T clears his throat. Then, flipping something up on top and holding the gadget close to his mouth, he presses the button in the center and takes a breath before speaking into it.

"We've just arrived at Hollow Pines Plantation in Georgetown. Established in 1718, Hollow Pines was once one of the top producers of rice in South Carolina. It now stands deserted, forgotten, the remaining buildings in ruins."

Mateo gives his forearm a quick and loud mosquito smack. His maybe-twin sister and T both shoot him a glare.

*Sorry,* he mouths back.

Cousin Cornelius chuckles under his breath, but low enough that only I can hear. Mateo motions for T to keep going.

"Hollow Pines Plantation," he says into the gadget, his voice sturdy and serious, like Walter Cronkite's on the *CBS Evening News.* "The last place Will Perkins was ever seen."

I gasp. *Out loud.* It startles Cornelius, who stops rocking *and* puffing. The visitors look over in our direction, their eyes wide and searching. I'm not sure if they're staring at the empty rocking chair that suddenly stopped moving or looking for the source of the strangled sound that just escaped my mouth. I'm usually much better about flying under the radar when living folks are around, but I just couldn't help it. The name hit me like a ton of bricks.

*Will Perkins.*

I know that name. It echoes in my ears and shakes loose tiny crumbs of the bad memories from that day at the winnowing barn, memories I thought were buried so deep in my mind that they were gone forever.

*Will Perkins.*

He was there that day.

*Will Perkins.*

He was the boy who got hurt.

More questions than answers tumble around in my head. Starting with—how do these visitors know about Will Perkins? And more importantly, *what* do they know about him? Do they know what happened here that day? Because I sure don't. I just remember that something bad happened to Will and it was my fault.

The visitors stare over our way another silent couple of seconds. Cousin Cornelius and I stay completely still and quiet, which isn't hard for me at all, still in shock as I am. Finally, they look away, Mateo giving T urgent hand signals to keep going. He glances down at the shiny gray-and-black gadget and pulls it a little closer to his mouth.

"I'm Thomas Padgett," he says, his voice serious again. "And this . . . is *Finding Will.*"

# 4

**I KEEP MY** distance following the visitors as they ride up Live Oak Lane to the manor house. I'm still shaken from hearing the name Will Perkins for the first time in I don't know how many years. My mind races with questions, one of them being, *What the heck is* Finding Will? Now the visitors are talking about looking for *clues* and saying things like *foul play* and *prime suspect.* They don't have any idea that their prime suspect is following them right now, watching them, and listening to everything they say.

Grandma said it's rude to eavesdrop on other people's conversations. But if the way to move on from Hollow Pines has anything to do with remembering exactly what happened to Will Perkins, these visitors might be my one chance to put the pieces of the puzzle back together and find out. A spark of hope like I haven't felt in all my time here at Hollow Pines ignites somewhere deep inside me. Hope of maybe seeing my sister again. Hope of moving on.

The visitors slow to a crawl as they approach the manor house, hopping off their bikes one by one and walking them the last few feet forward. They stop at the largest live oak at Hollow Pines, which stands directly in front of the manor house—The Reaper, as some of the lost souls around here call it. The tree's sprawl of soaring branches matches the manor house in height and width. The two stand facing off against each other like giant alien soldiers locked in an eternal battle for the soul of Hollow Pines. The visitors barely give The Reaper a second glance as they lean their bikes against its massive trunk and walk over to the front porch.

The manor house has been invaded by an army of twisty vines and bright green moss, which is almost pretty until it's not. A lot of the windowpanes have been broken out, and the front door hangs cockeyed from the hinges. The visitors stand on the porch, arguing about whether or not they should go inside. They shouldn't.

I stand at the bottom of the porch steps, putting plenty of space between me and them. Sometimes visitors can sense our presence if we get too close—a chill in the air, hair on their arms standing up, a brief spell of nausea for some. Dogs usually sneeze when they get too close. I don't why. But if the visitors get a sense of me, it might scare them off. I'm not ready for them to leave yet. Not before I find out what they know about what happened to Will Perkins, and if it helps me remember what my part was in it all.

A low rumble of thunder sounds in the distance, drawing their attention. I look up too. The sky has dimmed a good bit since they got here, but the morning sun peeks through cracks in the fat clusters of gray clouds where it can, like it's trying real hard to do its job. The result is a sky that's dark and shadowy one minute and bright and sunny the next.

"What if that storm *is* heading this way?" the girl says, staring up at the sky, a wary look creasing her face. "Maybe we should head back."

"It's just a little thunder," Thomas says. "Last night on the news, they said that the storm was heading toward Charleston. That's an hour and a half south of us. We should be fine."

The girl rolls her eyes at him. "You can't control the weather too, Thomas."

"Got it covered." Mateo pats his backpack with a big grin. It feels like he's trying to melt the ice in his sister's voice. "I brought a pocket umbrella in case it rains."

Thomas turns to him. "Only one?"

"Dude, nobody stopped you from bringing your own supplies," he says. "I'm carrying the Tascam, the headphones, and all the food and water as it is. You guys should thank me for being your pack mule."

The rigid lines in the girl's face ease into a soft smile when she looks at her brother. She leans on the handrail, settling her dark eyes on him. "You're the Eagle Scout, little brother. We figured you like carrying everything. You know, 'be prepared' and all that."

Mateo takes a step back from the door. "I'm not an Eagle Scout yet. And I'm prepared for *me*. You guys are on your own."

The girl and Thomas laugh a little at that. I stifle a chuckle, even though it wasn't *that* funny. It just feels nice being *in on the joke*, as Grandma used to call it. She always said, *A joke is better shared* with *friends than* at *friends*.

Goldie sniffs around the trunk of The Reaper before squatting to pee. She trots over to rejoin Thomas and the others on the porch, stopping to sniff the ground near my feet. This is the closest I have been to the dog, so I stay *very* still. Goldie gazes up at me, like she's staring me right in the face. I look away. It's best for us not to look dogs directly in the eye, or else we might spook them. Goldie kind of neighs and snorts like a horse. Then she backs up, barks once, and sneezes. Like I said, I don't know why they do that. I figure maybe dogs are allergic to lost souls, like I used to be allergic to grass when I was little.

Thomas sticks his head through the front door, peering into the shadows of the manor house. I hope Miss Rebecca's not roaming around in there. And Thomas needs to be careful of those shadows.

"Give me the Tascam again," Thomas says over his shoulder. "We should record as we go inside."

The girl spins Mateo around so his back is to her.

Then she goes fishing down inside the backpack, pulling out the gadget that Thomas just called a Tascam and the headphones.

Thomas slips on the headphones and plugs the cord into the Tascam. He looks back at the girl, a smirk twisting his lips. "Maya, you go in first. I know *you're* not scared."

"That's right, dude," Maya says with a little forward snap. "Mateo's the one who still sleeps with a teddy bear, not me."

"Whoa, whoa, whoa," Mateo protests, hands raised. "Pooh isn't just any old teddy bear. He's a legend."

That makes Maya and Thomas laugh. I can't help smiling, because I used to love Winnie the Pooh, too, when I was little. I can tell the visitors are worried about going inside the manor house, because their feet are still planted firmly in the doorway, and no one looks like they want to go in first. They're smart to be worried, though. Miss Rebecca's not the only lost soul in there, and she's the nice one.

A muted groan of thunder sounds overhead, closer than before, but the visitors pay it no mind. I guess because it's sunny now. People don't usually take thunder too seriously when the sun is shining. It's a warning that's easy to ignore.

Thomas holds the Tascam close to his face and starts moving inside.

"We're now entering the manor house of Hollow Pines Plantation," he says, his voice low and kind of whispery. "The front door hangs off its hinges and the inside is draped in shadows."

Mateo and Maya share a glance and a little smile. *Draped?* Mateo mouths to his sister with scrunched eyebrows. She stifles a giggle.

They're all careful getting around the wide door hanging in the frame by only the top hinge. It does look like one wrong move and the door would come crashing down on their heads, but I sail right on through without a problem. The spotty sunlight meets us inside, peeking in through the windows like a nosy neighbor. Dust covers just about everything in sight. Vines creep in through the missing windowpanes like some kind of alien plant monster trying to swallow the house whole.

Only a few pieces of furniture are left over from the Culpepper days—a couple of wooden chairs in the front sitting room, three in the dining room, an overturned card table in one of the bedrooms upstairs, and a ratty old mattress in Miss Rebecca's room. Emma told me once that Miss Rebecca had the house jam-packed with all kinds of fancy chairs, tables, armoires, and cupboards a lot of years ago. But I guess it all got picked over by her family or visitors through the years, because this is the way it was when I got stuck here.

A huge mirror framed with elaborate gold-and-black swirls hangs over the fireplace in the sitting room. It's cracked in three places and looks like it has chicken pox or some such, with all those small dark spots covering the glass.

The visitors split up, walking through the rooms real slow and quiet—like they're in church, or a library. Thomas talks into the Tascam a little here and there, mostly just describing what he sees. The way he pitches his voice with a constant hint of anticipation makes everything sound more interesting than it looks. I'll bet he could be a real live newscaster one day if he wanted. I used to imagine taking over for Walter Cronkite on the *CBS Evening News* after he retired. But that'll never happen now—the growing up *or* being a news anchor. But maybe Thomas could.

The visitors avoid the shadowy areas of the first floor, sticking to the rooms with the most sunlight instead. It's best to stay in the light at Hollow Pines—something easier said than done when darkness falls over the plantation and the moon is your only salvation. And you can't always depend on the moon either. Every now and again, it takes the night off.

"This place is sick," Maya says, looking up at the chicken-poxed mirror over the fireplace in the sitting room.

It's an odd thing to say. That a house is *sick*. But she said it with wonder in her eyes, so I don't think she meant it in a bad way. Goldie pants her way into the dining room, which sits across the hall opposite the front sitting room. She sniffs around one of the overturned chairs in the corner. I watch her and wonder for a second if she's going to pee on it, like she did to The Reaper. Miss Rebecca wouldn't like that. I guess Goldie wasn't raised in a barn, though, because she doesn't pee on Miss Rebecca's chair.

Mateo slips his backpack off his shoulders, letting it fall to the floor in the hallway. He picks up one of the many soda cans littering the floor and looks at the label. The last visitors left a mess. But I scared them off before they did any real damage. Or before any real damage was done to them.

Thomas runs a hand along the edge of the fireplace mantel, small mounds of dust collecting on his fingertips. "This place isn't *sick*. It's *sad*."

Maya and Mateo don't say anything. I don't either, mainly because that would scare the living daylights out of the visitors. But my breath catches in my throat. No visitor that I know of has ever called Hollow Pines *sad*. They usually use words like *scary*, *spooky*, *eerie*—even *cool*. But never *sad*. That's the way I've always thought of it.

"Yeah," Mateo says. "Think of how the people who lived in this house treated the enslaved people who worked here."

Maya nods in agreement. "True." Then she gets a snarky look on her face. "According to Mrs. Cole in South Carolina history class, they treated them like family."

Thomas rolls his eyes. Maya and Mateo shake their heads, Maya adding a little huff. It's obvious that they don't believe what Mrs. Cole said. And they're right not to. I heard the same thing when I was in school, but I know better now, having spent so many years here with Retha Mae, Cousin Cornelius, and the others. The visitors seem to understand the truth about this place too.

Thomas wanders from room to room, describing everything he sees into the Tascam. I stay close to him—studying every nook and cranny of his face. Dark freckles are scattered across his nose, and his large brown eyes are bright, consuming everything in their path. There's something familiar about his eyes that I can't quite put my finger on. I stare at him, hoping it will come to me, but it doesn't.

As I watch him, I'm also keeping an eye on the shadows shifting ever so slightly in the corners of each room he enters. Luckily, he doesn't linger in any one room long enough for the shadows to touch him. I see them trying—reaching out for him when he's not looking but never quite making contact before he moves on. I'm sure Thomas doesn't even notice their advances. The shadows here are sneaky that way. You never realize how close they are until it's too late.

A more present boom of thunder sounds, stopping Thomas in his tracks. Goldie answers the coming storm's call with a throaty growl of her own.

"It's okay, girl," Thomas says, patting her head. "Come on."

"That didn't sound like *a little thunder*," Mateo says to Thomas as we enter the front sitting room. "Maybe we *should* head back."

Normally that would be exactly what I'd want too—for them to leave as soon as possible. But I don't, not yet. Not until I find out what they know about Will Perkins. This might be my only chance to jog my long-buried memories loose. Also, it just gets so lonely here and it's been a real long time since we've had visitors my age. Or maybe the reason I don't want them to leave is something more—like that familiar something in Thomas's eyes that I can't quite put my finger on.

Thomas lets out a frustrated sigh. "Guys, the media fair is next Saturday. I think we'll have a better chance of winning if we investigate and record the rest of our story here, where it all happened."

"Um . . . actually *we don't know* what happened here, T," Maya says, resting a hand casually on her hip. "All we know is that Will Perkins left his house on his bike on a Saturday morning, April 10, 1971, and never made it back. And it was reported that he was seen here the day he disappeared. That's all. The police searched the place but never found any trace of him."

"Yeah," Mateo says. "Will could have left here and gone anywhere. Or been *taken* anywhere."

"I don't know," Thomas says. "That doesn't feel right."

Maya shakes her head at him and then peeks out the front window, a worried look tightening her face. "I'll bet it wouldn't take too much rain to wash that road out."

Thomas joins her at the window. "Maya, it's not even raining yet."

"*Yet,*" she repeats, turning to face him.

Thomas and Maya fall into a silent stare-off, and neither looks like they're going to give in anytime soon.

Mateo glances back and forth between them. "Um . . . while you guys fight this out, I'm going to eat lunch."

"Lunch?" Maya says, finally turning away from Thomas. "It's not even ten o'clock."

"Pack mules eat when they're hungry," Mateo shoots back. "And this one is starving."

Thomas rubs his stomach absently, giving Maya a softer look now. "I don't think Sheila even knows how to cook breakfast food. I could eat too."

Maya exhales loudly. "Fine."

I breathe a quick sigh of relief, for the moment. I can't let them leave until I know more about *Finding Will*. All I have so far is a name that I haven't thought about in I don't know how many years—Will Perkins. I still don't know what happened that day. How did Will Perkins get hurt? And how was it my fault? All I know is that I can't let them leave until they help me remember more.

While the visitors dig into Mateo's backpack, I run down the hallway, sneak out the back door, and cross the yard to the kitchen house.

I need to borrow Retha Mae's carving knife.

# 5

**WILL SCANNED THE** cafeteria for Ronnie, anxiety gnawing away at his insides. He did *not* want to sit alone at lunch on his first day at Winyah Junior High School. He and Ronnie had eaten lunch together every day at school since third grade, so why would today be any different? But Will hadn't seen his best friend most of the summer because Ronnie had gone to the beach for a month with his family and then straight off to football camp in Charleston. Ronnie had made the junior varsity team. It was a dream of his, so Will was happy for him. He couldn't wait to hear all about Ronnie's time at camp.

Across the room, Will spotted a mass of wavy dark blond hair topping a set of broad shoulders in a navy-blue-and-white jersey with the name Cribb and the number 63 printed on the back in big block letters. He exhaled. He realized he hadn't been breathing much the whole time he'd been searching for his friend. But this Ronnie—whom Will hadn't seen in nearly two and a half months—already looked different to him, even from the back. He was thicker all over, had grown taller, and his shoulders and back sported the hills and valleys of actual muscles easily noticeable through this jersey.

*What did they do at football summer camp?* he wondered. *Eat bacon double cheeseburgers and lift weights all day?*

To be honest, Will was a little envious. His own body had yet to sprout the way the bodies of some of the other boys his age had. And his father was always eager to remind him that he was sure to be a late bloomer.

Will walked straight over to the table where Ronnie was sitting with some other boys wearing similar blue-and-white jerseys. Frankie Dimery, a year older and a lot bigger than Will, sat on Ronnie's right, tearing into his lunch like he hadn't eaten in a week. A metal folding chair sat empty on Ronnie's left, and although Will didn't know the other boys at the table, he thought sitting beside his best friend at lunch on the first day of junior high school was worth the trade-off. Will stood there, holding his tray piled with paper-thin slices of roast beef, lumpy mashed potatoes with watery brown gravy, and candied carrots—waiting for Ronnie to notice him. He didn't. Will cleared his throat.

All the boys at the table, seven of them, mostly eighth and ninth graders, stopped eating and looked up at Will with unsettling blank stares. Ronnie's eyes widened instantly at the sight of him. Frankie's face, though, stretched into a smile. And not the friendly kind either.

"Will," Ronnie said, surprise making his voice shallow. "Um . . . hey."

"Is this seat saved?" Will asked with a hopeful smile, desperate eyes locked on Ronnie's deep blue ones.

But Will easily read Ronnie's next expression. Panic. "Um" was all Ronnie got out before Frankie chimed in.

"Yep," Frankie said decisively, leaning back in his chair so much that his jersey rose up, exposing a sliver of flat, tanned stomach.

Will caught himself staring and looked away quickly.

"It's saved for *real* men," Frankie kind of snarled at him. "Not queers."

Everyone at the table started laughing—except for Ronnie. He stared down at his lunch tray and didn't say a word. Will's mouth went dry. His face heated from the inside out. He tightened his grip on the tray so he wouldn't drop it, his hands beginning to shake. Ronnie had told them. He'd told them Will's secret. Will couldn't believe it. Not in a million years. Ronnie had sworn he would never tell anyone. And Will had trusted him.

"Yeah," Frankie continued, his arm draped lazily over the back of Ronnie's chair. "Ronnie told us at football camp how you said that you loved him, and that you tried to kiss him."

The other guys at the table laughed at that too. Even harder. Students at nearby tables noticed the growing ruckus and stared over at Will.

"Come on, Frankie," Ronnie said quietly, still straight-faced and gazing blindly down at his tray.

Will locked his eyes on the side of Ronnie's head, feeling like he'd surely pass out any minute. It had been last summer. They'd been camping in Ronnie's backyard. He lived only a few houses down the road from Will. And Will had never tried to kiss Ronnie, and he hadn't said he *loved* him either. He'd said he *liked* Ronnie so much he sometimes *thought about* what it would be like to kiss him. And then Ronnie had been quiet for a moment or two before he'd said, "I like you too, Will. But not like that. Can we still be best friends?" And he'd said it with such kindness and with such a warm smile that Will hadn't even felt weird about the major confession he'd made, the first time he'd ever let anyone in on his secret. He'd just told Ronnie that it was okay, that sure they could still be best friends. And Will believed they could. Of course they could.

And after he'd said those things to Ronnie, it all kind of fixed itself in Will's head. He started seeing Ronnie only as a best friend, and not as someone he wanted to kiss. He'd even told Ronnie as much a few weeks later. But that night in the tent in Ronnie's backyard, Will made Ronnie promise not to tell anyone that he thought of other boys that way. And Ronnie swore he wouldn't. But Ronnie had.

Will finally snapped out of his stupor, tears edging his eyes. Before they could fall, he turned on his heel, his sneakers marking his shame with a sharp squeak as he hurried away. He walked all the way back across the cafeteria, which might as well have been ten miles, with what felt like a hundred eyes following him to an empty table with eight empty metal folding chairs. He fought back tears every step of the way. He couldn't believe Ronnie had told them. He couldn't believe he'd been called a queer and made fun of for "that" on his first day of junior high school. What if his father found out?

Will sat there, alone. Staring down at his roast beef. Feeling like if he took even one little bite, he'd vomit it right back out. The snickers at Ronnie's table across the room finally died down. The other students stopped staring at him. But Will was numb all over, a darkness cloaking him like a heavy quilt.

Sarah walked over and plopped down in the chair across from him. She boldly rested her feet on top of the table, crossed at the ankle, the flare of her bell-bottom jeans swallowing her platform shoes entirely. She studied Will's face a moment without saying anything, like she was reading him. Sarah was in ninth grade but wasn't embarrassed to be seen with a seventh grader. She'd always been cool that way. Finally, she sighed, slinging her long, wavy blond hair over her shoulders. He'd seen her do that a thousand times, at least.

"Told you the first day sucks," she said. "Something always goes wrong."

Will didn't say anything. He really didn't feel like talking. To anyone. Even Sarah, who was best friends with Ronnie's older sister. She knew how close he and Ronnie were.

"I saw you over there with Ronnie," she said. "Looks

like that didn't go too well. Shannon told me her brother had changed over the summer. I should have warned you. Not that you would've believed me *or* Shannon—not when it comes to Ronnie."

Will didn't say anything. He loved Sarah, but sometimes he thought she talked too much. And having grown up with her, he'd been on the receiving end of her endless observations of life, people, religion, school, himself—a lot. But at least *someone* wanted to talk to him. She took her shoes off the table and rested her elbows there instead, leaning in close to him. Will swallowed back a sob that had suddenly tried to jump right out of his throat.

"I'm sorry," she said, a sweet smile tugging at the corners of her mouth and not bothered at all by his silence. "Tomorrow will be better. I promise."

A tight, fake smile and a little nod was the best Will could offer in return. It was a nice thing for her to say. Sarah had always been that way to him—understanding, encouraging.

But she shouldn't make promises she couldn't keep.

-:-

WHEN I REACH the kitchen house, Emma's voice drifts through the open doorway. She's reading from the Gullah Bible that I gave her.

A while back—I'm not sure how long—a group of visitors came to Hollow Pines in a gray-and-white miniature bus with *Lowcountry Tours* printed on the side. It had to be

47

a good long while ago, because those kinds of buses don't come out this way no more.

One of the tourists left the Bible on the altar inside the slave chapel. She was an older Black lady dressed to the nines, with a beautiful crown of silver hair. She had tears in her eyes as she knelt at the altar, placing the Bible there all careful-like. I watched the woman real close as I stood quietly in the back of the room. I don't know why she left the Bible, but it seemed like it was real important to her. All the other visitors were milling about, some more respectfully quiet than others, while that woman dabbed her eyes with a white linen handkerchief and prayed there all by her lonesome.

After those visitors left Hollow Pines in the gray-and-white miniature bus, I took the Bible and gave it to Emma and Retha Mae to help them pass the time. I'm sure the woman who left it would've wanted them to have the Bible rather than for it to stay in the chapel to collect dust and rot, or maybe get stolen or worse by some ne'er-do-well visitors with sin and mischief in their hearts.

I wait for Emma to stop reading before I go inside, because I don't want to be rude or disrespectful. When I do step over the threshold, she jumps in her chair with a start, slapping the Bible closed. Seeing that it's just me, she exhales long and slow.

"Lord, have mercy," she says, slipping the small Bible into the front pocket of her apron. "Boy, you 'bout scared me clean to death. I thought you was the boss."

I figured out a while back that "the boss" and "the

overseer" that Emma talks about when she ponders the missing index finger on her left hand are the same person. What I eventually learned from Retha Mae is that Deacon Pope was a mean-as-a-snake white man who worked for Jackson Culpepper the Third in Emma's before time here at Hollow Pines. Retha Mae said Pope was in charge of the enslaved folks, making sure all the work on the plantation got done. But from what I hear, he wasn't like any pope or deacon of the church that I've ever heard of.

I watch Emma as she stands. She's wearing her usual faded beige floor-length frock with a dingy white apron tied around her waist. Her hair is short with tight curls, and in her eyes she carries both a youthful glow and something like an ancient weariness.

"Sorry," I say. "Didn't mean to scare you."

Emma doesn't say anything, just reties her apron in the back. I watch how she does it without her index finger, but her other fingers are working so fast she's done before I can focus on the movement at all.

One time when Emma wasn't around, I asked Retha Mae about Emma's missing finger. She mumbled something about Emma being a favorite target of Pope's, who saved his wrath for the ones who didn't stand a chance of defending themselves even if they had a mind to. Retha Mae said Emma's missing finger was the result of her pointing it at him one time. Just because she pointed at him. *One time.* Those are the kind of things there weren't no mention of in our South Carolina history textbooks in school. When we studied the time before the Civil War, it was a bunch of facts about all the rice and indigo that were produced on plantations like Hollow Pines, and the grand lives of the planter and his family, and how the citizens of South Carolina fought real hard for states' rights, and such.

I scan the room for the carving knife. Retha Mae is nowhere in sight, which is good. She doesn't like it when I take stuff out of the kitchen house, so my timing is perfect.

Emma has her hands planted on her hips, staring at me. "What are you doing here, boy, all up in my way?" She grabs the straw broom from the corner and starts pushing all the dust on the floor from one side of the room to the other. "And who's that up at the big house. Miss Rebecca ain't gon' like all that racket and carrying on up there. You best get rid of them before they get Culpepper riled up."

I'm afraid she's right. I look through the doorway and back up to the manor house. The shrieks and laughter of the visitors echo out the broken windows of the house and drift across the yard. Jackson Culpepper *usually* only shows up at night. But he's always taken an interest in visitors, especially children, who get past Cornelius and all the way up to the manor house. I'd better get back before he gets interested in Thomas, Maya, and Mateo. Or before Miss Rebecca gets agitated and starts making a fuss. It's all very stressful to manage for a twelve-year-old.

I search around the room for the carving knife while

trying not to look like I'm up to no good. "I'll take care of them."

Emma eyes me suspiciously.

"What's Retha Mae cooking for supper?" I ask, trying to distract Emma from my thieving ways.

A few tin plates are stacked up neat on a crooked shelf, but the knife isn't anywhere to be found.

"Chicken-and-sausage pirlou," Emma says, still side-eyeing me.

I stop a moment, letting myself imagine my mouth watering the way it used to when I was part of the living world. What Retha Mae and Emma call *pirlou* is what my family called *perlo*. It's a Lowcountry rice dish, with chicken, sausage, onions, and tons of black pepper, that's cooked up in big old cast-iron pots and served at about every wake, wedding reception, and church potluck in Georgetown County. I haven't had any non-pretend perlo in a long time. Grandma made the best perlo in town. Well, after she stopped making it with squirrel meat that is.

"Can I borrow the carving knife?" I just come right out and ask, feeling anxious about being away from the manor house for too long.

Emma leans her weight on the broom handle. "And what does a little boy like you need with a carving knife? It's too rusty to do anybody much good anyway."

I'm not *that* much younger than Emma in living years, and she knows it. But sometimes she calls me a little boy to keep me in my place. I let out a defeated huff, playing on her soft spot for me. I know she has one.

"Please," I say, dragging out the word with a put-on whine.

Emma sighs. She goes over to the counter and grabs the knife from underneath Retha Mae's small collection of rusted and dented utensils.

"You better bring it on back before Retha Mae goes looking for it," she says, pointing the knife at my face, holding it so the blade sticks out where her left index finger should be. "You hear me, boy?"

"Yes, ma'am," I say all respectful-like as I reach for it. "I will."

Once the knife is in my hand, I inspect it real close. Emma's right—it *is* rusted and a little dented, but it still has a pretty sharp point. Sharp enough to get the job done anyway.

"Emma?" I say, quietly. "What happened to your finger?"

She jerks around and looks at me like I just slapped her across the face. I think she's gonna bite my head off, but she takes a deep breath and exhales slowly.

"You never asked me that before," she says, staring down at the broom. "Why now?"

I shrug. "The visitors maybe. Been thinking about lots of stuff I usually don't since they got here."

She gives me a quick nod. Fiddles with her hair. Tightens the ties of her apron. She's definitely not comfortable talking about this, but she doesn't seem cross with me for asking. Maybe she's been waiting for me to ask for a long time.

"Was it the boss who did it?" I ask cautiously. "Deacon Pope?"

Emma glances over at me and then sits down in a chair at the table, shoulders sagging. She finally nods.

"He was dragging my sister Maisy out into the woods," she says, gazing into a corner of the room at nothing. "We all knew what that meant. She was real sick. Wasn't able to plant rice no more, all that stomping around barefoot in those swampy fields, copperheads and gators lurking about always ready to strike." She looks over at me, pain and regret weighing down her eyes. It's a look I recognize. "I tried to stop him. Ran after them. Put my hands on him when I shouldn't have. Shoved my finger in his face, and he took it off with one strike of his machete. He pushed Maisy to the ground and commenced to kicking me in the stomach until I couldn't breathe or move. I just lay there watching him drag Maisy off to the swamps. By the time I could pull myself up, it was too late."

My tongue is tied in ten different knots. If I needed to breathe, I wouldn't be able to right now.

"I failed her," Emma says, her voice broken. "My own baby sister."

I open my mouth to speak but nothing comes out.

"I pray every day that she can forgive me," Emma says softly. "Wherever she is."

Again, I try to think of something to say that might be of comfort to Emma, but I'm still coming up short.

She clears her throat. "Don't know how she could, though, when I can't even forgive myself."

"Emma," I manage to get out, my voice small and insignificant. "There wasn't anything you—"

Emma stands, cutting me off. "Is there something else you needed, boy?"

Her face is hard, and her eyes are cold.

She starts sweeping again. "'Cause I got work to do."

I don't say anything. Just shake my head, turn, and head out to meet the approaching storm.

# 6

"I THINK WE'VE got a bunch of thugs here, Dan."

That's what Mr. Walter Cronkite said on the *CBS Evening News* one night a couple of years before I got stuck here at Hollow Pines. I'm pretty sure the year was 1968, because I'd just had my tenth birthday. There was some big ruckus at a convention of Democrat folks in Chicago, where things got out of hand both outside and inside the building. Mr. Walter Cronkite's friend Dan Rather was there, reporting from inside. Mr. Rather got socked in the stomach and pushed down to the floor while he was trying to tell Mr. Cronkite and all of America what the heck was going on.

That's when Mr. Cronkite said, "I think we've got a bunch of thugs here, Dan."

I wonder if Mr. Cronkite would call me a thug on the *CBS Evening News* right now if he saw me running across the yard with a carving knife in my hand and mischief on my mind, like those rowdy folks in Chicago. I'd like to think that Mr. Cronkite would understand that I don't mean the visitors any harm. I just need them to stay a little while longer so I can find out if they know what happened to Will. And on top of all that, Emma's awful story is gnawing away at me.

When I get back inside the manor house, I find the visitors spread out in the middle of the dining room floor—open bags of potato chips in front of them and half-eaten sandwiches in their hands. The handheld recorder and headphones are on the floor close to Mateo. Goldie lies on her side behind Thomas, her back pushed up against his like she doesn't want anyone or anything sneaking up on him.

Cans of soda and a half-empty sleeve of peanut butter cookies sit in the center of their little indoor picnic. There's even a plastic bowl full of water for Goldie. Thomas, Mateo, and Maya are all mustard-stained smiles, and their easy laughter sounds like music echoing around the dining room. I stand in the doorway, listening to them, watching them, gripping the carving knife at my side.

"Remember when she told your mom she was changing her name to Maya?" Thomas says to Mateo while pointing at Maya, his mouth full up to the brim with turkey, cheese, bread, and mustard.

Maya covers her mouth like she's about to spew soda all over the place. Finally, she recovers. She looks up, raising her shaking fists in the air with a little crack and cry in her voice like the women on Grandma's favorite afternoon soap opera, *As the World Turns.*

"Dios mío, ¿por qué me estás castigando?" she says.

They all go hysterical with laughter, Thomas doubling over and Maya and Mateo lying back on the dusty wood plank floor, their stomachs heaving up and down. I don't know what Maya just said, because I don't speak Spanish. But I know it was Spanish because when I was a little kid, I learned a few Spanish words from watching *Sesame Street.* I wonder for a moment what Maya's name used to be and why she changed it.

Thomas snorts, making Maya and Mateo crack up even more. I can't help but smile with my whole face, because I imagine this is how it's going to be now that the visitors are going to stay awhile—me and Thomas and Maya and Mateo, telling stories and making one another laugh until we snort and almost spew soda everywhere. They'll have to teach me more Spanish than *Sesame Street* did, though. That is, if I get up the nerve to let them see me.

A sharp crack of thunder silences them instantly. Goldie scrambles to all fours, growling at the ceiling. Thomas gets up off the floor and I follow him to the window, standing just behind his left shoulder. I tighten my grip on the handle of the knife so I don't get nervous and drop it. That would be a disaster.

Thomas doesn't have any idea how close I am, but I wonder if he can sense my presence. His light brown hair is damp around the edges. He smells like sweat and fresh-cut grass, and the combined scent reminds me of home.

Maya joins us at the window. "It's starting to rain."

She says it like an *I told you so*.

"Not too bad, though," Thomas says. "Come on, let's check out the upstairs. Maybe there's some evidence of Will being in the house up there."

Mateo pulls a white plastic trash bag out of his backpack, throwing the empty potato chip bags, soda cans, and plastic wrap inside. The leftover cookies he stuffs into his backpack. He wasn't kidding about that Boy Scout *be prepared* thing, and I really appreciate him cleaning up. Most visitors don't do that. They treat the manor house like a garbage dump. I usually tidy up after them so Miss Rebecca doesn't get upset. Every now and then, I find something cool or interesting they leave behind and hide it in the slave village chapel under the third floorboard from the back wall, with the rest of my treasures. Preacher doesn't seem to mind as long as I show up for Sunday services on time.

I've collected all kinds of things over the years—a couple of magic pocket phones, a watch with no hands or winder knob, a wallet full of credit cards with the name William Brockington on them, a funny-looking orange-and-black pistol, a couple of flashlights, tons of matchbooks with the names of restaurants and hotels printed on them, and some other cool stuff too.

After Mateo finishes cleaning up, he ties a knot to close the garbage bag and sets it on the floor beside his backpack. Then he moves Goldie's water bowl over to the wall too. Thomas picks up the Tascam and the headphones, leading Goldie and the twins into the foyer. He stops in front of the staircase.

It's definitely *not* a good idea for them to go upstairs. Even though she's a nice person once you get to know her, Miss Rebecca has never liked visitors poking around her house, and she has given some nosy folks a good fright more than once over the years. She doesn't have to do very much to scare them either. Sometimes she just appears in front of the window when they wander into her bedroom. Even with her back to them, they still about pee their pants before hightailing it out of there. Then there're the shadows that aren't like regular shadows at all. And there're a lot more dark corners for them to hide in upstairs.

Thomas plugs the headphones into the recorder and lets them rest around his neck. He puts his free hand on the wobbly wooden banister, taking the first step real careful-like. He takes another, stopping, and then pressing down on the next step with his foot. Another rowdy clap of thunder stops him cold.

Thomas looks over his shoulder at us. "Just take it slow and watch where you step."

I let Maya and Mateo go after Thomas, because Grandma always said it wasn't polite to rush in front of others like an ill-behaved fool. Thomas, Maya, and Mateo all hold on to the banister and ease their way up the stairs, watching every step they take, because some of the boards are broken and others are missing altogether. Carefully, I move past Goldie and follow them. The dog doesn't budge from her spot at the bottom of the staircase. Thomas notices when he's about halfway up.

"Come on, Goldie," he says, looking back at her and coaxing her with excited eyes and a nod.

But Goldie's not buying it, not one little bit. She sits staring at the ceiling like she can see right through it and into the rooms on the second floor. Maybe Goldie doesn't like what she sees up there, and who could blame her? A deep growl forms in her throat. The visitors all stop climbing the stairs at once, looking back at Goldie with something like fear twisting their faces.

Thomas's sharp brown eyes cut right through me, but I know he can't see me. He's looking at his dog below. He watches Goldie another second or two and then sighs in defeat.

"Okay, fine," he says to her, like she can understand him. I wouldn't be surprised if she can. "Stay right there, then. Don't go anywhere, Goldie. Stay."

Goldie answers him by shifting her low growl to a more helpless-sounding whine. I'll bet if she could talk, she'd be saying something like, *Hey, you idiots! Don't go up there. We need to hightail it out of here pronto!* And she'd be right about that.

"Okay, if Goldie doesn't want to go up there, maybe we shouldn't either," Mateo says.

"You can stay down here if you want, but I'm going," Thomas says.

A line of sweat dots Mateo's forehead. He wipes it away. Maya does the exact same thing at the exact same time. That must be one of those creepy twin things.

"Well, you're not going up there by yourself," Mateo says, resigned. "And I'm not staying down here by myself. Let's go."

"It'll be okay, little brother," Maya says to him with a playful tone. "I'll watch out for you."

Mateo starts moving up the stairs again. "Stop calling me that. You're only nine minutes older than me."

"Yep," Maya says. "And I always will be."

Thomas laughs at that, but Mateo just shakes his head. I'll bet Maya reminds him that she's nine minutes older a lot. Thomas presses the button in the center of the Tascam and holds it close to his mouth.

"We're moving up to the second floor of the manor house now," Thomas says into the small, silver flipped-up microphone on top of the recorder. He doesn't bother sliding the headphones up over his ears. He's speaking slower than he did before, barely above a whisper.

The visitors finally make it safely to the landing at the top of the stairs. I ease by Maya and Mateo—not rushing like an ill-behaved fool—and stand protectively beside Thomas. I have an uneasy feeling, and the every-now-and-again rumbles of thunder outside aren't helping. The rain has picked up, steadily pelting the roof of the house. The wind sings an eerie song through the broken-out windows.

There are four bedrooms on the second floor—Miss

Rebecca's at the end of the hall on the right, Jackson Culpepper's across from it, a nursery beside Miss Rebecca's room, and a guest room just to the left at the top of the stairs. From what Emma and Retha Mae tell me, Miss Rebecca and Jackson Culpepper the Third had only one child, a boy they named Jackson Culpepper the Fourth. They called the baby Ford. He died in his crib before his first birthday.

I can't imagine how Miss Rebecca must have felt after losing her only child, a child that I'm told they had been trying to have for a long time. Retha Mae said that Jackson Culpepper wanted nothing more in the world than to have a son and heir, and that losing baby Ford sent the man into some terrible dark places.

"Made a mean-as-a-snake man even meaner," she'd said.

After baby Ford's death, Culpepper started drinking more, gambling more, and taking his wrath out on anyone in his path, especially the enslaved folks at Hollow Pines. Miss Rebecca was never the same after losing her child, so torn up with grief was she. She blamed herself for the baby's death, having left him alone in his crib while she attended to the house. She had forgotten to remove the miniature wooden horse that Ford loved to hold tight in his tiny grip. Unfortunately, the horse was small enough to get stuck in the baby's throat. Culpepper also blamed Miss Rebecca for the death of his only heir. And soon after, in a fit of drunken rage, he strangled her for it.

I find Miss Rebecca in the nursery sometimes, sitting

in the rocking chair, humming a sad lullaby, and holding a ratty old baby doll like it's her real live baby Ford. I hope she's not doing that right now, because it's real creepy and I don't want her to scare off the visitors.

"Did Will Perkins come inside the manor house the day he disappeared?" Thomas asks the Tascam, overselling the question on purpose, I think. Mr. Cronkite did that sometimes. "Did he come up to the second floor?"

*I don't know if he did or not, Thomas. Because I can't remember what happened to him!*

That's what I want to say, right into the small silver microphone on top of the Tascam. Thomas turns the recorder off and holds it at his side.

Maya coughs into her elbow. "Dang, it's dusty up here."

"Darker too," Mateo says. "Maybe I should go get a flashlight out of my backpack."

"Of course you brought a flashlight in the middle of the day," Thomas says, rolling his eyes.

"Dad's not here to be impressed, you know," Maya says.

Mateo ignores her, but he doesn't go back downstairs for the flashlight.

All the bedroom doors are closed. I keep them that way to discourage visitors from poking around where they shouldn't, not that it ever works. I think Miss Rebecca appreciates the effort, though. I *never* go into Jackson Culpepper's room. I don't know how much time he spends in there, but I really don't want to know either. Most of the time he keeps to the swamps, way out in the woods.

Retha Mae says that when Culpepper was part of the living world, he loved hunting alligators out there. And he didn't even hunt them with a gun, because he thought it was more exciting to use an ax. I can't for the life of me understand why anyone would want to go looking for gators in the first place, never mind hunt them with an ax. But Grandma used to say, *Bad men chase after like-minded demons.* And I guess she was right about that.

Thomas moves quietly from door to door, placing the palm of his hand in the center of each like he's trying to feel what's on the other side, making his choice carefully, almost prayerfully. He stops at the door of the nursery, and my uneasy feeling returns. Of all the rooms in the house, Miss Rebecca especially doesn't like anyone going into that one. Maya and Mateo stand close behind Thomas as his hand finds the doorknob in the dim light. I'm keeping an eye on all those shadowy spots around us. But so far, the shadows are keeping to themselves.

Another boom of thunder sounds, vibrating through the walls and floorboards and stoking my nerves. Thomas pauses before turning the knob, looking up as if he can see the stormy sky through the ceiling. Rain beats down on the roof like it ain't got nowhere else in the world to be. I watch Thomas's hand on the doorknob, wishing with all my heart that he wouldn't turn it. I wonder if she's in there. Rocking the ratty old baby doll. Humming the sad lullaby.

Thomas looks back down at the doorknob, turning it slowly, with Maya and Mateo huddled around him. I stand right beside Thomas, clutching the carving knife at my side and holding my breath. Goldie growls from somewhere below. The door creaks open a little just as an ear-numbing crash sounds downstairs. The visitors whip their heads around toward the staircase, Goldie calling them in a frantic cry.

"What was that?" Mateo whispers, fear choking his words.

"Goldie!" Thomas calls out.

But Goldie's cry has turned into snarls. She sounds like she's about ready to tear somebody or something apart down there. I check the dark corners around us, and my throat closes up.

The shadows are on the move.

Thomas darts over to the staircase, leaving the door of the nursery ajar. Maya and Mateo follow him down the stairs, being a lot less careful than they were going up. They don't even see the gang of shadows following them down, nipping at their heels every step of the way. I quickly pull the door closed, making sure I hear the latch click into place before I chase after them.

About halfway down the stairs, a long, thin shadow slithers between Maya's feet. She loses her balance and teeters forward, grabbing the banister with both hands to steady herself. Without thinking, I sail down and reach for her with my free hand. I only graze her arm for a second at the elbow before stopping myself and pulling back, but she looks over her shoulder with a little gasp. Her reaction startles me so much that I accidentally loosen my grip on the carving knife. It slips through my fingers, clattering down the stairs all the way to the bottom.

Now they can see it.

Mateo looks back at his sister. "You okay?"

Maya nods, reaching for his outstretched hand. "What was that?"

Mateo leads her safely down to the foyer. She pulls her hand away from him to rub the spot on her elbow where I just barely touched her. The shadows near her feet scatter away, retreating into their dark corners and hidden spaces. Goldie has finally calmed now that Thomas is back by her side. He stands in the middle of the foyer, holding the dog's collar and staring at Retha Mae's carving knife lying at his feet. Goldie sniffs at it cautiously.

"A knife?" Mateo says, looking bug-eyed at the thing.

Thomas picks up the knife, turning it over in his hand. Mateo, Maya, and I circle around to inspect it too. I act like I'm seeing the thing I dropped for the very first time, even though they can't see me acting like I'm seeing the thing I dropped for the very first time.

"Where did that come from?" Maya asks. "It wasn't here before, was it?"

Part of me wants to speak up. Just let them see me, introduce myself, and explain everything—why I had the knife, how as soon as it left my hand it became visible to them—*That's how things work around here, don't ask me why!*—and tell them it's not a good idea to go into the nursery, and that they really need to be mindful of the shadows. But the visitors seem shaken enough as it is right now. I think it would be rude to make it worse by just appearing out of thin air.

"I don't know," Thomas says. "Maybe it was lying on the steps all along and you kicked it down when you tripped."

Mateo takes a step back, like the knife has ghost cooties or some such.

"I didn't see that thing when we were going up the stairs," Mateo says. "And I was watching those janky steps pretty closely."

They're all quiet for a second or two, no good explanation to be found among them. None that their living brains can easily process, that is.

"Whatever," Thomas says, still holding on to the knife. "Come look at this."

Thomas leads us into the front sitting room. Maya lets out another little gasp when she sees the big mirror that was hanging over the mantel now lying on the floor in front of the fireplace—the frame broken all to bits and what looks like a million shards of chicken-poxed glass scattered around it.

"Whoa," Mateo says in a reverent whisper.

"I guess it fell somehow," Thomas says.

"Um . . . okay," Maya says, looking at him suspiciously. "So, it just fell? After being up there for who knows how long?"

She looks at Mateo for backup, but he just shrugs at her.

"Maybe the way the thunder was shaking the house caused it to fall," Thomas says.

As if it heard Thomas talking about it, thunder like the voice of God roars overhead. But God's got no business at Hollow Pines. I go over to the window and look out into the front yard. It's still early in the day, probably around ten or eleven in the morning, but it's dim and dusky outside like it's almost nighttime. The clouds are eerie shades of black, gray, and purple. Lightning streaks through them like electric veins. Wind whips the Spanish moss in the tree branches around in a frenzy, and the rain has already made a dark, muddy mess of the usually powdery-white Live Oak Lane. Hollow Pines is throwing a temper tantrum. And there's no reasoning with Hollow Pines when it's in a tizzy like this.

"Guys," Maya says, "I really think we should leave."

I turn back to the visitors. If I *did* speak up, maybe I'd be able to change Maya's mind about leaving. I could explain the reason the mirror fell—that they just got Miss Rebecca all riled up by trying to go into the nursery, is all. I'd bet all the treasures I have hidden away in the chapel that she's the one who caused the mirror to crash. And she must be real upset, too, because she's not usually so showy. That's more Jackson Culpepper's thing.

"Wait, do you hear that?" Thomas says, staring up at the ceiling.

And speaking of Miss Rebecca, I guess she's not done with the show just yet.

Maya and Mateo stay quiet, following Thomas's gaze. It's faint, but I hear it too. It's her, all right. Upstairs. In the nursery. Humming the sad lullaby. And probably rocking the ratty old baby doll.

Mateo is breathless. "Someone's here."

The visitors lock eyes for a silent moment.

"Maya's right," Thomas says, breaking the brief spell, finally convinced. "Let's get out of here."

He drops the knife.

As soon as it hits the floor and they turn away, I grab it, making it invisible again. Maya pulls Goldie by the collar to the door. Thomas hands the Tascam and headphones to Mateo, who grabs his backpack and stuffs them inside. In about two seconds flat, all three of them are running out into the pouring rain and heading for their bikes.

I'm not too worried, though. The visitors aren't leaving anytime soon. Not with flat tires.

# 7

I WATCH THEM from the doorway, standing side by side in front of The Reaper, rain beating down on their uncovered heads as they stare blindly at their useless bicycles. It only took a good hard stab of the carving knife's point in each tire to puncture a hole big enough for all the air to escape. The visitors are quiet—I guess while their brains catch up to what their eyes are seeing.

Goldie sniffs around the bikes like she's a dog detective searching for clues. I hope she doesn't pick up my scent—if I even have a scent anymore. I tighten my grip on the knife at my side. I can't drop it again. I need to get it back to the kitchen house before Retha Mae goes looking for it.

Thomas backs away from the bikes like they're some kind of alien hatchlings in a science fiction movie. "What the—"

"How are *all* the tires flat?" Maya yells over the wind and rain, panic rising in her voice.

Thomas looks around—from The Reaper to the manor house to the stone columns way down at the end of Live Oak Lane—shielding his eyes from the thickening downpour. A crack of thunder makes him jump a little, and a lightning flash of fear widens his eyes. His frantic gaze finally settles on the front door of the manor house.

"Come on," he says, jaw fixed. "We have to go back inside."

Goldie rushes ahead of him to the house like she can read his mind. Either she knows what *inside* means or she doesn't like getting wet.

Mateo wipes the rain from his eyes. I guess it could be tears he's wiping away. It's hard to tell out here.

"I'm not going back inside," he says, voice cracking, head shaking. "Someone's in there. You heard it too."

Thomas nods real fast, like that will calm Mateo. "I know. I don't want to go back in there either. But we can't stand out here in the rain." He points to the bikes. "And we're not going to get very far with these."

Thomas turns, running back toward the front door of the manor house, where I stand, and follows Goldie inside. I almost reach out and touch him as he passes me. Make him see me. Apologize for messing up their bikes. But I don't. Besides, I'm really not *that* sorry for what I did. I just hate that the visitors might be scared.

Maya hesitates a moment or two before heading back to the manor house. Mateo stands there watching his sister sprint away, rain soaking him. I know he really doesn't want to go back inside the house, but I'm sure he doesn't want to stay out here in the storm by himself either. I look up. Violent streaks of lightning rip through dark gray clouds. It doesn't look like the middle of the day should look. It doesn't look like any part of the day should look. It looks unnatural—like most things at Hollow Pines. After a few more stubborn moments, Mateo follows after his sister in a huff.

Back inside the house, the visitors stand in the foyer, dripping all over the floor and gazing up at the ceiling, listening. But Miss Rebecca isn't humming the sad lullaby anymore, thank goodness. The only sounds disturbing the quiet of the house are the rain, the wind, and the now less muted rolls of thunder vibrating through the walls.

"I don't hear anything," Thomas says, shaking the rain off his clothes. "Maybe it *was* just the wind."

But Thomas doesn't look convinced by his own words. Neither do the twins.

Mateo lets his backpack slip off his shoulders and eases it down to the floor. "Dude, since when can the wind carry a tune?"

"He's right," Maya says. "It sounded like someone was singing, or humming, or something up there."

"Well, whatever it was, it stopped," Thomas says. "At least it's dry in here."

"But what happened to our bikes?" Maya says, her eyes simmering with unease.

She pinches the front of her soaked T-shirt, pulling it away from her skin. Her hair is matted and the small pink bow at the end of her short braid is drooping and crooked but still hanging on for dear life.

Thomas leads them back into the front room. "Maybe we rode through some broken bottles covered in the sand. Or nails." He shudders a little. "Is it colder in here now?"

A knot tightens in my stomach. It could be chillier in the house because of the wind and rain. That and the fact that the visitors are soaking wet. But it could also mean other things. I wonder if Jackson Culpepper is close by. I check the corners for shadows. All clear for now.

"I didn't see any broken bottles or any nails," Mateo says. "Someone *did* that."

"I don't know, dude. Okay?" Thomas sounds exasperated. Like he's tired of them expecting him to have all the answers.

Something passes over Thomas's face, a change of expression that I can't read. He digs the Tascam out of Mateo's backpack but doesn't bother with the headphones this time. He flips the two small silver microphones up before pressing the button in the center and launching right into recording.

"After being inside the manor house at Hollow Pines for a little over an hour, some . . . *unusual* things started happening," Thomas says, his voice settling into that professional newscaster mode he'd had when recording earlier. He paces around the room as he talks into the recorder, shoulders up around his ears. "First, a large mirror that hung over the fireplace fell, crashing into pieces. We thought it could have been from the thunder shaking the house."

"*You* thought it could have been from the thunder shaking the house," Mateo mutters under his breath.

Maya shushes him.

Paying Mateo no mind at all, Thomas continues. "Second, we thought we heard humming or singing coming from upstairs."

Mateo looks over at his sister and mouths, *Thought?*

Maya shakes her head at Mateo. And I don't know if her eye roll is meant for him or Thomas. Maybe both.

Thomas stops pacing. He relaxes his shoulders and stands at the front door, peering out into the storm. "Even though we haven't been here that long and had only just started recording this episode, we decided we should leave. But when we got outside to our bikes, all the tires were completely flat. We don't know what happened to them. It's raining pretty hard now, so we came back inside to figure out what to do next. For now, we're stuck here."

His last few words are like a punch to the gut. I've been trying to move on from this place forever, and I just caused the visitors to be stuck here like I am. Well, not exactly like I am, but stuck nonetheless.

Thomas turns, walking over to Maya. He holds the recorder between them.

"I'm here with *Finding Will* producer Maya Lopez," Thomas says.

Maya's eyes go wide with surprise.

"Maya, what do you think is going on here?"

Maya looks down at the recorder and back up at Thomas before answering. "I don't know. Maybe we imagined the humming upstairs, or maybe it was the wind. But we didn't imagine the mirror falling or our tires being flat. Maybe someone else is here, trying to scare us."

"Someone?" Thomas asks with a glint in his eye. "Or some*thing*."

Maya narrows her eyes at him. "What are you saying, T?"

"I'm just saying," Thomas replies with a noncommittal shrug, "maybe whoever or *whatever* was responsible for the disappearance of Will Perkins all those years ago is still here. Still haunting this place."

I freeze, as if any movement at all will be a full confession to Thomas's accusation.

Mateo walks over to stand beside his sister. "What?"

"Haunting?" Maya makes a chopping motion on her open palm. "Cut!"

Thomas lets out a heavy sigh as he presses the button to stop the recording. "Dang it, Maya, I was on a roll. And technically the director is the one who's supposed to yell 'cut.'"

"Then *cut*!" Mateo says, sounding a little annoyed.

"What are you doing?" Maya says to Thomas. "This is a true-crime podcast, not a campfire ghost story."

"But what if it's both?" Thomas says, his eyes gleaming. "Think about it, Maya. That would really make the podcast stand out. Adding a . . . *sensational* element. We'd be sure to win the media fair."

"Hold up," Mateo says. "Are you saying you think some kind of ghost or spirit did something to Will Perkins?"

Thomas shrugs. "I don't know. Maybe."

"No, Thomas," Maya says decisively. "You can't just make stuff up. We have to stick to the facts and follow the evidence. *That's* what will make the podcast stand out."

"What evidence?" Thomas says. "There isn't any evidence. That's why nobody knows what happened to Will." He sets the Tascam and the headphones down on the floor. "All we know is that Will left his house on his bicycle on Saturday morning, April 10, 1971, and never came back, like you said. And that kid Frankie Dimery from his school said he saw Will here. That's it. I think we have to try and fill in the blanks."

I take a few steps back, like a guilty person sneaking away from the scene of a crime. The memories of that day swirl around in my head in one big blurry blob, refusing to take form. But I know that name.

*Frankie Dimery.*

I remember him.

Maya hugs herself, rubbing her arms. "Filling in the blanks is one thing. Making stuff up to make a story more exciting is another. That's not journalism, T."

"Yeah," Thomas says. "But we can't ask Will what

happened, so we have to speculate a little. And what's wrong with keeping an open mind?"

Maya points a finger at him. "You've been explaining away every weird thing that's happened since we got here. So I know you don't really believe there's anything . . . *supernatural* going on." Her teeth begin to chatter. "Oh my God, I'm cold."

Thomas and Mateo look at Maya, concern building in their eyes as she starts shivering all over and can't seem to stop.

Thomas walks over to the fireplace. "We should build a fire while we wait out the storm."

"Dude," Mateo says. "That chimney has probably been clogged up for a hundred years. Do you want to burn the house down?"

Thomas kneels in front of the fireplace. He picks up a mostly burnt piece of wood, half of it tinged with bluish-gray ash. "This wood doesn't look a hundred years old."

Thomas would be right about that. A few visitors over the years have started fires in the fireplace. And nobody has burned the house down. Yet.

Mateo throws his hands up, letting them fall right back to his sides with a loud smack. "What we *should* be worried about is how we're going to get home, not getting all warm and cozy here."

Maya walks over to Mateo, putting a hand on his shoulder. "Calm down, little brother. We can walk our bikes home as soon as the storm dies down."

"Calm down? Walk home?" Mateo's eyes widen almost cartoonishly. "Are you serious? How many miles is Hollow Pines Road, if you can even call it a road?"

Thomas kicks some of the broken mirror glass away from the hearth. "At least a mile. Probably a mile and a half."

"Yeah," Mateo says, his voice higher and his breathing shallow. "Then another mile or so home. And that dirt road will be like quicksand after the rain." He points at Maya accusingly. "You said yourself it could get washed out."

Mateo doubles over, hands on his knees, taking in deep breaths. Maya and Thomas share a tight look.

"Hey," Maya says, rubbing his back. "Just breathe. Did you bring your medicine?"

Mateo inhales, letting it out slowly. "I didn't think we'd be gone long enough to need it."

"Did you take it this morning?" she asks hesitantly.

Mateo looks up at her a little sheepishly and shakes his head.

Maya rolls her eyes at him and then pulls her magic pocket phone out again. "Still no bars. And my battery is getting low."

"Great," Mateo says. "That's just perfect."

He looks like he's about to cry, which causes a pesky lump to lodge in my throat.

"Mateo, deep breaths," Maya says. "Slowly in through your nose, hold for five, and out through your mouth. You know the drill."

Mateo does as he's told. And I'm starting to worry

about him. It's like he's having some kind of spell or something.

"Dude," Thomas says to him, his voice smooth and calm like Walter Cronkite's. "I know you're scared. We're all scared."

"*I'm* not scared," Maya says, crossing her arms. Like she's trying to convince everyone, including herself.

Thomas ignores her. "We'll figure it out, okay? I promise. We'll be home before dinner. You and Maya will be eating your mom's amazing enchiladas, or your dad's tamales, or—"

"It's taco night," Maya interjects, wringing the rainwater out of the hem of her T-shirt and right onto Miss Rebecca's floor.

"Or tacos," Thomas continues, shooting Maya a look. "And I'll probably be eating canned tomato soup and a fried baloney sandwich with my dad and Sheila. Or those baloney, mashed potato, and cheese cup things she bakes in the oven. I guess I should give her more credit. She's a real baloney expert."

Mateo's tightly wound face softens a little, and he lets out a long exhale as his face breaks into a smile. Sheila must be Thomas's stepmother, and it sounds like he doesn't like her very much. But those baloney and mashed potato cheese cups sound kind of good to me. Baloney, mashed potatoes, and cheese are three of my favorite foods.

Thomas leans down, carefully grabbing the damaged mirror frame at one corner and pulling it over to the wall.

He kneels in front of the hearth of the fireplace and peers up the chimney chute, careful of the ash and soot.

"I think the flue is open," Thomas says, his voice echoing a little up the chimney. "I feel a breeze on my face."

With a defeated sigh, Mateo rummages through the front pockets of his backpack and pulls out a box of matches.

"Yes!" Thomas exclaims when he looks back and sees what Mateo is holding. "Are they dry?"

"Of course they're dry," Mateo says. "My backpack is waterproof. Duh."

"Great," Maya says. "Now if only we had some firewood."

She's still shivering, hugging herself and rubbing her arms. Thomas's searching gaze lands on a couple of old wooden side chairs piled in the corner. He goes right over and pulls one out into the center of the room. The chair looks like it's seen finer days. It's dusty and has only three legs left, and there's a hole in the seat. Thomas raises the chair over his head, bringing it down hard on the floor. Goldie jumps up, scampering to the other side of the room. Mateo flinches at the sound of the crash, even though he was watching the whole time and saw exactly what Thomas was about to do. Maya wasn't really paying attention, so she about jumps out of her skin. She mutters something in Spanish, something I never heard on *Sesame Street*.

The chair is so old and rotted that the remaining three legs break off easily, and what doesn't, Thomas brings a foot down on until the whole thing is just a pile of wood. I brace for a disturbance from upstairs, but Miss Rebecca is still quiet for now.

"Firewood," Thomas says, like it isn't plain as day.

"Nice, dude," Mateo says, seemingly back to his old self again.

Maya kicks broken glass away from the front of the fireplace. "I'm afraid Goldie is going to cut her paw on all this glass. I'm going to go see if there's an old broom around here somewhere."

I tense up. Maya shouldn't go snooping around looking for a broom that isn't there. Because there's no telling what else she might find instead. If I hurry, maybe I can stop her. But I hate to leave the visitors alone in the house again. I eye the still shadows in the corners of the room. If I think about it too long, I'll change my mind, so I leave them. I head out the front door, making my way quickly across the yard toward the kitchen house.

–:–

IT WAS FRIDAY afternoon and Will couldn't have been happier about that. He sat on the floor of his bedroom listening to 45s on his Mickey Mouse record player. It was white with a red turntable and had a little handle so you could close it up and carry it around like a briefcase. It also had a picture of Mickey on the inside of the lid. He was smiling that Mickey Mouse smile of his and wearing a blue-and-white-striped shirt with a blue bow tie. The arm on the turntable was made to look like Mickey's out-stretched arm, his white-gloved hand holding the needle just so. Will knew it was a record player for little kids, not a seventh grader, but it was the only one he had.

It had been a gift from his mother on his eighth birth-day, two days before she left. He woke to pee in the middle of the night and found a note on his nightstand.

*I have to go away for a while.*
*I'll be back for you as soon as I can.*
*Don't forget to say your prayers.*
                    *Love,*
                    *Mama*

He guessed that the longer she stayed away, the eas-ier it was for her to do just that, because she never came back. He knew it was because of Daddy's temper. And things only got worse after that.

Will flipped through a stack of white-sleeved records, some his and some that Sarah had let him borrow—the Beatles, the Jackson 5, the Partridge Family, Bobby Sher-man, Carole King. He finally decided on "Close to You" by the Carpenters. It was Sarah's favorite, and she'd threatened to knock him into next week if he got even one scratch on it. He secured the 45 on the turntable and carefully placed Mickey's hand on the outer edge. The piano intro started, and Will immediately felt calmer.

Will and Ronnie used to listen to records together all the time—Bobby Sherman was their favorite. They both knew all the words to his songs and would always sing them at the top of their lungs and laugh at each other, but only when Will's father wasn't home. He and Ronnie hadn't done that in a long time, though. Will doubted they ever would again. That made the heaviness in his head feel even heavier. All he wanted to do these days was play his records and sleep. Definitely *not* go to school, where the teasing had gotten a lot worse over the last few months.

There had even been some pushing and shoving added to all the name-calling. And exaggerated kissing noises when some people passed him in the hallway. Frankie Dimery had been telling everyone he could about Will's secret. That he liked boys. Wanted to kiss them. Will didn't see things changing anytime soon. The thought of all that continuing through the rest of his time at Winyah Junior High and then through high school was just too much to think about.

The back door of the house slammed shut and Will's whole body tensed up. His father was home from work early. And the last thing he would want was to find Will on the floor of his bedroom, sitting with his legs folded under him, listening to the Carpenters on a Mickey Mouse record player that his mama gave him. He would say Will needed to be spending his time doing "boy things"—hunting, fishing, playing football or baseball with his friends. But his father didn't know that Sarah was his only true friend now, and neither of them liked doing boy things much at all.

Will lifted the needle off the record, careful not to

scratch it and stopping Karen Carpenter right after she sang, "Why do stars fall down from the sky, every time you walk by?" He quickly shifted to sitting cross-legged, but his father pushed through his bedroom door before he could put everything away. Will swallowed hard as he looked up into cold, hard eyes. His father was a tall, bulky man, with large calloused hands that Will had felt the sting of on his face many times.

"The school called me at work today," Will's father said, with a healthy dose of annoyance in his voice. "At *work*. Said you've been picked on or something."

What could Will say? It was true. Even kids other than Frankie and his friends had started teasing him. Kids he didn't even know and who didn't know him. Sarah stood up for him when she could, but she was in ninth grade, so really the only time they saw each other was at lunch or once in a while in the library, where he would go to hide from his tormentors. And Ronnie never tried to stop Frankie either. He'd even started laughing along with Frankie. But he would never look Will in the eye when he did. Ronnie's sister was right. He had changed since he'd joined the football team. A lot.

"The principal said they've been calling you names— 'homo' and 'sissy' and other stuff." His father almost spat the words out, like they tasted nasty on his tongue.

Will never told on Frankie or anybody else for bullying him, because he worried it would be even worse if he got them in trouble. But one of his teachers, Mrs. Collins, saw

Frankie in action yesterday and had broken it up. She must have reported it to the principal, even though Will had begged her not to. He couldn't be too mad at Mrs. Collins, though. She thought she was helping.

Will's father stormed over to him, kicking the Mickey Mouse record player out of the way, and Sarah's 45 of "Close to You" along with it. Will heard the needle skid across the record right before his father reached down and slapped him hard across the face, about as hard as he ever had. Will was stunned, the breath knocked out of him and his cheek on fire. His eyes immediately itched with oncoming tears. He fought them back by instinct. He knew better than to cry.

Sometimes he could tell when his father was going to hit him. It had started not long after his mama left. But Will wasn't expecting it this time, because he was the one getting picked on. He hadn't done anything wrong.

"No son of mine is going to be queer," his father said in a low and threatening tone.

Then he swore, calling Will a name worse than any Frankie Dimery had used so far—a biting, hateful word that stung Will's ears. The word hung in the air between them as his father stared him down, not a trace of fatherly love to be found in his eyes. Will wondered where the man who used to rock him to sleep when he was little, read him bedtime stories, and built him a tree house in the backyard had gone. But Will knew. After his mama left, things changed. And the older Will got, the more he disappointed his father. Will was just glad his father never acted this way when Sarah was around.

"You understand me, boy?"

Will's cheek throbbed. But he swallowed hard and nodded slowly. A tear blurred the vision of his right eye. Almost as an afterthought, his father reached down and grabbed the record player and all the 45s, including the ones that belonged to Sarah.

"And this sissy music is going in the trash," his father said.

"Daddy, no!"

Will didn't mean to say it, definitely didn't mean to yell it. It just popped out of his mouth, with a little cry in his voice that he knew was going to make things worse. He couldn't hold back the tears anymore either. He wished his mama was there to protect him. But after years of being the target of his father's temper, she had fled and Will had become the new one.

The second slap was much harder than the first. But at least Will was expecting it. He closed his eyes and braced himself for the third.

# 8

AS I RUN across the yard, I can see and hear the storm raging all around me, but I can't feel the wind or the rain. It's as weird as it sounds, but I've gotten used to it. When I touch something, I know that I'm touching it, but I wouldn't call it *feeling*—except when I touch the living, that is. That's a really amazing feeling, and one that I don't get to have very often, because of the effect it has on them.

I touched a visitor a while back. She must have been eighteen or nineteen. She came to Hollow Pines with three of her friends—another girl and two boys. They thought it would be a great idea to play hide-and-seek in the manor house. Well, they were almost dead wrong about that.

The girl hid in the closet in Culpepper's room upstairs. She must have thought that was a real good hiding place, but she didn't have any idea whose room she was disturbing. Out of nowhere, Culpepper appeared and began pounding on the closet door. He hissed that sinister hiss of his and growled through the door like a rabid dog. That poor girl screamed and cried like a wounded animal, she was so scared. Then Culpepper locked the closet door, leaving the room to go mess with the girl's friends. I guess he figured he would save her for later torment.

I waited in Miss Rebecca's room until Culpepper went downstairs before I sneaked across the hall to his bedroom. I unlocked the closet door and opened it to let the girl out, but she just sat there on the floor, crying as she stared through the open door. I'm sure she was wondering who or what had opened it, and who had been doing all the pounding before. She was really frightened. I was just trying to help her, not scare her even more by opening the door. But the girl was frozen, wouldn't move for God or nobody.

I had to get her out of there before Culpepper came back, so I reached out and gently touched her arm. She screamed, jerking away from me like she'd been bitten by a snake or some such. I'm sure it was scary for her because she *felt* something but didn't *see* something. But for me, the touch was so warm. No, not just warm, exactly. More like grabbing on to the handle of a cast-iron skillet sitting on a red-hot stove burner, only it didn't hurt like that would. The brief touch sent blazing flames of her living spirit through my fingers and arm and down through my whole body. It was like fireworks going off deep inside me somewhere. I felt *alive* again.

The girl finally came to her senses and went running out of the room and down the staircase screaming like the house was on fire. I felt terrible, because like I said, I was only trying to help her. And it worked. She and her friends hightailed it out of the house as fast as they could. And that was the whole point, really.

I haven't touched another living person since then, and I miss that feeling so much. That's one way you know for sure you don't belong in their world anymore. When a friendly touch sends the living running away from you, it's a cruel reminder.

I'm just passing the schoolhouse when Teacherman steps out onto the porch, calling me back. I don't have time for this, but I can't be disrespectful to Teacherman either. I stop and back up a bit so that I stand facing him. A staggered flash of lightning draws his attention. Teacherman is really tall, and he stands with his arms crossed high on his narrow chest. He's wearing the same gray suit he's worn since the day we met. It's a real nice suit, though, not frayed and rotted like the one Jackson Culpepper the Third wears.

Sometimes when I see Teacherman, I think, *well-dressed, young white man*, because that's how Mr. Walter Cronkite described the man seen running from the scene of the crime when he told us about Dr. Martin Luther

King being shot on the *CBS Evening News*. It was 1968, the very same year that Mr. Cronkite's friend Dan was punched in the gut at the convention of Democrats in Chicago. I always thought it was weird that the police described the white man who killed Dr. King as *well-dressed* and *young*. Made him sound like an honor roll student and not the stone-cold killer he was.

Teacherman's fine blond hair grazes the peaks of his bony shoulders, and a matching blond mustache curls at its ends over thin, ruddy lips. He's a nice-looking man, I reckon. I've never heard Teacherman talk about a wife or a girlfriend or anything like that. He told me he came to Hollow Pines a couple of years after Miss Rebecca left the living world and Jackson Culpepper remarried a widow named Miss Joanna, who was twenty-five at the time. She had two young sons from her previous marriage, who needed educating, so Culpepper hired Teacherman to do the job. The way Teacherman's eyes go all dreamy when he talks about her makes me think Miss Joanna was someone he was real fond of.

"Good afternoon, sir," I say all polite-like and not like he's a bother at all, which right now he definitely is.

"Boy," he says in his usual to-the-point manner. "What are you doing running around out in this storm? Get inside here this instant."

I glance up at the angry sky. I can see the rain pouring down all around me, but like I said, we lost souls can't really feel it or get wet. Teacherman knows this, but the ways of the living are sometimes hard to shed.

I rack my brain for an excuse *not* to go inside the schoolhouse. Grandma used to say, *Sometimes the truth works wonders,* so I give it a whirl and see if it does this time.

"I can't, sir. I'm heading over to the kitchen house," I say, stammering a little. "Need to get Retha Mae's carving knife back before she misses it."

Teacherman eyes the knife at my side suspiciously. "Is that so?"

"Yes, sir," I say in my most respectful tone.

He stares at me like he's either going to ask me why I have a knife in the first place or make me go inside and have a lesson right this very minute. Probably history, because that's his favorite subject to teach, even though he's never even heard of the *CBS Evening News with Walter Cronkite.*

With his finger and his thumb, Teacherman smooths out his mustache on one side into a long thin line. When he lets go, it pops right back into a curl. I glance at the manor house, because I'm worried about being gone for too long. I hope Maya's not searching all over for a broom. There aren't any sounds of kids screaming their lungs out yet, so that's a good thing, I guess.

"Why haven't you scared off those young visitors up at the manor house?" Teacherman asks, twirling the other end of his mustache and narrowing his eyes at me.

"Working on it, sir," I lie.

Teacherman gazes at the manor house. "You know how Culpepper is about children. They aren't safe here."

I swallow hard at the reminder. Jackson Culpepper the Third has always been obsessed with the younger visitors. The loss of baby Ford, his only son and heir, damaged the man forever, from what the other lost souls around here tell me. Rotted his soul and hardened his heart to pure stone. After Culpepper died by the pistol of a rival planter over an unpaid gambling debt, he stuck around, turning his attention to the living folks who came to Hollow Pines, especially the younger ones. He fed on their souls. It made him stronger. And the stronger he got, the more he wanted.

Teacherman uncrosses his arms, casually sliding his hands into the pockets of his britches. "Answer one question, and if you get it right, you can go."

*I don't have time for this!* I want to scream, but I don't.

"Yes, sir," I say instead.

Teacherman rocks on his heels, staring up at the menacing clouds for inspiration or some such. "I'll ask you one that you missed on your last oral exam."

I look down the way to the kitchen house, longing for my freedom.

"Pay attention, boy," Teacherman says sharply.

"Yes, sir," I say, looking up at him. "Sorry, sir."

A satisfied smile curls his lips to match his mustache. "In what year did the War of Independence begin, and in what year did it end?"

That's really two questions, but I don't think it's a good idea to argue with him if I want to be on my way anytime soon. I just need to get this right, so I rack my brain. I love history, and I'm usually pretty good with dates. I remember my wrong answer from my oral exam, which was 1776 until 1783. I was real bummed that I missed that one. I'm pretty sure the war ended in 1783, so that means I got the year the war began wrong. I know the Declaration of Independence was signed in 1776, so I thought that was when the war started. Maybe it was either the year before or the year after.

"Give me an answer, boy," Teacherman says impatiently. "And if you get it wrong, we will have a lesson right now on the events leading up to the war."

I definitely don't have time to sit through a lesson. I need to get back to the manor house before the visitors run into Miss Rebecca, or Jackson Culpepper, or the shadow snakes. I'll just have to trust my gut on this one.

"The War of Independence started in 1775 and ended in 1783, sir," I say with as much confidence as I can muster, like *mustering* could make a wrong answer right.

Teacherman gives me one of his blank stares for what seems like forever, but he doesn't say anything. On the *CBS Evening News*, Mr. Cronkite never made you wait to hear the facts. But Teacherman lived and died long before Mr. Cronkite was around. Too bad, because Teacherman could have learned a thing or two from watching the *CBS Evening News*.

Finally, he relaxes his rigid stance and leans against the porch railing. He grins a little. Or is it just the mustache?

"Very well done, boy," he says.

I exhale. That was close. A small explosion of thunder sounds, making me jump a little and drawing my attention upward. Teacherman doesn't seem fazed by the storm, but he scans the yard, another kind of worry clouding his eyes.

"What's wrong, sir?" I ask.

"Culpepper's about," he says.

Teacherman can usually sense Jackson Culpepper's presence better than most of the lost souls at Hollow Pines. And he always gets a hard look in his eye when he talks about Culpepper.

"Who are those visitors up at the manor house anyway?" he asks.

The last thing I need is Teacherman getting curious and going over there and giving the visitors a scare by demanding they recite the preamble to the Constitution or some such. That's about as terrifying as he gets, but still, to a living person, that's plenty.

"Just some kids, sir," I say, smiling as best I can. "I'm taking care of it."

I hope the lie doesn't show on my face.

"You know, I had a child one time," Teacherman says, kind of distantly. "A little girl."

I just stare at him with my tongue tied up to Jesus and back. This is the first I've heard anything about Teacherman having a child. I know he was never married. He's told me so himself.

"You had a daughter, sir?" I ask, even though I need to be moving along. But as it's been known to do, my curiosity has gotten the better of me. My sister didn't used to call me *Nose-ella* for nothing. "I never knew, sir."

Teacherman looks like he wishes he could remember

how to cry right about now. That's one of the most awful things about being stuck at Hollow Pines—that we can't cry anymore. I mean, I didn't much like doing it when I was part of the living world. But I never understood how useful crying was until I forgot how to do it.

Teacherman nods a little. "Yes, I had a daughter. Until Culpepper . . ." His voice trails off, and after a quiet moment he gives me a pained look. "You be careful with yourself, boy. Stay out of his crosshairs."

The rain picks up around me. Shadows move across the yard in unnatural ways, ghostly soldiers advancing on the enemy, getting closer and closer to the manor house.

*Stay out of his crosshairs.*

"Be on your way now," Teacherman says.

His eyes are glued to the tree line in the distance, just another dead end for us lost souls.

"A reckoning is coming," he adds softly. "I can feel it."

I take a step back, turn, and run toward the kitchen house, Teacherman's words chilling me to the bone.

# 9

RETHA MAE SITS at the table in the center of the kitchen house in her black frock and white apron, her hair wrapped up tight in a faded red headscarf. She's humming a haunting melody as she goes through the motions of shelling a bushel of butter beans, even though there's not a bean in sight. I understand, though. The familiar rhythms of our before times are often hard to shake. Normally I would sit right down and help her, because Grandma taught me how to shuck and shell just about everything.

*The best part of a thing is always on the inside,* Grandma would sometimes say as we worked. I'm not sure if she was talking about butter beans or people, but I always hoped the same was true about me.

"Close the door, boy," Retha Mae says softly. "Don't be bringing the storm in here with you."

"Yes, ma'am," I say, pushing the door closed.

I keep the knife hidden behind me and ease over to the counter where I got it. Retha Mae watches me the whole time, but that doesn't slow down her handiwork. I imagine butter beans popping right out of the open shells as Retha Mae runs her thumbnail from bottom to top, just like Grandma used to do.

"What you got behind you, boy?" she asks, curious.

"Nothing," I lie, which I feel kind of bad about, because I've done a lot of it today. "I was just wondering if I can borrow the broom. Some visitors up at the manor house made a mess and I don't want Miss Rebecca getting upset."

She lets out a grunt. "Maybe she should clean up her own house for once." Her mouth is a tight line across her face, her eyes going distant and cold. "When we was part of the living world, she'd have Emma up there at the crack of dawn seven days a week, cleaning, polishing silver, scrubbing the floors, and washing clothes, all before I could even get breakfast on their table. Run that poor girl ragged." Retha Mae glances around the room. "And this here was my jail cell—up at four in the morning, building the fire, heating the water, making breakfast, cleaning the dishes, wringing a chicken's neck for dinner, cleaning *those* dishes, the evening tea and supper, and more dishes to be cleared and cleaned, dough to be made for the next morning's hoecakes." She stops her shelling and looks off into a corner, shaking her head. "They always had so much food; the scraps were given to the animals, you see. And all of us living on a bit of cornmeal, a few ounces of salted fish, and what vegetables we had time to plant and tend to. And God forbid you was late with Culpepper's evening cigar and whiskey. Deacon Pope would have you out for lashes before you could bank the fire for the night."

I stand there staring at her, taking in every troubling word. I swallow down a lump the size of my fist, wishing I still had my old South Carolina history textbook so I could burn it page by page for all the ugly truths it left out. Retha Mae, Emma, Cousin Cornelius—they're the only textbooks you really need.

"Yes, ma'am," I say with a respectful nod. I clear my throat. "I thought I would take care of the mess this time. You know how Miss Rebecca can get. I just don't want her taking it out on the visitors. Then there'll be more stories. And like you always say, 'More stories, more visitors.'"

Retha Mae meets my gaze, her cold eyes warming again. "Ain't that the God's honest truth. The more boring this place is, the more folks will just leave us be." She gives me one more suspicious glance. "What'd you say you needed, boy?"

"The broom," I say. "If it ain't too much trouble."

She nods once and even smiles a little. "All right, then. Let me go see where I left it. Memory ain't what it used to be, you know."

"Yes, ma'am," I say. "I absolutely know."

Retha Mae wriggles herself out of the too-small chair, planting both hands on the table to push herself up. She's a large woman for her height, and the limp causes her to stoop when she walks. She disappears into the closet on the back wall. I quickly put the knife with the other utensils on the counter, turning to face her before she comes out with the straw broom in hand.

"Not much left to it," Retha Mae says, holding the ratty old thing out to me. "But you better bring it back just like you find it. You hear me, boy?"

I take the broom. "Yes, ma'am. I hear you loud and clear."

Retha Mae sits again at the table and resumes her shelling. I glance over at the door and then back to her. I need to get on up to the manor house, but I just can't help myself.

"Miss Retha Mae?"

"Lord, I can't get no peace," she mumbles, and then looks up. "What is it now, child?"

"Did you know that Teacherman had a daughter?" I ask, sounding as innocent as I possibly can.

A look of surprise widens her eyes. "He told you 'bout that, did he, now?"

I nod. She stares at me a silent moment.

"I knew," she says, falling easily back into the rhythm of her work, not offering any more on the subject.

I watch her hands. They're knotty and swollen, calluses ridging her palms like a miniature mountain range of hard, crackled skin.

"What happened to her?" I ask. "Teacherman's little girl."

Retha Mae looks up. "Jackson Culpepper—that's what happened."

She doesn't say anything else, so I prod a little more. "Who was the girl's mama?"

"And what business is that of yours?" she snaps, eyeing me.

For a second, I don't think she's going to tell me, but I know Retha Mae is just as much of a Nose-ella as I am. Maybe more.

"Miss Joanna," she finally says. "Culpepper's second wife. But he'd been over in England a few months when she got round with child, so we all knew the baby probably wasn't his, even though she carried on like it was. The little girl was born early, right before Culpepper returned."

"Oh," is all I can say as I take in the information.

"Culpepper drowned that poor baby in the canal the day he got home," Retha Mae says, shaking her head again. "Then he went after Teacherman. And you see how that turned out."

I stare at her dumbly, because I don't know what to say. Culpepper killed Teacherman? After a few moments of heavy silence, Retha Mae lets out one of her weary sighs.

"I had children too," she says almost dreamily. "A boy named Daniel and a girl named Lettie."

Retha Mae gets quiet again and I'm almost afraid to ask her what became of her children. But it seems like it would be rude not to after all that she just told me.

"What happened to them?" I ask in a cautious whisper. "Daniel and Lettie."

Retha Mae stops her shelling and stares up at me like I just knocked the wind out of her with my question. But she recovers real quick-like and her eyes go flat and hard.

"That devil Culpepper sold them off," she says in a near growl. "Their daddy too. Said he needed some quick cash to pay off a gambling debt. And there weren't a thing I could do to protect them but keep that demon fed and myself alive so I could find them again one day. Never was able to, though. Even though I promised them I would."

Now I feel like *I've* had the wind knocked out of me, but I know it can't be anywhere near as bad as how Retha Mae feels—to have your whole family sold off like cattle, and then you're forced to stay and work for the man responsible.

After a good long stare, Retha Mae clears her throat and glances down. "Get on out of here now and let me have some peace, boy."

"Yes, ma'am," I say.

"And get them living children on their way, you hear me?" she says a little louder. "This storm didn't just come up out of nowhere. Dark things shaking loose 'round here."

I nod, swallow hard, and hurry out the door.

—:—

WILL'S GRANDMOTHER DIED in early March. Sarah stayed with him that night while his father was at the hospital, because Will didn't want to be alone. He appreciated Sarah sitting with him until he fell asleep, but all he could think about was how much he wished he could talk to Ronnie—the old Ronnie. Will knew Ronnie would understand what he was feeling.

They were both close to their grandmothers and used to trade funny stories about them all the time. They were also always trying to convince the other which grandmother was the better cook. Neither of them ever gave in on that one. They even had a fried-chicken taste test with both women present, which turned out to be way more stressful than they had imagined. They called it a tie, even though each suspected the other was lying. They didn't want their grandmothers at each other's throats, after all.

Will's head rested in Sarah's lap, and she stroked his hair as she softly hummed a Karen Carpenter song. The lavender-and-lilac scent of her favorite shampoo filled his nose, calming him, lulling him closer to sleep. His tears had dried and he lay there feeling numb and empty, all cried out as he was. He didn't think he had a single tear left anywhere inside him. First his mother left him and now his grandmother was gone. Just the thought of it made his head feel heavier and his chest feel tighter. At least he still had Sarah.

"Sarah?" he said softly.

"Yeah?" she answered, a finger curling strands of his hair.

"Promise you won't ever leave me," he said, his voice cracking.

She was silent a moment. No humming or anything. Finally, a sniffle.

"I promise," she said, her voice scratchy and shaky.

He smiled for the first time all day. But Will was glad she didn't ask him to promise the same. Because he honestly didn't know if he could. He didn't know much of anything anymore.

He just wanted to sleep.

# 10

I TOOK WAY too long getting back to the manor house, but thankfully I made it just in the nick of time. Maya stands ready to climb the stairs, I guess still in search of a broom. It's in my hand, but I can't drop it right here in the middle of the foyer. It would look to the visitors like it appeared out of thin air, and they're already suspicious about the knife.

I dart down the hall, clutching the broom as tightly as I can. There's a small closet behind the staircase that's easy to miss, because it doesn't have any regular kind of door with a knob. It was made to look like part of the wall, and you have to push on the top left corner for it to pop open.

I open the door the way living folks have to, because it's a creaky old thing and I want to draw the visitors' attention to it. Quickly, I place the broom inside. The noisy hinges do the trick. There're whispers down the hall, and then hesitant footsteps are heading my way. I back away from the closet, leaving the door ajar just enough to see inside.

Maya is the first to round the corner. She stares inside the closet. "OMG!"

Thomas, Mateo, and Goldie catch up to her.

"What is it?" Mateo says, appearing next.

Maya points at the broom. "Look."

"Whoa," Thomas says. He reaches in and snatches the broom, like there might be spiderwebs or monsters lingering inside, before handing it off to Maya.

"Okay, that is too weird," Mateo says, almost backing into me. "You're looking for a broom, and then a secret door under the staircase opens and there one sits?"

They're making too big of a deal out of this. Trust me, it would have been way weirder if I had just walked in the front door and let the broom drop to the floor. I thought this was a pretty smart idea.

"And what was that you were saying about this not being a ghost story?" Thomas says with a little sass in his voice.

Maya rolls her eyes at him and then leads them back down the hallway, with Goldie and me following. The dog looks over in my direction with a wary but curious gaze. I know she can't *see* me, but she knows I'm here, so I smile at her just the same.

A small fire crackles in the fireplace in the front room. Thomas goes right over to it, arranging broken pieces of the side chair into a tepee shape over the flame. He adds some of their used napkins, and the fire catches hold pretty fast, slipping in and out of the woodpile, its flickering orange-red light zapping away the worrisome shadows clinging to the edges of the room. It reminds me of something Grandma always said—*The one thing darkness cannot abide is light.* And I guess Grandma was right about that.

Mateo sweeps the broken glass into the corner. Maya stands close to the fire, hugging herself, lines of worry creasing the smooth, golden-brown skin of her face. They're all still damp from the rain. I hope they dry out soon. I don't want any of them getting sick, or *catching their death,* as Grandma would say.

The visitors huddle close together in front of the fireplace. They look like a painting—all standing there reaching out for the warmth. Goldie lies at their feet, her eyes locked on the dancing flames like the fire is putting a spell on her.

The storm has settled down for the moment, but it hasn't completely died off. A steady but less irritable drumbeat of rainfall plays across the roof, filling the house with an easy and constant rhythm that's almost soothing.

Thomas is the first to ease down onto the floor. He sits facing the fire, leaning against Goldie's back and hugging his knees. It doesn't take long for his friends to join him, so I reckon I should too. I sit next to Thomas but not close enough to get Goldie all riled up. She's already sending plenty of sideways glances and curious sniffs my way, but luckily, she doesn't seem overly bothered by me now. I hope she can sense that I'm one of the good ones.

"Things still bad at home?" Mateo asks Thomas kind of cautiously. "With Sheila?"

Maya jerks her head in Thomas's direction, like Mateo's prying just gave her permission to ask a question she's been holding in for a while. "Do they still make you call her *Mom?*"

Without looking her way, Thomas nods. A darkness passes over his face.

Mateo lets out a long sigh. "Dude, that is so messed up. I mean, just because your mom died doesn't mean she never existed."

The weariness I saw in Thomas's eyes when the visitors first got here has returned, and now I understand.

"Don't use that word, little brother," Maya says.

"What word?" Mateo asks, looking at her with scrunched eyebrows.

"*Died,*" Maya says, bumping his arm with her elbow.

"What's wrong with *died?*" Mateo asks.

"I don't know." Maya shrugs. "It sounds harsh."

"Well, what am I supposed to say?" he asks. "I don't think *kicked the bucket* is a very nice way of putting it."

Thomas winces at that, but he doesn't look away from the fire. I want to reach out and touch him, put a hand on his or something. I don't think it would make him feel any better, though. It would just scare him.

"Shut up," Maya snaps. This time she doesn't bump her brother with her elbow—she punches his shoulder. "Just say *deceased* or *passed away*."

Mateo looks at her a second or two like he's deciding if she's right about this or not. He turns to Thomas. "I'm sorry, dude. I didn't mean any disrespect. You know how much we liked your mom."

Thomas glances over at him for a second and then back to the fire. "It's okay. It doesn't really matter what you call it. She's gone. The family I've always known is gone too." Thomas pushes his hair away from his forehead. His eyes with their long, lazy lashes go hard on a dime. "My dad has certainly moved on." The hard edge in his eyes is slipping into his voice. "He only waited a year before he started dating Sheila and only four months more before he married her. Now there's a stranger living in our house, sleeping in my mom's bed, moving everything, changing everything."

When neither of the twins respond, he shakes his head a little. "Sorry." He looks over at Maya, shifting their attention. "How are things with your parents these days?"

Maya lets out a heavy sigh. "Mom is trying. She *mostly* gets the pronouns right."

"But not Dad," Mateo adds quickly. "He still calls her Marco sometimes. It's messed up."

Maya doesn't look at her twin. Just keeps staring into the fire, her eyes getting glassier by the second. I can't tell if it's the reflection of the flames or something else. After a quiet moment, her jaw stiffens, and her eyes lose their gloss.

"Dad says it's a phase and that I'll grow out of it," Maya says. "I tell him it's not, but he won't listen."

I look from one glowing orange face to the next. I really want to speak up and ask the visitors what the heck they're talking about.

*Pronouns?*

What *phase?*

*And why would Maya's dad call her Marco?*

"It's hard enough at school with all the teasing and name-calling," Maya adds. "It should be easier at home." She peers into Thomas's eyes. "And with my best friend."

Thomas stiffens, averting his gaze from Maya. I shift a little on the floor, feeling like I'm intruding on something very private. After a few moments of waiting for a response from Thomas but not getting any, Maya seems to let it go with a resigned sigh.

"Besides," she says, her tone instantly lighter, "I can't compete with Mateo when it comes to Dad anyway."

Mateo rolls his eyes and shakes his head.

Thomas relaxes, now that the attention is off him, and his mouth eases into a grin. "Your dad *is* a little obsessed with you, dude."

"I wish he wasn't," Mateo says.

"You're his last hope for a son, little brother."

A sheepish grin creeps up on Mateo's face. "Yeah, thanks for that, sis."

Thomas and Maya both chuckle. I feel bad for Mateo, though, so I don't.

"Seriously, though, it really stresses me out," Mateo says.

"Your dad?" Thomas asks.

Mateo nods, eyes glued to the fire. "Dad, my grades, the sports, the Scouts, my sister being trans."

Mateo stops himself and looks over at Maya. "Sorry, you know what I mean."

Maya gives him a shy smile and nods. "I know. And I'm sorry. Not for the being-trans part, but that it affects you too—not always in fun ways."

I ponder the unfamiliar word. *Trans?* No idea what it means, but it sounds like something important. Something that Maya *is*.

Mateo nods at his sister, his face softening. "My anxiety is just through the roof lately. My head feels like it weighs a hundred pounds sometimes."

Mateo's words rattle something loose deep inside my brain. I remember Will feeling that way sometimes. He talked about his head feeling heavy and his chest feeling tight. I wonder if he had the same thing that Mateo does.

"Is the new medication helping?" Thomas asks.

Mateo shrugs. "I can't tell a difference yet. Other than this one makes me sleepy a lot."

Thomas nods at his friend and then they all go back to

staring into the flames, soaking in the warmth of the fire and silently comforting one another. I look at them one at a time, realizing that they're not all easy laughter and playful ribbing. They're too young to have such complicated lives. But I guess all kids are. I know I was.

Maya gets up to retrieve Mateo's backpack. "Well, since we're stuck here, we might as well get back to *Finding Will*." She digs out the recorder and the headphones and passes them over to Thomas.

"Right," Thomas says, plugging the headphones into the recorder. He slips them over his head, letting them rest on his neck.

The brief tension between Thomas and Maya seems to have disappeared for the moment.

"Maybe you should talk about what we know about Will Perkins—before he came to Hollow Pines that day," Maya says.

"Yeah," Mateo says, his excitement level rising instantly. "Like what kind of student he was, if he had any friends, and who might want to hurt him and stuff."

The hair on the back of my neck prickles to attention. I know I didn't *want* to hurt Will that day. Things must have gotten out of hand. And if Frankie Dimery was here, like the visitors said earlier, I could see that happening.

"Who was Will Perkins?" Thomas says in his newscaster voice.

He has the headphones over his ears now and holds the recorder close to his mouth as he paces in front of the fire.

"Will was a straight-A student at Winyah Junior High. His favorite subjects were language arts and history. He held a perfect attendance record for Sunday school at Prince Street Pentecostal Holiness Church and he loved riding his bike. According to those who knew him, even though Will didn't have a lot of friends, he was nice to everyone he met."

I watch Thomas with my mouth hanging open a little. It's almost like he's reading from a script about Will's life, but he's not reading at all. He has the facts about Will memorized. It's true that Will didn't have many friends, now that I think about it. But Will and I were friends— once. Before I turned on him.

A low hum sounds upstairs. Soft at first, then louder— slowly morphing into a familiar sad melody and drawing the visitors' frozen stares to the ceiling. I'm not even sure if they're still breathing, because their faces have turned to stone. I should have known that Miss Rebecca wouldn't stay quiet for long with strangers wandering around her house, breaking her furniture and starting fires in her living room and such.

Maya slowly rises to her feet. "Okay. That is *definitely* not the wind."

Mateo stands, backing away from the fireplace, like that's where the humming is coming from. "I told you." His voice cracks. "Someone *is* in the house."

Goldie pushes up on her haunches, directing a menacing growl upstairs.

Thomas stands. Looks at the ceiling but doesn't say anything.

"What do we do?" Mateo asks, panic tightening his voice.

"I think someone is trying to scare us off," Maya says, looking from Mateo to Thomas with more questions in her eyes than answers.

But Miss Rebecca's not just trying to *scare them off.* She's upset. Agitated. Her broken spirit has been disturbed again. And if Miss Rebecca gets all riled up, there's a good chance Jackson Culpepper the Third will too.

Maya picks up one of the broken-off chair legs that hasn't been thrown into the fire yet. She grips it in her right hand like a club, even though she doesn't seem one hundred percent certain about her next move. Thomas lifts the recorder toward the ceiling as he eases over to the staircase.

"Dude," Mateo exclaims in an urgent whisper. "What are you doing? Let's go!"

Thomas shushes him with a finger to his lips.

Maya nods. "Yeah, I have to agree with Mateo on this one."

But Thomas pays them no mind. He stands at the bottom of the staircase, holding up the recorder.

"Thomas!" Mateo whisper-shouts.

Thomas turns back to them. "What if someone *is* up there and they're hurt? What if they need help?"

Maya shakes her head, still gripping the chair leg like

a club. But she hesitates. "I don't know, T. I don't like this. I don't like this at all."

Mateo edges toward the front door. "Come on. Let's just get out of here."

"And go where?" Thomas says, lowering the recorder and pressing the center button to stop it. "Are you really going to walk all the way home in that storm?"

Mateo clenches his jaw. His nostrils flare. "Yes."

But his eyes don't look so sure. And if I can see that, I'm sure Thomas can too. Both boys look at Maya— waiting for her to choose sides, I guess. Gritting her teeth, Maya stomps her foot a little. I don't know who's going to win this standoff, but I have to be prepared.

I sail around Thomas and Goldie, and I'm up the stairs and at the nursery door before I hear Thomas take another step. I don't know how I'm going to persuade Miss Rebecca to stay quiet and out of sight. I just need to calm her down and convince her that I can handle the visitors. And I'm pretty sure I can, but it'll take what Teacherman sometimes calls *extreme measures*.

I need to let them see me.

# 11

MISS REBECCA DOESN'T even look up when I pass through the door of the nursery. I find her right where I knew she would be—sitting in the rocking chair by the window and holding the ratty old baby doll in her arms like it's the real living baby Ford. She's wearing the dingy white nightgown that she died in and she's humming the lullaby. Sometimes it sounds more like a moan than a hum—or like a record player slowed way down. Her messy hair is piled on top of her head like a big mound of dried Spanish moss. Her pale face is still kind of pretty, but her eyes are cold, resting lifeless and gray in their sockets.

"Miss Rebecca," I say quietly, not wanting to startle her. We lost souls can be startled too, you know.

She stops humming and looks up at me, a sad smile stretching out her face.

"Boy?" she says. "Is that you? Come over here and look at baby Ford. He's sleeping like a precious little angel."

I do as I'm told, slipping in beside her and peering down at the baby doll's cracked, bald head. Moldy patches dot its face, a chunk of plastic is missing from its left cheek, and one eye hangs out of the socket by a thread. A small black spider crawls out of the empty eye hole, skittering down the doll's good cheek like a creepy giant teardrop with eight furry legs.

"Yes, ma'am," I say. "He sure does look like a precious little angel to me."

Footsteps sound downstairs, moving toward the staircase. I guess Thomas won the standoff. The visitors will be here soon.

"Who's in my house?" Miss Rebecca asks, a hard look quickly replacing her somber smile. "You get them out of here this instant, boy, before Jackson gets ahold of them."

"I'll take care of it, ma'am," I promise.

She forgets me for a moment and looks back down at the baby doll, the lullaby trapped inside her tightly closed mouth.

I put a finger to my lips. "But you have to be quiet, Miss Rebecca. And it'd be best if you made yourself scarce."

She jerks her head in my direction, eyes accusing. "I will not leave my baby unattended ever again, boy." She pauses. A flash of anguish darkens her eyes. She looks down at the doll. "I left him once and I'll never forgive myself for what happened."

I stare at her a silent moment and swallow hard, trying to imagine what Miss Rebecca must have felt when she found baby Ford lifeless in his crib. The sound of footsteps on the stairs rouses me out of my grim thoughts.

I touch her arm. "Just for a bit, while I talk to them. I need to explain things to the boy who's about to come through that door. He'll understand. He's really smart."

She trains her cold, dead eyes on me. "No one is allowed in this room. You know that."

"Please, Miss Rebecca," I say. "Give me a few minutes alone to talk with him. Make him understand. I'll get him out of the nursery as fast as I can."

The footsteps land right outside the door, a set of two and a set of four.

"Well," Miss Rebecca says, "I suppose I could give you a few minutes alone with him. But you'll have to keep rocking baby Ford, so he doesn't get fussy."

I stare at her, waiting for her to bust out laughing.

*That was a joke, right?*

She stands and nudges me into the rocking chair, easing the doll down into my arms.

"Watch his head, boy," she snaps.

I place one hand under the back of the doll's head. "Oh, sorry, ma'am."

I can't believe that the first time Thomas is going to see me, I'll be rocking a spider-infested baby doll. It's not exactly how I imagined our first face-to-face meeting would be.

"Just a few minutes, now, you hear me?" Miss Rebecca

points her index finger in my face. "I'll be over in the corner, watching. And you take real good care of my Ford or I'll take a switch to you. Biggest one I can find."

I nod real fast, but I don't say anything, because the doorknob is already turning.

"Hello?" Thomas calls from beyond the door. "Is someone in there? I'm coming in."

I start to panic, because Miss Rebecca is still visible, patting the top of the baby doll's head. I hope that spider is gone. I may be dead, but I hate spiders. She's as good as her word, because the moment the door swings open, Miss Rebecca is nowhere to be seen, at least by the living.

Thomas stands in the open doorway, staring at me, because I let him see me now. And what he sees must look pretty strange to him—a boy about his own age sitting in a rocking chair, holding a busted-up baby doll. Goldie stands next to him, the hairs on her back rising to attention. She growls at me. I think she was just starting to get used to me when I was invisible. But seeing me is a different thing altogether. She calms down at Thomas's touch. He holds on to her collar just in case, and I think that's really nice of him to do. I'm sure Goldie will like me this way just fine once she gets to know me.

"Hello?" Thomas says, like he's asking.

Maybe he doesn't believe his own eyes. I can understand. I realize that a few seconds have passed and I haven't said anything back, which is rude of me.

"Hello," I say finally.

Thomas steps inside the room, still holding on to Goldie's collar with one hand and the recorder with the other, the headphones resting around his neck. "We heard moaning or humming or something. Are you okay?"

I give him my best I-am-not-a-scary-ghost smile. "I'm fine. Thank you for asking. Are you okay?"

His forehead creases. "Um. Yeah. I guess so."

Thomas eases closer, pulling Goldie along with him. She sneezes with her whole head.

"What are you doing here?" Thomas asks. "Are you alone?"

I ignore the second question and answer the first, glancing down at the baby doll and back up. "I was sitting here, rocking and singing."

Another step closer. Another Goldie sneeze.

"We were just looking around. We didn't know anyone else was here." Thomas's eyes linger on the doll a moment. "What's that you have there?"

My cheeks go hot in an instant and I stand. I take the baby doll over to the rickety old crib in the corner of the room. Gently, so Miss Rebecca doesn't get upset, I give the doll a kiss on the forehead before laying it down inside the crib on its back, the way Grandma said you're supposed to. That should make Miss Rebecca happy, but it probably looks real creepy to Thomas. That can't be helped, I guess.

"Are you sure you're not hurt or anything?" Thomas asks.

I stand in front of the window, hands clasped in front me. "Yes, I'm sure, Thomas."

His eyebrows shoot up. "Wait. How do you know my name?"

I panic a little. I don't want Thomas to know I've been spying on them since they got here. He might find that creepy too.

"I heard someone downstairs say that name," I say, hoping that will cover me.

He takes another step in my direction. Goldie seems a bit less agitated now, but when Thomas lets go of her collar, she sits and doesn't come any closer.

"Do you live close by?" Thomas asks.

I think about how to answer that question. Should I say I live *here* at Hollow Pines? I've been here so long—is *this* my home now? I sure don't want it to be. But I guess I waited too long to answer, because Thomas asks me another question.

"What's your name?"

I know it sounds like an easy question, but it really isn't. I'm sure I used to have a name. But I can't for the life of me remember what it is any more than I can remember what happened to Will Perkins.

"I don't have one."

It's the only way I know to answer his question.

"You don't have a name?" Thomas asks, his forehead creasing again.

I shake my head.

He comes closer, only a few steps away now, his eyes trained on me. He fidgets with his hands and scratches the back of his neck as he scans the dusty room. His gaze lingers a little too long on the baby doll in the crib.

"How long have you been here?" Thomas asks, a little more cautiously this time.

I look down at the floor, because I'm embarrassed to give Thomas the same dumb answer a second time. But what else can I say?

"I don't know that either."

Thomas doesn't respond, just stares at me with crinkled eyes and his mouth stretched into a thin, straight line. Goldie swings her big old head back and forth between Thomas and me, a soft whine cradled in the back of her throat. I don't know if it's Goldie's sympathetic whine or the concern brimming in Thomas's half-squinted eyes, but I muster up enough courage to ask Thomas a question that's been nagging at me for a long time. And if I don't ask right now, I might chicken out altogether, because I'm not a hundred percent sure I want to know the answer. But I manage to get it out anyway.

"Thomas," I say. "What year is it?"

–:–

WILL LOOKED UP and spotted Sarah walking toward him across the yard. He was sitting in one of the rubber-seated swings of the old, rusted set in the backyard. His father wouldn't be home for a couple of hours, so he was enjoying the peace and quiet before the storm.

"Hey," Sarah said as she took the swing beside him, tucking one foot under her.

"Hey," he said flatly.

Normally he was always happy to spend time with Sarah, but he really just wanted to be alone. He'd felt that way more and more lately, closing himself off to everyone around him. They sat in silence for a minute, each using a foot to push the swings in a slight rocking motion.

"Want to talk about it?" Sarah asked cautiously, staring straight ahead.

She always knew when something was bothering him. But he didn't want to talk about it. He couldn't. What was he supposed to say to her? That his best friend had betrayed him and his father hits him because he likes boys? And then there was the constant bullying at school, which Sarah had only witnessed once or twice and not during the worst of it by far. No. He'd trusted Ronnie with his secret and look how that had turned out. He wasn't about to make that mistake twice.

"Not really," he said, staring at his own shadow on the ground—the dark and cloudy Will that felt more right than what he saw in the mirror.

"Look," she said. "I know something's been bothering you for a while now. Did something happen at school?" She nodded over to the house. "Or here?"

Will's right cheek stung with the memory of the last time his father slapped him. He never did that when anyone was around, and Will had never told anyone, for fear it would make things worse.

"I said I don't want to talk about it, okay?" Will said, not even trying to mask the irritation in his voice.

He immediately felt bad. Sarah didn't deserve that. But he didn't have the energy to apologize. So he stayed silent, letting his words keep their sharp edges.

Sarah let out a long sigh. "Okay, then." She stood, slipping her fingers into the back pockets of her cutoff denim shorts. "What've you got going on this weekend?"

Her long, wavy blond hair danced in the warm breeze, and Will got a whiff of her shampoo—lavender and lilac.

Will shrugged and looked up at her, the bright spring sun forcing him to squint. "Thought about riding my bike to Hollow Pines maybe."

"By yourself?" she asked, an eyebrow raised.

He nodded. "I've done it before. Lots of times."

Sarah did a little whole-body shiver and shook her head. "You're braver than I am. That place gives me the creeps."

Nobody had ever called him brave before. He didn't feel very brave. If he were brave, he would trust Sarah with his secrets. If he were brave, he would stand up to Frankie Dimery and the others at school. If he were brave, he would tell someone that his father hit him, a lot. But he wasn't brave.

Sarah started walking away backward. "I'm going down to Shannon's. Just be careful out there. Okay?"

"Okay," he said. "I will."

Sarah smiled at him and walked away. Will watched her leave, feeling desperate inside, wishing Sarah knew everything that was going on with him but without him having to tell her. He thought about calling her back, but he didn't. The words were too painful to get out.

# 12

**HEARING THOMAS SAY** what year it is and it starting with the number *two thousand* is too much for my brain to process, I guess, because I really don't hear anything he says after that.

It seems impossible that I've been stuck here at Hollow Pines for fifty years. *Fifty years.* My sister would be in her sixties now. And if I was still part of the living world, I would be too. My sister could still be out there somewhere. Sixty is old, but it's not *that* old. If I could leave Hollow Pines, I still might be able to find her.

Thomas and I stare at each other in silence for I don't know how long. An extended rumble of thunder that goes on forever sounds overhead, like Hollow Pines is reminding us of who's in charge here. But the rain's steady patter on the roof is almost comforting now.

Thomas sits cross-legged on the floor in front of me.

Goldie plops down beside him, resting her head on his knee. She gives me a leery glare, but at least she's not growling at me, or barking at me, or peeing on me. I feel awkward standing now, so I sit too.

Thomas inhales real deep. For the first time, I notice a tiny red light between the two small silver microphones when he presses the center button on the recorder.

"Are you here all alone?" he asks cautiously.

I nod. A lie. But it's better to have him think I was the one making all the racket earlier. Not that you should call Miss Rebecca's humming *racket*. I'll bet she used to sing real nice in her before time. But Hollow Pines has a way of stealing all the joy out of a song, and out of the singer too.

Thomas is still staring like he can't quite figure me out, and I guess that's fair. I mean, he finds a boy alone in the manor house of a deserted rice plantation who says he doesn't know his own name or how long he's been there. But now I know how long—*fifty years*.

"Our bikes," Thomas says. "Was that you?"

I break my gaze on him, hanging my head. I nod. "I'm real sorry."

"But why would you do that?" Thomas asks, with an edge in his voice that stings. "Now we'll have to wait out the storm and walk home, which will take forever. Our parents don't even know where we are. We could get into a lot of trouble."

I could try and explain that I wanted to find out what they knew about Will Perkins, help me fill in the blanks about that day. But then he might figure out that I had something to do with what happened to Will. That I betrayed Will. That I hurt him.

I can't look Thomas in the eye, for fear of giving myself away, and I don't have a good answer for him anyway. Not one that I think he would understand. I keep my eyes glued to Goldie's fat, hairy paws. I really want to reach out and touch them. I haven't felt the silky softness of a dog's fur in I don't know how long—well over fifty years, I reckon. But I don't think Goldie would like the feel of my touch one little bit.

"What's *Finding Will?*" I finally ask, changing the subject.

Thomas stares blankly at me. "Huh?"

I nod to the recorder. "You keep talking into that thing and saying *Finding Will.*"

Thomas looks down at the recorder like he's been caught red-handed. "Oh. That's the Tascam—it's a digital recorder." His voice has lost the edge it had before. "My friends and I are making a podcast for a school project."

He must be able to tell from the look on my face that I don't know the word.

"It's sort of like a radio show," Thomas explains. "Except it's not on the radio—it's on the internet. And you can download episodes to your phone or whatever. Our podcast is called *Finding Will.* It's about a boy who disappeared a long time ago. His name was Will Perkins."

Thomas looks at me as if waiting for me to say something. I don't. I want to ask, *What's the internet?* But he mentioned it so casually, like it's something living folks should know about. He might get suspicious if I ask what it is.

"Have you ever heard of him?" Thomas asks. "Will Perkins?"

I hate lying to Thomas. "No."

He lets out a little defeated sigh. "A lot of people don't know about him. Or they've forgotten. That's why we're doing this podcast. To bring attention back to his case."

"His case?" I ask cautiously. "Like a police case?"

Thomas nods. "Yeah, it's called a *cold case*, because the police never found Will or figured out what happened to him."

That's a really nice thing the visitors are doing for Will. But the last thing I want is for people to find out my part in all of it.

Footsteps drum up the stairs, stopping on the landing.

"T?" Maya whispers from out in the hall. "Thomas."

"It's okay," he calls back in a normal volume. "I'm in here."

Within seconds, the twins are standing in the open doorway of the nursery, Maya holding the chair leg like a baseball bat and Mateo beside her holding out a Swiss Army knife, every tool in it splayed open, from the can opener to the corkscrew.

"Dude, who the heck is that?" Mateo asks, pointing at me with his tiny weapon.

Thomas gets up off the floor and goes over to them. Goldie stays behind, probably to keep an eye on me.

She rests her head on the floor and just stares up at me like she doesn't know what to make of me. I guess I can understand that.

"I don't know," Thomas says. "I found him in here. He was the one humming earlier." Thomas glances over his shoulder at me and back to Maya and Mateo. "He says he doesn't know how he got here or how long he's been here."

I never said I don't remember *how* I got here. I came the same way they did—on a bike. They walk over to me guardedly, Maya and Mateo, still holding their weapons out in front of them like I'm dangerous or something.

"Did he hit his head?" Maya asks.

Her baggy *Born This Way* T-shirt is finally dry, and her hair looks a lot fluffier now.

"Did you hit your head?" Thomas asks me, like he's translating Maya's question, but I understood her fine since she said it in English and not Spanish.

I shake my head as a flash of lightning fills the room. Only a few seconds pass before a clap of thunder follows.

"Do you have amnesia?" Mateo asks me in a whisper—like *amnesia* is a bad word that needs to be whispered. It's not. People got it all the time in Grandma's afternoon stories on the television.

I shake my head again. Then wonder if maybe I *do* have amnesia. But I don't think lost souls can get such a thing. I just can't remember some stuff.

Maya lowers her chair-leg club. "Does he talk or just hum?"

She says it kind of bossy. But I don't think she's trying to be mean.

Thomas sits on the floor in front of me again, setting the Tascam down between us. Maya and Mateo sit on either side of him. I feel like I'm on trial and they're the jury. Thomas turns the recorder on again.

"Is it okay if we interview you for our podcast?" he asks.

I think it's real nice of Thomas to ask, even though he didn't before. I nod, but then realize nodding doesn't work too well for tape recorders, which I guess is what the Tascam sort of is.

"It's okay," I say, leaning forward a little to make sure the thing heard me.

Thomas nods and then says clearly and slowly in his serious newscaster voice, "We're here with . . . a kid we came across inside the manor house, in the nursery on the second floor. He doesn't appear to be injured, but he can't remember his name or how long he's been here at Hollow Pines. We don't recognize him from our neighborhood. The boy has agreed to let us interview him for *Finding Will.*"

Thomas looks me in the eye. "So, can you tell us what're you doing here?"

"I live here."

My throat tightens around the words as the truth behind them lands on me like a ton of bricks.

"By myself," I add, and I feel bad for lying about that part a second time.

They exchange quick glances. I can't tell what they're thinking. I've never talked like this with any visitors before. It's like they're having a whole conversation with just their eyes—a conversation that I'm not a part of. I'm not too good at reading people's faces.

"So, are you, like, homeless or something?" Mateo finally asks.

Thomas knocks Mateo with his elbow. "Dude."

"What?" Mateo says. "It's a perfectly good question."

Maya says, "Don't be rude, little brother."

The visitors all stare at me, Thomas the hardest—like he's searching my face the same way I've been searching his. I wonder if he finds something familiar about me the same way I do about him. I can't hold his gaze for too long, so I glance down at his jeans with the neatly placed raggedy holes, like they're meant to be there or some such.

"What do you mean, you *live here?*" Thomas asks. "Did you run away?"

I glance back up at him, not sure if I should tell them the truth or not—about knowing Will Perkins, or about what happened to him. I'm sure they would like to have a firsthand account for their podcast.

Thomas lets out a disappointed sigh when I don't answer him, but his eyes are so chock-full of kindness that I can't stop myself from smiling at him.

"Look, we're just trying to help you," he says, a concerned look on his face. "That's all. You can tell us."

I look at each of them. And I believe him, that they want to help me. I hope they can.

"I can't leave," I say, like that should explain everything.

"What do you mean you *can't* leave?" Mateo asks.

It's a fair question but not an easy one to answer. And Grandma always said, *Fair and easy are two entirely different things.* But I know I'm not making a whole mess of sense to them. I know it would help if I just came out and told the visitors that I'm not part of the living world anymore. But how do you say something like that to people you just met?

"I don't know," I say.

It's kind of true, because I don't rightly know *why* I can't leave Hollow Pines. Just that I can't.

The visitors are back to staring at me and silently exchanging glances with one another. A sudden surge of rain pounds the roof, and the wind forces The Reaper to scrape its sprawling limbs against the windowpanes like some kind of tree monster trying to get inside the house.

Something changes in Thomas's eyes, almost like a light goes on in them. He touches Maya and Mateo on the arm. "Hey, guys, can I talk to you outside a second?"

They look confused, but they get up anyway.

"We'll be right back, okay?" he says to me in a soothing tone.

I notice him glance down at the recorder, but he doesn't move to pick it up, and the red light stays on.

"Okay," I say.

Mateo and Maya follow Thomas out the door. Goldie stays behind to keep me company, which I think is nice of her. Thomas pops his head back in, grabs the knob, and pulls the door closed behind him. Then the whispering starts, the voices rushed and tense. I don't go to the door to try and listen, because that would be rude and I'm trying real hard not to be a Nose-ella.

But I do make out a *You can't be serious* and a *What if* and a *That's insane, Thomas.* And then I hear one thing clear as a bell—a name. It opens up some hidden doorway in the back of my brain, knocking the wind right out of me.

*Ronnie Cribb.*

# 13

THE VISITORS ARE still out in the hall, whispering, and I'm still sitting on the floor, rolling the name over in my head.

Ronnie Cribb.

It's as familiar to me as the names Will Perkins and Frankie Dimery. For some reason, though, this name—Ronnie Cribb—was buried even deeper in my brain. I don't know why, but the sound of it in my ears rattles something deep inside me.

Goldie sits staring at me, her head cocked in that curious look that dogs are sometimes known to give. She whines a little, like she can hear my thoughts. Actually, her laser-like stare is making me a little uncomfortable, so I get up and go over to the crib to check on baby Ford. I pat the doll's head and make a few cooing noises. It's all for show so Miss Rebecca doesn't think I'm not taking care of her baby like she told me to. She's watching me from the corner of the room. She's been here the whole time, but the visitors don't know, because they can't see her. I can tell by the anxious look in her eyes that she's itching to get back to tending baby Ford herself. I need to get the visitors downstairs before she can't control herself any longer.

I walk over to the door, just about to open it, when I hear them again, clear as day.

"Okay, I think you have officially lost it, dude," Mateo says, not even whispering anymore.

"Wait," Maya says. "Let me get this straight. You're saying you think we were just in there talking to a ghost?"

I freeze, as if they'd caught me listening. But mostly because they've already figured out at least one of my secrets.

Someone makes a shushing noise—Thomas, I think.

"He doesn't look like a ghost," Mateo says. "He looks like a kid. Just like us. Though his clothes do have kind of a retro vibe. But that doesn't prove he's a ghost."

I feel bad for eavesdropping, but it's hard not to when they're talking so loudly.

"And how would you know what a ghost is supposed to look like?" Thomas asks.

"Okay. Solid point," Mateo says. "But I still think we should get out of here. Like now."

I move across the room to the window and look out. It's still windy and rainy, but the lightning has stopped for the moment. It must be early afternoon now, but I can't be sure, the way the sky looks. If I'm right, in a few hours the sun will go down. But right now, the storm clouds still hang fat and low in the sky, making it look later in the day than it probably is. One thing is for sure, though—Live Oak Lane looks like one long swamp full of quicksand. So it stands to reason that Hollow Pines Road does too.

"Let's just ask him," Thomas says, nearly at shouting level.

Goldie scrambles to all fours and goes over to the door, sniffing at the bottom of it.

"Maybe I don't care, and we need to get out of here," Mateo says, the volume of his voice rising to meet Thomas's.

"Mateo, calm down," Maya says.

"Don't tell me to calm down," Mateo shoots back. "You're always telling me to calm down. It's not that easy sometimes, okay?"

I pick up the handheld recorder on my way back across the room. When I pull open the door, they all jump a little. Mateo even lets out a little high-pitched yelp.

"Sorry," I say. "I didn't mean to scare you." After Goldie trots out of the nursery, I close the door behind her and give the Tascam back to Thomas. "We should go downstairs now. The baby is sleeping."

I don't know why I said it, other than I needed to find an excuse to get them out of the nursery and back downstairs. But I'm sure it sounded weird. The visitors all look at me differently from how they did before, with a whole lot more suspicion. Even fear. It's not a good feeling.

I smile real big at them, hoping that helps, and head down the staircase, also hoping that they'll just follow me without any questions. At first, they're silent, but then they fall in behind me. I try to make my footsteps as normal as a living boy's would be, because I don't want to freak them out any more than I already have. I don't really have to touch the ground to walk, but it creeps me out when I see some of the other lost souls floating above it, like Miss Rebecca. I prefer the old-fashioned way.

I lead the visitors back into the front room. The fire lights the space with a flickering golden haze. Mateo goes right over to the window, I guess to check the weather. Thomas and Maya stand in front of me, Thomas with wonder-filled eyes like I'm Santa Claus or some such, and Maya still holding the chair leg at her side, eyeing me with a healthy dose of suspicion.

"So, what was the last show you watched on TV?" Maya asks, arms crossed and shoulders squared.

That's easy.

"The *CBS Evening News with Walter Cronkite*," I say.

"Who the heck is Walter Cronkite?" Mateo says, joining us.

I gasp a little without meaning to. "He's only the most trusted man in America."

There's a little sass in my voice that I didn't mean to put there. But, come on, who in the world doesn't know who Mr. Walter Cronkite is? Then I remember fifty years have passed. *Fifty years!* Of course they're not going to know who Walter Cronkite is.

"Or, he was, at least," I add.

"What's your favorite song?" Maya asks, one eye kind of squinting.

Another easy one.

"'Easy Come, Easy Go,'" I say proudly.

The song instantly makes me think of Will. He loved that song. The visitors stare at me like they've never heard of it.

"Bobby Sherman?" I say, but I can tell that the name doesn't mean anything to them either. "You know, 'Little Woman'? 'Julie, Do Ya Love Me'?"

Still nothing.

"You've never heard of Bobby Sherman?" I ask.

Thomas shrugs. Maya and Mateo shake their heads. Wow. I can't believe the visitors have never heard of him. Even though fifty years have passed, some singers deserve to be remembered forever—like Elvis Presley, Frank Sinatra, and Bobby Sherman.

Thomas steps forward. "Wait, who was the president of the United States when you came here?"

"Richard Milhous Nixon," I say confidently.

Of course I know that. I even did a report on him in school not long before I came here to Hollow Pines for the last time. The assignment was on modern-day American heroes.

They pass funny glances around from one to another,

but Thomas looks satisfied enough with my answer. Maya looks even leerier of me now, and Mateo looks like he doesn't know what to think. Goldie sniffs my butt. I think *she's* warming up to me, at least.

Mateo reaches his hand out to me cautiously, like he's going to touch me, but also like he's sticking his hand right into a fire. I step back, because he's already scared of me, and I don't want to make it worse.

"Oh," he says. "Sorry. I guess I should have asked."

I don't know what to say to that and I'm kind of embarrassed, so I don't say anything. I think it's time to just *show* them what I am.

I walk over and pick up the broom, which is lying on the floor. I stand in front of them, holding the broom in both hands, parallel with the floor.

"Try not to be scared," I say calmly.

"Scared of what?" Maya snaps back.

Then I show them.

# 14

"OH, BOY! WHEW! Boy!"

That's what Mr. Walter Cronkite said on the *CBS Evening News* on July 20, 1969, when he showed me and the whole entire country live video of the *Eagle* spacecraft landing on the moon with Mr. Neil Armstrong and Mr. Buzz Aldrin tucked away inside. I remember because it was my eleventh birthday. I was pretty excited about the whole thing, because I thought maybe Mr. Armstrong and Mr. Aldrin would find Will Robinson and his family out there in space somewhere and finally bring them home safe. But Grandma reminded me that *Lost in Space* was a made-up show and that the moon landing was happening in real life. When that really sank in, I repeated what Mr. Walter Cronkite had just said right there on the television.

"Oh, boy! Whew! Boy!"

That's what I imagine the visitors are thinking right now. Because I just made myself invisible, but not the broom.

Mateo lets out another high-pitched yelp. Maya jumps back, slapping a hand over her mouth. Goldie drops into a crouch, growling like she's going to attack the broom floating in midair, I guess. Thomas's eyes widen and a grin curls his lips like he's just seen the coolest magic trick in the world, which I guess it kind of is.

"Whoa," Thomas whispers.

He reaches out to grab the broom and I let him take it from me. He holds it at arm's length, staring at it, repeating the *whoa*. He's acting like the broom did the cool magic trick and not me, but he can't see me right now, so I guess that's fair.

Mateo keeps inching away from me. I let them see me again and their reactions are about the same as when I disappeared. Goldie tucks her tail between her hind legs and hurries off into the dining room. None of them say anything, and it's starting to feel awkward. I hope I didn't just make a huge mistake.

"I don't believe it," Maya says with a stutter. "It can't be real. We can't be standing here talking to a ghost." She looks at Mateo and Thomas. "Can we?"

I think I really spooked her, which I feel bad about. But at least now she believes me, even though she just said she doesn't. It's funny how people say *I don't believe it* at the exact moment when they finally do.

Thomas doesn't waste another minute on the proving-

I'm-a-ghost show. He turns the recorder on and holds it in front of me.

"You said upstairs that you can't leave Hollow Pines. What did you mean by that?"

I shrug. "Whenever I try to leave, past the stone columns, I'll walk through but then find myself walking right back into the plantation. Same with the woods around Hollow Pines. I walk away from the plantation through the tree line, and when I come out, I'm right back where I started."

"So, you're what?" Maya asks. "Like trapped here or something?"

I nod but then remember the recorder and lean into the microphone a little. "Yes. That is exactly what I am. Trapped."

I hope that sounded professional.

"Well, that sucks," Mateo says, slowly recovering from his shock.

"Yes," I say for the recorder. "That's what it does."

"Do you know *why* you're stuck here?" Maya asks, keeping her distance.

I think about that for a moment. The truth is, I'm not sure of anything when it comes to being stuck here. The other lost souls don't really discuss it with me, though I get the feeling they have their theories. But we're all still stuck, so I guess nobody has the *right* theory.

"I've been trying to figure that out for fifty years," I say to Maya.

A sad smile takes hold of Thomas's face. But then his expression changes altogether on a dime.

"Wait," he says. "The last president you remember is Richard Nixon, and he was president in the early seventies. Will disappeared in 1971. You look about the same age as he would have been. Are you sure you didn't know him?"

I take a deep breath. I don't think I can keep the lying up. The visitors are too smart. Plus, if it helps me leave this place, I guess I'll have to face up to what I did. Eventually. If I'm able to jar those memories loose.

I hang my head. "Yeah, I knew Will. Sorry I lied about that."

Thomas looks confused. So I share a little bit more.

"I was here," I say. "That day."

The stunned look on their faces spooks me a little, making me wish I could take the words back immediately.

Thomas swallows hard, pushing the Tascam in my face. "Um . . . okay . . . wow. Just to be clear, are you saying we're interviewing an eyewitness to what happened to Will Perkins the day he disappeared?"

"I guess so," I say with a shrug. "Sort of."

Maya narrows her eyes at me. I don't think she believes me yet, believes anything about me. Her brother is shifting, though. I can see the curiosity in his eyes—that he wants to know more.

"Maybe it would help to tell your story, about what happened that day," Thomas says, holding the recorder even closer to me. "Help you move on, or something, I mean. That's what you want, right?"

I stare at Thomas's familiar eyes and then down at the recorder. I wonder if he's right. I thought maybe just remembering might do the trick. But what if I need to *tell my story*, confess to my part in all of it? Maybe that's what will help me finally leave this place once and for all.

I've never told anyone about what happened that day— the other lost souls, I mean—because I've been burying those memories, and my guilt along with them, for what I now know has been fifty years. I don't know if I can, though. Confess, that is. I don't even know exactly what I would be confessing to. I have to remember first. But I know it must be something terrible—what I did. What would the visitors think of me if they knew the truth? What would the whole world think of me? What if my sister ever heard this podcast? What would she think of me? But if I'd finally be able to leave this place, to move on for good, to be free, it would be worth it. Right?

"I don't remember a lot about that day," I say to Thomas and the Tascam. "That's the God's honest truth, I promise. I heard you talking about Will Perkins when you got here, and I thought maybe you knew some things that could help me remember. That's why I've been following you around all day."

"All day?" Maya says sharply, a hand planted on her hip. "Okay, I'm sorry. That is too creepy."

Mateo says, "Yep, got to agree with sis on that one. Way creepy, dude."

"I'm sorry," I say, hoping they'll forgive me. But it *is* kind of creepy, now that I think about it.

Thomas doesn't seem bothered at all. "So, what *do* you remember?"

I take a deep breath. "All I remember is being here that day. And that something bad happened to Will Perkins. And it happened over at the old winnowing barn."

I left out the confession part on purpose—that I was responsible in some way for what happened to Will. My mouth is having a hard time saying it *on the record*, as Walter Cronkite used to say on the *CBS Evening News*.

Thomas squints his eyes at me. "The winnowing barn?"

He looks over at Maya. She shrugs at him.

"There wasn't anything in the sheriff's report about a winnowing barn," she says.

Thomas looks down, shaking his head.

I look back and forth between Maya and Thomas, hoping they have more facts than I do to share.

"Guys," Mateo says, fear raising the timbre of his voice. "What is that?"

We all look over to find Mateo backing away from the wall and into the center of the room, his index finger pointing to a dark corner where there is movement. The shadows are following him.

I've been so distracted that I haven't been keeping an eye on them. And I didn't even notice that the fire has died down to almost nothing. I check the corners of the room and find shadows slithering toward us from all directions. Goldie lunges at them, a chilling growl erupting from the depths of her chest, but there's nothing she can do to stop them.

"What is happening?" Maya says, alarm rising in her voice as she takes in the shadows advancing on them.

Snakelike extensions of the shadows form, boldly striking at the heels of the visitors. They manage to dodge the attacks, panicked yelps flowing freely from their mouths.

A door slams upstairs and we all jump. Even Goldie is momentarily distracted from the shadows, her attention and her ears pointing upward.

Thomas looks back to me, his breath short and his chest heaving. "You said you were here by yourself."

I stare blankly back at him. There's no time to explain now.

A woman's shrill scream fills the house. It's so loud that Mateo buckles, covering his ears. Maya's eyes are wide, her mouth hanging open as she stares up to the ceiling. I've heard that scream before. It was Miss Rebecca. And there's only ever one reason for it—Culpepper's in the house.

"We have to get out of here," I say in an urgent whisper. "Now!"

–:–

WILL HAD ONLY just ridden past the stone columns of the old entrance gates and rolled into the old slave village of

Hollow Pines when he spotted them. Two boys over in the field at the winnowing barn. They were too far away for him to see their faces, but he recognized the mass of straw-colored hair of the taller one right away. It was Ronnie. So the other boy had to be Frankie Dimery, because ever since Ronnie had joined the football team, you never saw one without the other. That's the way Will and Ronnie used to be, and it pained Will to his bones to watch Ronnie and Frankie cutting up together over there, doubled over laughing, throwing their arms around each other.

It made Will heartsick for his former best friend. In that moment, Will would have forgiven Ronnie for everything—telling Frankie his secret, standing by silently while Frankie and his teammates called Will the most awful names and while they shoved Will around on the schoolyard. And even, lately, joining in on the teasing himself, which hurt Will the most—to hear those words coming from Ronnie's mouth directed at him.

*Sissy.*

*Homo.*

*Queer.*

But he knew he would forgive Ronnie if he asked. Anything to get his friend back. He still hoped it was possible.

Will didn't want to be there anymore. This was not going to be the peace and quiet he was looking for, so he turned his bike around. But before he started pedaling back the way he'd come, he heard his name being called from over at the winnowing barn, Ronnie's voice echoing across the field. Will's heart almost burst out of his chest at the sound of it. He'd heard Ronnie call out his name so many times when they used to be friends—that crack of joy in his voice when Ronnie had called out to him in the hallway in elementary school, or in the cafeteria, or when they ran into each other unexpectedly at the Five & Dime in town. Will couldn't resist it.

He looked over their way, shielding his eyes from the blinding sun. He spotted Ronnie in the distance, waving him over with one hand, then two. And then Frankie waved him over. They were both smiling. Friendly-looking, even.

Will bit down on his lower lip. That always seemed to help him decide what to do when he was confused. At first, Will didn't trust the invitation. Why should he, after all Frankie had put him through at school this year? But what if they wanted to apologize? What if they really did just want to hang out? Being way out here, far away from school, where Frankie was always showing off for his friends, Will didn't see him as the same threat somehow.

So Will decided to give them a chance, and turned his bike toward the winnowing barn.

# 15

**A WRITHING MASS** of shadows has blocked our path to the front door.

As frightened as the visitors are right now, seeing normal shadows moving in such abnormal and aggressive ways, they don't have any idea how dangerous the things really are. The shadow snakes are part of Culpepper's dark army, and they've been roused into battle by his presence in the house.

"Don't let them touch you," I call out.

"Why?" Thomas calls back urgently. "What can they do?"

"Just trust me!"

I look over at Mateo standing beside me. His breathing is shallow, and the color has drained from his face, but not by the grip of a shadow snake. His eyes are hazy, like he's having trouble focusing or like he might pass out. His sister holds on to his arm, and Thomas holds on to hers.

I run and sail over the shadow snakes blocking our exit.

"Jump over them," I yell back at the visitors. And then to the dog, "Come on, Goldie!"

They follow my commands without question, Goldie leading the charge with two decisive barks. She runs in my direction and leaps over the shadows, but they don't seem all that interested in her. Thomas and Maya help Mateo into position. His breathing still labored, he stumbles a little. He locks his gaze on me. Letting go of Thomas and Maya, he takes a few quick strides in my direction. A shadow snake coils in front of him, striking just as Mateo jumps. The thing misses his foot only by a couple of inches. He makes it over with a messy landing.

Thomas and Maya hold hands. They're going to go together, and it's a good thing, because the shadows are closing in. They run and jump. Thomas makes it over. So does Maya. But she lands too close to the border of shadows. One of them reaches out, snatching her ankle and coiling around it. The thing jerks her downward. She lands hard on her stomach, losing her grip on Thomas's hand. She immediately starts clawing at the wood floor as the shadow slowly drags her back into the front room by her ankle. She opens her mouth to scream, but nothing comes out. Her face is a mask of terror as she looks up at us, her eyes pleading.

Thomas and Mateo lunge for her, each grabbing a hand and trying desperately to pull her back into the foyer. They don't gain any ground at all, as now a second shadow snake coils around Maya's other ankle. A wave of panic rolls over me. I have no idea what to do. I can't help the boys pull Maya free. Me touching her would just make things worse. I watch her eyes closely. They're beginning to gray. Thomas and Mateo probably don't even notice it, but a tiny bit of her soul is already gone.

Goldie hasn't stopped barking and jumping around since the shadow snakes began their attack, and now it's like she's barking orders at the boys about how to save their friend. Finally, Maya starts moving in the right direction. Thomas and Mateo scoot backward on their butts, using their whole bodies in the struggle. But they don't give an inch of the ground they've gained. Their faces strained and sweating, they pull with everything they have.

Finally, Maya rockets forward, the shadow snakes losing their grip on her ankles. They all scramble to their feet, though Maya is moving a little slower than usual.

I lead them through the front door and out into the storm. Or, I guess I should say, away from one storm and right into the middle of another. But I'll take nature's fury over Culpepper's and his dark army of shadows any day of the week. I just need to get the visitors somewhere safe.

The Reaper stands its ground, facing down the storm, branches snapping violently back and forth, slinging gobs of soaking Spanish moss here and there. The rain has turned the sandy yard into a swampy mush. Goldie and Thomas run beside me, the boy's shoes sinking and then rising from the soggy ground with each step. Like two big suction cups trying desperately to keep hold of the earth. Or like Hollow Pines trying to pull him down to hell.

The rain seems to have picked up since the moment we left the manor house. Thunder growls at us from above. Lightning brightens the dim sky, not with violent streaks anymore, but with quick, stuttered whole-sky flashes. Like the world's light bulb is dying and will soon leave us altogether.

I guide the visitors across the yard to the schoolhouse, because it's the closest building to the manor house. I'm sure Teacherman won't mind us hiding out there for a while. Plus, he knows Jackson Culpepper the Third better than most, himself once the target of Culpepper's rage and retribution.

"Where are we going?" Thomas shouts at me through a thick wall of wind and rain.

I look over at him, resisting the urge to grab his arm and pull him along faster. I point to the small brick structure in our path. Goldie trots ahead, bounding up the few steps. She waits for us on the porch of the schoolhouse, shaking the rain loose from her matted fur. The visitors scramble up the steps and take a second to catch their breath. Mateo leans forward, hands on his knees and chest heaving. He takes his time inhaling for a few seconds. He holds his breath a few seconds more, and then exhales. Maya pats his back, coaching him with soothing words. Her face has regained its color and her eyes are back to normal. The shadows didn't have hold of her long enough to do any lasting damage, I don't think. If they'd had her longer, they could have drained her of her soul entirely if that's what Culpepper commanded them to do.

"What were those things?" Thomas raises his voice enough to be heard over the noise of the wind, the rain, and the rumbles of thunder.

His chest rises and falls like his next breath might be his last.

"I call them shadow snakes," I tell him.

The visitors stare blankly at me.

"They're soul-stealers," I say flatly.

Thomas leans in. "They *steal* souls? How is that even possible?"

Maya hugs herself. "I felt them." Her voice is small. "I don't know how, but I felt them inside me. Like they were crawling around under my skin."

I nod at her. "They're a part of Culpepper, his darkness. Remnants of souls he's stolen over the years. They're bound to him. Like prisoners."

"Culpepper?" Mateo says.

I look back toward the manor house, feeling exposed. We've been out here too long. Goldie looks up at me with a cocked head and a little whine, like she agrees.

"We need to go inside," I say, with a hand on the doorknob.

"Wait—who was that screaming in the house?" Thomas asks, his voice raised and pitched higher.

"You said you were alone," Maya adds sharply. "You lied to us. Were you the one who slashed our tires too?"

Thomas looks from her to me. He already knows about the tires, and maybe he feels guilty for not telling Maya and Mateo. But I don't know what to say. I guess it's obvious to them now that I'm the one who did it.

Mateo looks up at me again. His eyes grow cold and angry as he glares at me. "You did that?" He straightens his spine as he takes one more deep breath through his nose. His lower lip trembles as he exhales through his mouth. "Why would you do that? Now we're stuck here. And there's someone inside that house. Maybe more than one someone. And are you even real or not?"

That last question surprises me. It stings a little too.

*Am I real or not?*

The thing is, I guess I don't really know the answer. So I don't say anything at all. And we don't have time for this anyway.

I push through the door, waving Goldie and the human visitors into the schoolhouse. Even though I don't think they trust me now, they hurry inside anyway, and I close the door behind us. Teacherman is there, as always. He's calmly writing dates on the blackboard. Looks like dates of wars or some such. Teacherman likes to teach about wars. He always says there's a lot to learn from wars, but that doesn't make any sense to me. Seems like the only thing we should learn from wars is not to have them.

"Ah," he says before turning around, already visible to the living. He prefers that state of being. "Lessons aren't until tomorrow, boy, but if you are so eager to learn,

I suppose we should put that curiosity to good use."

He places the chalk on the ridge at the bottom of the blackboard and turns to face us. He takes us all in, one by one. Goldie inches over to him, sniffs his hand, and sneezes.

"Goldie," Thomas calls to her.

She trots obediently back to him and sits at his side.

"Um . . . who is that?" Mateo says with a shaky voice.

At least his breathing is back to normal and the color has returned to his face. Maya stares at Teacherman like he has three heads. I walk up to the front of the class and stand beside him.

"This here is Teacherman," I say, like that should be the most obvious thing in the world.

I realize that I don't know his real name. Never had a need to know it. The lost souls around here have always just called him Teacherman, and I never thought to ask him.

"These are my new friends, sir," I say, all respectful-like. "Thomas, Maya, Mateo, and the dog's name is Goldie."

Teacherman strokes his pointy chin with his thumb and index finger. "I see."

The visitors don't move an inch. I know they're wondering if Teacherman is like me, even though they probably already suspect that he is. Why else would a teacher in old-timey-looking clothes be holding classes on a deserted plantation on a Saturday in the middle of a storm? I remember how strange I thought it all was, too, when I first came to be stuck here.

"Sir," I say, "Culpepper is about. I'm afraid he might be after the visitors."

That draws the attention of Thomas, Maya, and Mateo. They stare at me, eyes wide and tinged with fear.

"Who is Culpepper?" Thomas asks, a hint of irritation in his voice.

"And what do you mean, *after us?*" Mateo adds.

I sigh. "Jackson Culpepper the Third. He was once the owner of Hollow Pines. Now he's a dark spirit who preys on the living."

The visitors stare back at me. I can see on their faces that they're trying their best to process what I'm saying. But I know that to them it doesn't make a lick of sense. It didn't to me at first either.

"What does he want with us?" Maya asks a little timidly, hugging herself tight, as if she can still feel the shadow snakes crawling around inside her.

I glance up at Teacherman. He has a pained look on his face, and he doesn't offer me any help in explaining this to them. So I look back at the visitors.

"He collects souls," I say, an air of defeat in my voice that I didn't mean to put there. "He's especially fond of the souls of children. His son died when he was just a baby. Culpepper kind of lost it after that. He uses the shadow snakes to steal the souls and then he feeds on them. That's why he's so powerful."

Teacherman looks down his long, thin nose at me. "Miss Rebecca? Is she all right?"

I shrug, because I don't rightly know why Miss Rebecca

screamed earlier or if she's all right now or not. Culpepper has the power to wring a lost soul's spirit out like a dish rag, twisting and twisting until you're choking on all the sadness and bad memories of your time in the living world. He hasn't done it to me—yet—but it sounds just terrible. That could be why Miss Rebecca screamed. He's made her relive the moment she found baby Ford dead in his crib over and over again. Evil always preys on the weakest.

Teacherman nods once, looking at the door. "And these friends of yours? Have they met Culpepper yet?"

"No, sir," I say, shaking my head.

Teacherman rubs his chin like he's deep in thought. "Well, he doesn't *usually* darken my door, so you should all be safe here for the moment."

"*Usually?*" Mateo's voice cracks on the word.

Maya shushes him. She's back to herself now. So is Mateo. Thomas is still quiet, though.

"Thank you," I say.

Teacherman gives me a tight smile and a quick nod. "So, Battle of Hastings, boy?"

Teacherman can't help himself. He has to quiz me every time he sees me. But I also get the feeling he's trying to calm us down, distract us. And I think that's real nice of him.

"That would be 1066, sir," I say.

"The Battle of Waterloo?" he snaps back.

"The Battle of Waterloo was in 1815," I say, eyeing the door, hoping Teacherman is right about Jackson Culpepper not darkening it.

"And when was the Treaty of Paris signed?" Teacherman asks.

"September 1783," I answer confidently.

The visitors look back and forth between me and Teacherman. I guess this all seems pretty weird to them. But this is just normal Teacherman stuff.

"Excuse me, sir," I say to Teacherman. "But my friends are working on a school project of their own."

That seems to shake Thomas out of his stupor. He steps forward, kind of bowing a little to Teacherman.

"Yes, sir," he says, and then nods over at me. "We'd like to interview him some more. If you don't mind us taking up your time."

Teacherman narrows his eyes at Thomas, exhaling slowly. "Is that right? Well, I suppose that would be acceptable." He looks back at me, a haze of unease tinting his eyes. "But keep your voices down."

"Yes, sir," I say with a respectful nod.

I wave the visitors over to some old wooden desks in the front of the classroom. They all take seats, Thomas placing the Tascam recorder on top of his desk. I stand in front of Thomas, Maya, and Mateo. Thomas points one of the little silver microphones on top of the recorder in my direction and the other back at himself. Teacherman leans in cautiously to inspect the Tascam. Then he retreats to the blackboard, watching us closely. Goldie plops down on the floor at my feet with a weary groan, but it's nice that she chose a spot closer to me than anyone else. Another clap of thunder sounds outside. The wind rattles through the few remaining windowpanes, like chattering teeth. Goldie lifts her head to check out the noise and then lays it back down on the floor.

When the Tascam's red light comes on, I speak up before Thomas has a chance to ask me a question.

"You mentioned a name earlier," I say anxiously, not knowing how much time we have before Culpepper finds us. "Ronnie Cribb."

Thomas shares a look with Maya and Mateo that I can't read.

"Yeah," Thomas says. "Ronnie Cribb was here with Frankie Dimery the day Will disappeared."

The name Ronnie Cribb feels so familiar rolling around in my head, but I can't put my finger on why it feels so familiar. Memories start bubbling up to the surface of my brain as I ponder the names over and over.

*Will Perkins.*

*Frankie Dimery.*

*Ronnie Cribb.*

"You said something about a winnowing barn." Thomas with the newscaster voice is back in action. "What happened there?"

"I can't remember," I say, shaking my head. "Not everything, I mean. Just that I was there when Will Perkins died."

The word *died* fell out of my mouth before I had a chance to stop it. Before I even knew it was rising in my throat. Another bit of memory was loosed, and one I can't fully explain. I feel Teacherman's eyes boring into the side of my head. I turn to meet his gaze, but his face is like stone.

"Wait," Maya says, not letting me get away with my slipup. "The sheriff told us that a body was never found. How are you so sure Will died?"

Avoiding their eyes, I stare at the floor and stay quiet. But her words rattle something loose deep inside me.

*A body was never found.*

How could that be? I was there. And now I remember that Will died somehow because of me. A sudden wave of sadness washes over me as the memories buried deep in my brain fight to free themselves. Will never did anything to me, but I turned on him because I was scared. He didn't deserve that. He didn't deserve to die. He had his whole life ahead of him and I somehow robbed him of that. I stay quiet, hoping they will just drop it, so I don't have to say the words out loud that I now know are true, even if I don't remember the details. Maya won't let it go, though.

"How do you know he died?" she asks, louder and more impatiently now.

I look up at the visitors. They're all staring at me, waiting for me to say something. So is Teacherman. They're all so still it doesn't even look like they're breathing. And I can tell they're not going to let this go. So I take a deep breath and let it out slowly like Mateo was doing before.

"I know he died," I say finally, "because I killed him."

# 16

THE DOOR OF the schoolhouse crashes open, interrupting the painful memories and the story I was telling the visitors. The wind sails in through the gaping door, filling the room with a putrid, suffocating blast of air. Shadow snakes spill in, slithering in all directions. Maya, Mateo, and Thomas scramble out of their seats and we all crowd behind Teacherman at the blackboard. Goldie crouches in front of us, hair rising along her spine and a ferocious bark filling her throat as she snaps at the approaching shadows. Heavy footfalls sound on the porch, silencing Goldie on a dime. She whimpers, sidling up to Thomas protectively. The shadow snakes retreat to the corners of the room as quickly as they'd charged in.

And then, he's there—filling the doorway with his wide frame, his air of dread, and his murderous scowl— Jackson Culpepper the Third. His appearance matches his sour soul. His rotted, decaying flesh hangs from his bones like moldy, wet laundry. His vacant eye sockets are dark, but I know he can see us just fine, eyeballs or no eyeballs. His nose is gone too, and all that's left is a gaping, ragged hole in the center of his face. One ear hangs loose, making his already freakish face seem lopsided.

He's wearing the same filthy, threadbare black suit he always wears—his clothes ravaged by time the same way his face, hands, and body have been. He looks like he's been decomposing in a grave somewhere since leaving the living world, his rot revealing grim new designs every time I see him. But the most chilling thing of all is what hangs at his side, and the sight of it causes my frayed breath to catch in my throat. Culpepper grips the handle tight in his right hand—his gator-hunting ax.

The visitors don't make a sound, but their shallowed breathing tells me all I need to know about how they're feeling. They are terrified. Culpepper has that effect on the living—and the dead, too, if I'm being honest. I mean, he can't hurt us lost souls, not physically anyway. But that doesn't make him any less horrifying.

Teacherman clears his throat, probably so it won't crack when his fear betrays him. "Culpepper, you have no business here. Leave immediately."

Culpepper peers around Teacherman at the visitors with his grotesque empty eye sockets. His mouth creaks a little when he opens it, but the only thing that comes out is a sinister snakelike hiss, which gets the shadows in the corners to coiling and writhing around.

The visitors don't move, but I do. I have to do *something*. I step out in front of Teacherman. Goldie eases over and stands beside me, giving Culpepper a wolflike warning growl, teeth bared, untamed and unpredictable.

"These are my friends," I say, trying to keep the tremors out of my voice. "They got stuck here in the storm. They'll be leaving real soon. No need to bother yourself with them, sir."

I swallow my guilt whole. It's my fault the visitors are stuck here. It's my fault they're scared half to death right now. And it will be my fault if Jackson Culpepper the Third and his army of shadows cause them any harm.

Another hiss seeps out of Culpepper's mouth. The shadows in the corners respond, gliding forward and circling his feet as if commanded to do so.

"He's not real," Thomas says with a quiet concentration, trying to convince himself as much as he's trying to convince everyone else. "He's not real, so he can't hurt us."

"That ax looks pretty real to me," Mateo says, backing up.

As if to prove Mateo's point, Culpepper raises the ax high over his head, bringing it down hard, right in the center of one of the desks. The wood splinters easily and the desk collapses into a pile of rubble.

The visitors all flinch at the brutal show of violence. Goldie crouches even more, growling like she's ready to rip Culpepper to shreds. I hope she doesn't try, because she can't hurt him, but he can definitely hurt *her*.

Without thinking, I place my hand on her back, so she

doesn't charge him. The white-hot current of our connection immediately fills my whole body with Goldie's intense heat. The dog yelps, scampering away from me, ears and tail tucked. She darts for the door. Her sudden charge in his direction seems to surprise Culpepper, but he reacts by raising and bringing down the ax in her direction.

"No!" Thomas wails, the pain in his voice wild and raw.

The ax fails to connect with Goldie's head by mere inches. She sails out the door and into the storm, leaving Culpepper momentarily distracted.

"Children," Teacherman says urgently. "Go now. Hide. And hurry!"

Thomas grabs the Tascam, and Mateo his backpack, and I rush them past a disoriented Culpepper and out the door. We scramble down the porch steps, running away from the schoolhouse but in no particular direction. I look back to make sure Culpepper and his shadow army aren't following us. So far, so good.

"Where are we going?" Maya yells over the pounding wind and rain, her voice tight with panic.

"Goldie!" Thomas calls out.

The storm has reached a crescendo. The wind whips around us in a relentless fury. Thunder pounds on heaven's floor. Rain, drenching and deafening, soaks the plantation from end to end. The wind whips The Reaper around like a tree rag doll. Goldie barks somewhere in the distance. Seconds later, she trots right for us. She plows into Thomas's open arms, near about knocking him over. She eyes me warily as he kneels and hugs her tight around the neck.

"What are we going to do?" Mateo cries through unapologetic tears, his voice cracking and his shoulders shaking. I worry he's going to have one of those spells like he had before.

They're all looking at me now. No one has ever asked me anything like that. *What are we going to do?* Like I should know. I don't. Like I'm *a man*. I'm not. But I'm all the visitors have. And I have to help them. So, with a calm, reassuring tone that I think would make Mr. Walter Cronkite proud, I answer Mateo.

"Follow me."

–:–

**"HEY," WILL SAID** cautiously when he made it over to Frankie and Ronnie.

He got off his bike but hung on to the handlebars, keeping the thing pressed close against his body like a shield. Frankie and Ronnie didn't say *hey* back—just nodded at him with a look that Will couldn't read. He didn't know why they'd called him over. They never wanted to hang out with him at school. Frankie preferred to tease him and shove him around. And Ronnie preferred to stand by and laugh.

Frankie and Ronnie stood under the raised shed of the winnowing barn smoking cigarettes, like that was a normal thing for boys our age to be doing. He'd never seen

Ronnie smoke before. It made him look a lot older than he was. Ronnie stood straddling an old wooden ladder that was lying flat in the tall grass. Frankie leaned against one of the white posts supporting the shed above them. They probably thought they looked cool smoking cigarettes, but they didn't look cool at all to Will. The foul odor drifted over to him, slowly invading his lungs.

Will eased his bike to the ground on its side. Frankie and Ronnie still hadn't said anything, which made him kind of nervous. They just stared at him, puffing on those nasty-smelling cigarettes. Will walked casually around the shaded area under the shed, like that was something he'd done a million times before. He hadn't. He gazed up into the square opening in the floor of the shed above him, as if wondering what was up there.

He tried to act cool—not the smoking kind of trying to act cool, just the acting-like-you're-bored-and-looking-at-everything-under-the-sun-except-the-two-boys-staring-at-you kind. After all the bullying and Ronnie's betrayal, Will didn't know why he wanted them to think he was cool anyway. But something inside him did, and he hated himself for feeling that way.

"What're you doing way out here?" Frankie finally asked.

Will looked down, because even though Frankie's voice sounded friendly enough, his eyes rattled Will.

"I come here to hang out sometimes," Will said.

Ronnie knew that. They'd ridden their bikes to Hollow Pines before, when they used to be best friends. Ronnie was probably the reason Frankie was here now, which felt like another betrayal.

"Creepy place to hang out by yourself," Ronnie said with a chuckle, but not a teasing one, Will didn't think.

Frankie stared at Will, a slight smile curling his lips. But Will didn't know if he believed the smile. Smiles could mean a whole lot of things, and not all of them good. And Frankie's smile suddenly had a hint of danger in it—something about the tightness of his upper lip, the slight flare of his nostrils, and the way his pearl-shaded teeth glinted through the slight part of his lips. Will started to think that maybe this was a bad idea after all.

Frankie motioned up with his cigarette, a trail of smoke following his hand. "You know what this thing is?"

Will nodded. "It's a winnowing barn. After the field hands harvested the rice from the paddy fields, they would take the husks up there and drop the grain through the hole, letting the wind carry away the chaff."

Frankie's smile shifted again, causing Will to cut his explanation short.

"Or something like that," he said. "We learned about it in school, remember?"

He knew Ronnie remembered. They'd been in that class together—South Carolina history. But Ronnie snickered, as if paying attention in class was only for losers. Frankie silenced Ronnie with a hard look, almost like he was taking up for Will, which was weird. Will thought if anyone should be taking up for him, it should be Ronnie, not Frankie. He didn't know what to think. His head felt full and heavy again, like it weighed a hundred pounds. He was suddenly real tired too. All he wanted to do in that moment was sleep.

"You ever been up top before?" Frankie asked.

Will shook his head. "I'm afraid of heights."

He immediately wished he hadn't said it. It'd just kind of fallen out of his mouth, as words sometimes do. But Ronnie already knew about his fear of heights, and Frankie didn't laugh or make fun of him for it. He wondered for a second if Frankie had changed his ways and turned from the devil to Jesus on a dime. Will's preacher had said that happens sometimes.

"You should climb up there," Frankie said matter-of-factly. Like what he was suggesting was no big deal at all.

"Huh?" was all Will could say back.

Frankie pushed off the post and took a step toward Will, his shoulders relaxed, his body posture casual. Like he didn't have a care in the world. Will wondered what that must feel like—to go through your days without a tightness in your chest and the constant heaviness in your head making you sleepy all the time. And without fear.

"You know," Frankie said. "It might help you get over the fear of heights thing. Right, Ronnie?"

Will looked back at Ronnie and their eyes locked. He searched those ocean-blue eyes for his friend, hoping he was still in there somewhere. When Ronnie smiled at him, Will felt a glimmer of hope that he just might be.

"Sure," Ronnie said.

Ronnie took a long drag on the cigarette and blew the

smoke over Will's head. A rustling sounded behind Will and he turned quickly, half expecting to find Frankie grabbing him, or about to give him a wedgie, like he had in the school cafeteria in front of everyone about a month ago. But Frankie was just lifting the ladder off the ground—leaning it against one of the posts and up the side of the shed, his cigarette dangling out the corner of his mouth like a toothpick. Will was amazed by how Frankie and Ronnie handled lit cigarettes like they were forty-year-old men instead of twelve- and thirteen-year-old boys.

Once the ladder was in place, Frankie slapped one of the rungs like he was telling Will to hop on. Like this was a ride at Grand Strand Amusement Park in Myrtle Beach or something. A knot immediately formed in the pit of Will's stomach as he thought about how high up the roof was. He looked back at Ronnie, who gave him a reassuring smile. Ronnie took the cigarette from his lips and held it between the tips of his index finger and thumb at his side, flicking ashes away with the slight thump of his middle finger.

"Come on," Ronnie said. "We'll all go up." He dropped the cigarette and ground it into the dirt with the toe of his shoe. "It'll be fun."

# 17

THE ONE PLACE at Hollow Pines I'm pretty sure
Jackson Culpepper has never set foot inside is the chapel in the slave village. Maybe it's because he's afraid
to show his rotted soul in such a holy place after all the
bad things he did to the enslaved folks at Hollow Pines.

I don't hear Preacher's booming voice pouring out of
the windows this afternoon, but I don't know that I would
over the noise of the storm. I'm sure he's in there—he's
always in there. The chapel is also the place where I hide
all the treasures I've collected from visitors over the
years. And there's one thing in my stash that I hope can
help Thomas, Maya, and Mateo.

"Hurry," I say, looking over my shoulder at them as
I sail up the three rickety steps to the chapel door and
push it open.

There are only a few benches left inside, and a

pulpit at the front, where Preacher gives his sermons. Two figures sit side by side on the front bench, and I know by the massive shoulders of the man and the slight frame of the woman that it's Preacher and Emma. Emma reads slowly from her Gullah Bible, and Preacher nods on every word. Preacher and Emma have always been sweet on each other. Everyone here knows it.

Goldie trots right down the center aisle like she's answering the altar call to repent for her sins and pray for her eternal soul, but she only sniffs around the pulpit, paying Preacher and Emma no mind at all. I know she can't see them, but I'm sure she can sense them just like she sensed me.

"Come on," I say to the visitors. "I'll introduce you. And don't worry. They're not like Culpepper. They're real nice, like Teacherman."

"Who is?" Maya asks, looking around, but they follow me down the aisle all the same.

Preacher, still a young man when he left the living world, is wearing the Sunday-go-to-meetin' suit he always wears. Emma's still in her kitchen apron, but her hair is covered with a simple white bonnet, the straps dangling untied on her shoulders. Emma looks up from the Bible. She stares from me to the visitors and back to me, her lips sealed tight.

"It's okay," I say, impatience rolling my eyes. "You can let them see you. They've already met Teacherman."

"Boy," Emma says sharply. "What are you doing bringing these living children up in here? You was supposed to be scaring them off, not giving them a tour of the place."

By the end of her last sentence, Emma is fully visible to the visitors. Preacher appears a beat later. Thomas, Maya, and Mateo step back. I know that kind of thing takes some getting used to. Goldie, however, just walks over and sniffs Preacher's hand. And sneezes.

"They're my friends," I say, grinning wide at the sound of that, because I haven't had a living friend in over fifty years.

I turn to the visitors. "This here is Emma and Preacher. They've been stuck here a real long time—a lot longer than I have."

Mateo clears his throat, taking another small step back. "Um . . . to be fair, Miss Ghost Lady, ma'am, he's done an excellent job of scaring the heck out of us. Although he did let the air out of the tires on our bicycles, so I'm not sure how hard he was trying to make us leave."

If I could still blush, I probably would right about now.

Maya also inches back, her voice small. "We're stuck here too. At least until the storm passes. Then, I promise, we'll leave."

Thomas, unlike the twins, steps forward. "We're sorry to disturb your . . . um . . . Bible study."

He extends his hand to Preacher but thinks better of it when Preacher doesn't offer his own in return. Lost souls don't really go around shaking hands with the living. It's just not done.

"You children got names?" Preacher asks in his low-booming preaching voice.

"Yes, sir," Thomas says. "I'm Thomas. And this is Maya and Mateo." He points to Goldie, who's still exploring the room. "That's Goldie. Don't worry, she's housebroken."

Preacher nods. "I see. What's the reason for your afternoon visit to the house of God? Services aren't until tomorrow. And I sincerely hope you children are long gone from this place by then, for your own sake."

Emma stands, centering a worried gaze on me. "Is it Culpepper?"

I nod. "He's after the visitors."

Emma shakes her head and swallows hard.

"Well," Preacher says, "you are all welcome here. Culpepper knows he shouldn't come through that door."

I don't know if what Preacher says is true or not, or if he has what Grandma called *a fool's faith*, but I sure hope he's right.

Thomas steps in front of me, nodding politely to Preacher and Emma.

"Excuse me, ma'am, sir," he says before turning his attention to me. "In the schoolhouse, you said that you killed Will."

His words sting. But I guess they were really my words to start with.

"Wait." Thomas pulls out the Tascam and holds it up to me, the little red light capturing my attention.

"What did you mean when you said that you killed Will Perkins?"

Emma and Preacher share a questioning look and then move a little closer to us. I glance from Thomas to Maya to Mateo.

"I don't remember how it happened," I say. "I just know that Will died that day, and somehow it was my fault."

They all look disappointed in my answer.

"Could it have been some kind of accident?" Maya asks.

"What about the other two boys who were there?" Mateo says. "Frankie Dimery and Ronnie Cribb. Did they have anything to do with what happened to Will?"

I stare blankly back at him, rolling the names around in my head again to see if they are the keys to unlocking my memories.

*Frankie Dimery and Ronnie Cribb.*

*Ronnie.* That name more than the other one stirs something in me. I feel like I know Ronnie Cribb—know him in a way that you know your own self. And that's when it hits me. The floodgates of my brain open up, nearly drowning me with the revelation.

I look over at Thomas. "I think I'm Ronnie Cribb."

-:-

"WE'LL BE RIGHT behind you," Ronnie said.

Will looked from one boy to the other, trying to think

it through. Even though he was afraid of heights, he thought it would be kind of cool to see the plantation from the top of the winnowing barn. And Frankie and Ronnie would come up right after him, so he wouldn't be alone up there. Plus, if he did this, maybe they would think he was brave and stop calling him those names they called him at school. Maybe Ronnie would even want to be his friend again.

"Yeah, come on," Frankie coaxed, sounding friendly enough. And then he said something that Will had heard more times than he could count. "Be a man."

The words rang in Will's ears, badgering him.

*Be a man.*

His father said that to him all the time, anytime he thought Will was acting like a wimp or like a girl. He wished his father would remember that he was just a kid. He didn't have to be a man for a long time. And how would climbing to the top of a winnowing barn make you a man anyway?

"I'll hold the ladder for you, Will," Ronnie said.

He said it like a friend would. And Will so badly wanted to trust Ronnie again.

It was really Frankie who usually called Will all those bad names anyway. Ronnie just laughed and played along. That's what you have to do in school sometimes, play along so you won't be the target. Right? Maybe Ronnie hadn't turned into a bad person after all. Maybe he hadn't forgotten how close they used to be, how much fun they used to have together. So Will decided to give Ronnie a chance.

He walked over to the ladder, grabbed the sides, and put his foot on the first rung. Ronnie moved behind the ladder, so he was face-to-face with Will, and gripped the ladder from the other side. Both Ronnie and Frankie wore encouraging smiles. Will looked up. The sun blinded his view of the top of the winnowing barn, but it seemed really high up from where he stood. Will didn't want Frankie and Ronnie to think he was a wimp. He wanted to show them how brave he was, even though he didn't feel very brave.

Ronnie looked Will in the eye. "You can do this, Will. We'll be right behind you."

Ronnie's words and the kindness in his voice made Will feel warm all over. And safe. Just like old times. He took a deep breath to settle his nerves, tightened his grip on the ladder, and took the first step.

# 18

THE VISITORS ARE sitting on a bench in front of me. Goldie lies on the floor. Preacher and Emma stand behind the visitors, Emma with a hand on her hip and Preacher staring down at me with a real serious look.

Thomas looks like he wants to say something but doesn't know how to.

"What is it?" I ask him, feeling a little on guard.

Thomas looks at Mateo and then Maya. Maya nods at him. Thomas holds the recorder between us.

"So . . . your name isn't Ronnie Cribb," he says.

I squint at him. "It isn't?"

Thomas shakes his head and then glances down at the Tascam. "No, it isn't."

Maya leans forward. "Ronnie Cribb is still alive. We looked both him and Frankie Dimery up when we started working on *Finding Will*. Ronnie didn't want to be interviewed for the podcast. And we couldn't interview Frankie."

"Yeah," Mateo says. "Frankie grew up to be a pretty bad dude. He's in prison for all kinds of stuff."

"Frankie?" I say. "In prison?"

It's hard to imagine the thirteen-year-old boy I once knew being in prison. But I guess I shouldn't be too surprised that was where Frankie ended up.

"What about Ronnie?" I ask. "What happened to him?"

"He left Georgetown after he graduated from high school and never came back. We found out he lives in Dallas now. We tried calling him, but he wouldn't talk to us when we told him what we were doing."

I let the words sink in, so confused my brain hurts, and with one more question hanging on my tongue. "Then who am I?"

"Dude," Mateo says softly. "You're Will Perkins."

The answer clicks in my brain right before Mateo says it. But hearing it out loud somehow makes it more real. I am Will Perkins. The realization releases a flood of memories, painful ones. Memories I immediately understand why I buried so deep. I remember. Well, not everything. I still can't remember exactly how Will died. How *I* died.

Maya leans even closer to me, her eyes full of warmth. "There aren't really pictures of you around—your dad didn't keep any. He died several years ago. Kensington Elementary had your fifth-grade school picture on file, but you look a lot different in it, so we weren't sure at first."

She pulls something out of her back pocket and unfolds it in front of me. It's a sheet of paper with a small black-and-white picture in the center. It's a little grainy and blurry, but it's me all right. And the name printed under the picture reads WILL PERKINS, plain as day.

"We didn't want to say anything until we were sure," Thomas says. "Because you obviously didn't remember."

I look at him and nod. I know the Tascam can't record a nod, but I don't really know what to say, even if I could make myself speak. My brain is still sorting things out.

Thomas holds the Tascam closer to me. "Do you remember more about what happened that day?"

And I do. I nod slowly. "When I got here, Frankie and Ronnie were over by the winnowing barn. I remember they called to me—well, Ronnie did. He and I used to be friends, best friends, so I went. They said we should all climb up to the top—there was an old wooden ladder. I was going to go first and then they were going to follow me up."

That's where I run into another roadblock in my brain. Something stops me from going forward. But I know now that it's the painful memories that I have spent all these years forgetting. So I push through and find them, one by one.

The sting of Daddy's hand on my face. The names I was called at school—*sissy, homo, queer*. The heaviness in my head and the tightness in my chest. Ronnie. Ronnie's betrayal—twice.

–:–

**WILL'S FEAR OF** heights kicked into high gear, his heart-beat quickening with every step he took up the ladder. Sweat beaded on his forehead and trickled down into his eyes, blurring his vision. He had to stop every other step or so when he got dizzy and felt like he was going to fall. His father said that kind of stuff was all in his head, but it felt like it was all in his stomach, his chest, and his shaking legs. Still, he wouldn't let Frankie and Ronnie see the fear he knew must be twisting his face. He looked up. Not down. It was a little advice his grandma gave him one time when he was younger and afraid to go on the giant Ferris wheel at Grand Strand Amusement Park in Myrtle Beach.

She'd said, "Look up to heaven, where you want to go, not down to hell, where sinners glow."

It had helped then, and he hoped it would now too. Will made it to the top of the wooden post and stopped a moment to catch his breath. His heart was pounding away.

"Halfway there," Ronnie called from below.

Will didn't look down, for fear of losing his nerve or passing out. But it was nice hearing Ronnie's voice sounding so friendly and caring again. After Will steadied himself, he continued his climb, never once looking down. He climbed and climbed, looking only up. As Will reached for the next rung of the ladder, his hand instead scraped the scratchy shingles of the roof.

He'd made it. He'd reached the top of the winnowing barn.

He dug his fingers into the wood, the shingles, and

anything else he could use to pull himself the rest of the way. He was finally off the ladder, crawling on hands and knees up the slanted roof. About halfway to the peak, he stopped and turned over so he was sitting, knees bent and feet flat, on the roof of the shed. A wave of pride washed over him. He'd done it.

Will gazed up at the ocean-blue sky, which reminded him of Ronnie's eyes. Cotton candy clouds hung just above him, shuffling along like they weren't in any hurry to get to where they were going. He didn't think he'd ever been this close to the clouds, even though he knew they were really far away.

He scanned the plantation from one end to the other. He could see all of it from up there. The old slave village to his right, the manor house down at the very end of Live Oak Lane on his left, the kitchen house, the school-house—it all looked smaller from up here, so peace-ful. He'd have to talk Sarah into coming back with him and climbing to the top of the winnowing barn too. Will thought she would see Hollow Pines in a whole different way if she did. He lay back on the roof and breathed in the jasmine-scented air as he waited for Ronnie and Frankie to climb up and join him. Will knew that Ronnie would love it up here. Besides, he couldn't think about going back down that ladder yet anyway. Going down can be just as scary as going up, sometimes even scarier.

Will heard the scraping of wood and sat up quickly, expecting to see either Frankie's or Ronnie's head pop up over the ledge. But he didn't see either of them. All he saw was the top of the ladder moving back and forth, back and forth. And then just in one direction—away from the edge of the roof. Panic tied his stomach into knots. His eyes burned as he watched the top of the ladder sway slowly to one side, like a tall, skinny tree about to topple over as it's being cut down.

"No, no, no!"

The ladder finally fell away completely. It was gone. And with it, Will's only way down. He was dizzy. His heart raced and his breathing shallowed. His stomach turned and bile marched up his throat. He only barely managed to hold it back.

How could he have been so stupid? How could he have ever thought Frankie and Ronnie were just being nice and wanted to hang out with him? Or that Ronnie would ever want to be his friend again? The words that had taunted him at school floated up from the ground.

"Sissy."

"Homo."

"Queer."

It sounded like Frankie's voice. But both of them were full-on gut-busting laughing now—at him.

Will scooted higher on the roof so he could see Frankie and Ronnie below. For some reason, moving up to the peak of the roof seemed a lot less scary than easing down to the ledge. The boys walked backward out into the field until they could see him up there, Frankie pushing Will's bike by the handlebars over to the edge of the canal. He thrust the bike into the water, not too far. Will could still see it sticking out. But far enough that if Will didn't get it out soon, it would be taken by the rising tide and carried out to the river. He swallowed back a sob and willed his eyes to dry up.

Frankie and Ronnie were doubled over laughing. The sound of Ronnie's laughter hurt the most, slicing right through Will's heart. He shrank into himself, wishing he could disappear. Be anywhere else in the world.

"Ha, ha," Will called out, playing along like he thought what they had done was hilarious. He hoped maybe that would help. "That's real funny, y'all."

But it wasn't funny at all. Not even a little bit.

He forced a smile, even though he didn't know if they could see it from down there. "Okay. You got me real good. Now put the ladder back up."

"Hope you can fly, homo!"

"Fly, fairy, fly!"

Will couldn't tell which one said what, but that didn't seem very important anymore. He knew if his father saw him stuck up there, he'd expect Will to find a way down and then fight Frankie and Ronnie. But Will didn't even know how to fight. He'd never fought back. Not when Frankie and his friends were pushing and shoving him on the schoolyard. Not when his father hit him either.

Frankie's and Ronnie's taunts echoed across the field. Will put his hands over his ears to shut them out, but he could still hear them.

"Jump, homo! Jump!"

"Fly, fairy! Fly!"

Their voices drifted farther and farther away and the reality of Will's situation began to sink in. Frankie and Ronnie were really leaving him up there by himself. Even Ronnie had left him.

With the fading sound of the boys' voices and the sting of Ronnie's second betrayal, Will's heart broke in two.

# 19

"**HOW DID YOU** get down?" Thomas asks, sitting on the actual edge of his seat and still holding the recorder in my face. "Did Frankie and Ronnie finally put the ladder back up for you?"

That part is still foggy. How did I get down? How did I die? Neither Ronnie nor Frankie could have pushed me off the roof, because they weren't even up there.

"Did you fall, boy?" Emma asks. "Break your neck? Your head land on a rock or something?"

"I guess so," I say, looking up at her. "Or something like that."

An ear-pounding crack of thunder splits the sky, causing all of us to glance up at the ceiling. The wind sounds like a never-ending freight train passing by, and the rain is so loud that we all have to talk louder than normal to be heard over it.

Maya's eyebrows crease. "But if you fell, why didn't anyone find your body when the police searched the place?"

"Frankie and Ronnie didn't mention anything about the winnowing barn when they were questioned," Mateo says to her. "So maybe the police didn't look too hard over there."

Thomas stands. "We have to go to the winnowing barn."

His words twist my stomach into knots. I've avoided that place for fifty years, without truly knowing why. But now I do. I slowly shake my head at him.

"I can't," I say, my voice barely above a whisper.

Thomas's face sags a little, but he doesn't say anything.

"You have to, boy," a familiar voice calls from the back of the church.

Maya and Mateo join Thomas on their feet and spin around. I guess they thought it might be Culpepper, but it's not. Cousin Cornelius stands just inside the door. He holds his pipe in one hand and his straw hat in the other. I don't know how long he's been standing there, but long enough, I guess.

"Hey, Cousin," I say.

He nods once. "Cousin."

"Who's that?" Mateo stammers to no one in particular.

"That's Cousin Cornelius," I say.

"He's your cousin?" Maya asks, confusion lifting her words.

I don't have time to explain.

"But you got bigger worries," Cornelius says, and then

puffs on his pipe and blows out a small cloud of smoke, right here in the house of the Lord, like it ain't nobody's business but God's. "Culpepper's comin'."

"He wants the visitors' souls," I say, as calmly as I can. "And his shadow snakes have a taste for them now."

Maya rubs her arms, worry etched on her golden-brown face. "Can those things, like, really hurt us?"

"They can suck the life clean out of you if they get ahold of you for long enough," I say.

The visitors stare at me. Speechless.

"It's the devil's work," Emma says, crossing her arms with a little shiver.

"That's why we try to scare visitors away quick as we can," I add.

Preacher steps forward. "How long now, Cornelius?"

Cousin Cornelius draws the pipe to his lips.

"Headed this way now," he says, stopping halfway down the aisle. "Devil in his eyes, and ax swinging at his side."

Thomas, Maya, and Mateo don't say a word, but their eyes betray their fear. Goldie must be able to sense it, because she whimpers as she sidles up to Thomas.

"I have to hide the visitors," I say.

"Can't hide from the devil, boy," Preacher adds, shaking his head.

Emma nods. "If Culpepper wants 'em, he'll have 'em."

Cornelius eyes me curiously. "You remembering?"

I swallow real hard. "Some things. But not all."

He shuffles the rest of the way down the aisle. Thomas

grabs Goldie by the collar, and the visitors' eyes stay locked on the old man until he stops right in front of me. The leathery ridges and valleys in his face tighten as he smiles.

Cornelius points to my head. "It's all in there."

I swallow hard and nod, leery of the other memories I might dig up if I try too hard.

A woman's steady voice sounds outside in the distance. "I ain't seen the boy, I tell you. And you leave them living children alone, you hear me?"

It's Retha Mae. She must be talking to Culpepper. And she's trying to warn us. Giving us time to hide.

"He'll be here any minute," Maya says. "If we're going to go, we need to go now."

"But the preacher ghost said Culpepper couldn't come into the chapel, right?" Mateo asks, his voice cracking. "Won't we be safe if we just stay in here?"

"I didn't say he *couldn't* come in here," Preacher says, slipping his hands down into his pockets. "Just said he knows he *shouldn't*."

Thomas reaches for my arm, but I back away.

"Sorry," Thomas says.

I don't know what to say, so I shake my head.

He smiles but then glances over his shoulder at the door and back. Worry dulls the shine of his eyes.

"If we go to the winnowing barn, maybe you'll remember the rest of your story like Mr. Cornelius said. It might help you get free of this place."

I hear what Thomas is saying, but my mind is racing with questions.

*Where would I even go if I left Hollow Pines?*

*Could I still go to heaven?*

*Would I be sent to hell?*

*Are those even real places?*

"Go somewhere that's not here," Thomas is saying, I guess reading my face. "Someplace where you'll find peace."

*Peace.* I like the sound of that. That would be nice—as long as I wasn't alone. I'd rather stay stuck here at Hollow Pines than be somewhere else and all alone. At least here I have Cousin Cornelius, Emma and Retha Mae, Preacher, Miss Rebecca, and Teacherman.

"Hey," Thomas says, bringing me back. "Maya's right. We don't have much time. We have to get out of here."

"He'll see if you go out the front," Preacher says in a hurried whisper. "Use the back door. Behind the pulpit."

Before we leave, I go over to the floorboard three steps from the door in the back of the church. Kneeling down, I slip my fingers into the crack, and slide the board out. All my treasures are there. I guess now I'll need to find a new hiding place, since everyone is watching me. But there, under a couple of magic pocket phones and a black metal flashlight and some other stuff, I find what I'm looking for.

The orange-and-black pistol.

# 20

THE VISITORS AND I run across Live Oak Lane like our lives depend on it. Maybe theirs do and maybe my eternal soul does too. The sun hangs lower in the sky, peeking out through the storm clouds only now and then, like it's ready to call it a day. Who could blame it, really, after a day like this one. And it's not over yet.

Thunder grumbles all around us, warning us to turn back, but we keep moving toward the winnowing barn. I haven't been back there since the day I died, and I'm glad the visitors are here so I don't have to do this alone.

Raindrops the size of small marbles pelt the visitors as we race across the yard and out into the field. I haven't been concentrating too hard on making my footfalls much like a living person's. The visitors know what I am now, and it feels good to be able to be myself in front of them.

I don't know how much good the orange-and-black

pistol will do us if we have to face Culpepper and his army of shadow snakes, but I feel better having it tucked safely in the waistband of my pants.

I look over my shoulder and catch sight of a menacing, swirling dark cloud halfway between the kitchen house and the slave village chapel, moving close to the ground in an unnatural way. And that's how I know it ain't just any dark cloud; it's Jackson Culpepper the Third in all his sinister glory.

Retha Mae stands in his path, her hands held up in front of her like a human stop sign. The dark cloud barrels right over her and she disappears. A nauseating wave of panic washes over me. But then I see her form inside the dark cloud of Culpepper as she transforms into a ferocious cloud of her own, battling him with everything she's got.

"Hurry," I shout to the visitors through a wall of wind and rain.

"I'm running as fast as I can," Mateo yells back. He glances down at my feet. "Maybe you should carry us. It looks like you're about to take off and fly."

*Hope you can fly, homo!*

*Fly, fairy, fly!*

I shake the words out of my head as quickly as they come.

Thomas looks back at my feet hovering over the ground. His mouth is wide open, but nothing's coming out. I guess it must look pretty cool to him, but he needs to keep an eye on his own two feet.

"Watch where you step," I yell to him. "Lots of ruts in the ground out here."

No sooner are the words are out of my mouth than Thomas goes down. He cries out in pain, stopping us all in our tracks. Goldie gets to Thomas first, sniffing him, licking his face, and whining.

"What happened?" Maya says, doubling back through the tall weeds.

Thomas grabs his ankle. He rolls over on his side, his face creased in pain. "I think I sprained my ankle."

Mateo lets his backpack slide off his shoulders and down to the ground, but he just stares at it without even opening the flap. I guess he doesn't have anything in there that can fix a sprained ankle. At least that's what the look of disappointment on his face says, like he not only let Thomas down but the entire Boy Scout army, and his father too.

A crash in the distance behind us draws all our attention back to the slave village. The dark cloud of Jackson Culpepper is tearing through the chapel. I don't see Retha Mae anymore and I hope she's okay. Preacher's voice sails out of the gaping windows of the chapel, praying and preaching up a second storm. The splintering wood and booms of crashing furniture echo across the yard. No telling what the chapel will look like once Culpepper's done with it. Unless he's the one getting the Holy Ghost hide-whupping in there. Emma and Cornelius stand in front of the chapel door, blocking Culpepper's exit.

Maya and Mateo help Thomas to his feet, their worried gazes shifting back and forth from Thomas to the chapel across the field.

"Can you get my backpack, Will?" Mateo asks.

For a second, the name doesn't even register—it's been so long since anyone called me that. I grab the backpack.

The twins act as human crutches for Thomas, one under each arm. He manages to hobble along with them at a pretty good pace. Goldie leads us and I pull up the rear. I keep checking behind me, expecting any moment now to see Culpepper reaching out his long, bony, rotted fingers for me. But there's still a ruckus going on over in the chapel, so we have some time.

I glance to my right toward the manor house. I can just make out a figure standing in the far-left window on the second floor. Miss Rebecca seems to be watching the whole scene unfold from the safety of her room.

The noise coming from the chapel suddenly goes quiet. I stop in my tracks, but the visitors continue on toward the winnowing barn, Maya and Mateo doing their best to help Thomas along with his bad ankle. I look back. Culpepper appears in the doorway of the chapel, in his human form. He faces down Emma and Cousin Cornelius. They're so far away now I can barely make out what happens next. All I know for sure is that Culpepper roars forward, and his shadow army of soul-stealers is heading our way.

# 21

I STAND IN front of the winnowing barn, the visitors
panting beside me, rain beating down on us, Culpepper
coming, and bad memories rumbling around like an active
volcano in my brain, about to erupt at any minute, ready
or not. I gaze up. The winnowing barn doesn't look as big
and tall and scary as it did the last time I was here, the day
I died. I still wouldn't want to be stuck up there at the peak
of the roof with no way down, like I was that day. After
another moment, we all move under the shed to get out of
the rain.

"We could hide in there," Maya says, pointing at the
hole in the floor of the shed above. "If we can find a way
up."

I want to scream *no*, but I stand frozen, staring at the
square opening. It's like my mouth is full of molasses. Or

like I've forgotten how to speak altogether. But when I think about hiding inside the shed, I'm filled with dread, and I'm not quite sure why. I walk over to the edge of the covered area and spot what remains of the old wooden ladder I used to climb to the top fifty years ago. The one Frankie and Ronnie held in place for me, and then took away when I was on the roof. Time hasn't been kind to the ladder. It lies mostly covered in the grass, rotted and with just about every rung broken out.

I turn and hurry back to the visitors. Goldie roams around under the shed, nose to the ground. Mateo shifts Thomas's weight over to his sister and takes his backpack from me. He digs around inside for only a second or two before pulling out a rope. It doesn't look like the ropes I'm used to seeing, though. It's not as thick and it's tied up real tight and proper-like. It's also purple, which I've never seen in a rope before.

I look over my shoulder. I can't see where Culpepper and the shadow snakes are, because the overgrowth around the winnowing barn is almost as tall as I am. Mateo gets right to work, unraveling the rope, tying one end into a big bulky knot, and positioning himself directly under the square opening in the floor of the shed. Unlike before, when he had those breathing spells, he's calm, focused, confident in what he's doing. I step back to give him some room, wondering what he's planning. But I see soon enough when he hoists a handful of the rope and the big knot into the shed. It sails up, easily looping over the center beam of the roof, the knotted end falling right back down through the hole. He did it on his first try.

Mateo grabs both ends of the rope and pulls down, I guess testing the sturdiness of the wooden beam above. Once he's good and satisfied, he ties a few large knots spaced out like steps. He does all this with the kind of focus and concentration that would make you think we weren't being hunted down by an ax-toting evil spirit.

"Maya," Mateo says. "You go first."

Thomas lets go of Maya and hops on his good leg over to Mateo. He holds on to Mateo's shoulder for balance, his injured foot raised off the ground. Maya doesn't waste another second with questions. She grabs the rope like she's done this before and starts making her way up, using the knots Mateo tied to push herself up with her feet.

"What about Goldie?" Thomas asks.

It's a good question. What about Goldie? She's a real smart dog, but I'm pretty sure she can't climb a rope. Thomas, Mateo, and I stare at one another, but no one has an answer. The only idea I have is not the best one, but the only one I can think of.

"I'll get Goldie up there," I say, keeping my voice calm and even.

"Come on," Maya says, peering down at us from the opening in the shed floor. I didn't even realize she'd made it up there so fast.

I look down at Goldie. I barely touched her once before, and even that sent her running away from me. This time, I'll have to hold her tight with both arms wrapped around her. I don't have any idea how she'll react to that. It should only take a few seconds to get her up into the shed, though.

Thomas looks at me like he has the same worries I do. What if I scare her and Goldie freaks out? What if she yelps or barks, drawing Culpepper right to us?

"Try not to hurt her," Thomas says.

He might as well have socked me right in the mouth. The last thing I would ever want to do is hurt Goldie. I'm trying to save her. But I don't think Thomas meant it in a bad way. All I do is nod at him. Goldie stares up at me, tail wagging, which makes me feel a lot better about this whole thing. I kneel in front of her.

"Goldie," I say, gazing into her big brown eyes. "This might feel strange. And scary. But I'm just trying to help you. Okay?"

Goldie cocks her head at me and whines a little, like she maybe understands. So I don't waste any more time. I scoop her up in my arms and sail through the hole in the floor of the shed. She's a big dog, but I can't feel the weight of her at all. Only the intense heat running through my hands and arms and chest and every other spot on me where we touch.

Goldie yelps a couple of times, not too loud. But what she doesn't let out in sound, she makes up for with whole-body convulsions. As soon as we make it inside the shed, I ease her onto the floor.

"Whoa," I hear Mateo say.

Goldie shakes on her side for what feels like a full minute before her body goes completely limp. My breath catches in my throat.

Maya rushes over to her. "Goldie. Come on, girl. Wake up, sweetie. Please wake up."

Goldie is completely still a moment or so too long for my comfort. Maya and I exchange worried glances, but neither of us knows what to do. I drop to my knees beside the dog, but I don't dare touch her again. Her breathing is labored and dangerously shallow.

"Everything okay up there?" Thomas whispers from below.

Maya scrambles over to the opening in the floor. "Something's wrong with Goldie."

"What?" Thomas says, desperation raising his voice.

"Get up here fast," Maya says, and then hurries back to Goldie.

She strokes the dog's rib cage, as if wishing oxygen into her body. I take Maya's place at the opening in the floor and peer down.

Mateo and Thomas look at each other.

"You should go first," Mateo says. "I'll try to push you up as much as I can."

I know we're all thinking the same thing. *But what then?* Thomas can't put any pressure on his twisted ankle without screaming out in pain. It'll be impossible for him to use the knots in the rope to climb higher. He'll have to pull himself up with only his hands. And he'd have to be pretty strong to do that all the way up.

Mateo kneels on one leg, forming a makeshift step with his hands and entwined fingers. Thomas uses the rope for balance as he raises his leg, resting his good foot in Mateo's hands.

"Ready," Mateo whispers.

Thomas nods quickly.

A voice sounds from somewhere out in the field.

"Stop right there!"

We all freeze.

But I recognize the commanding voice—it's Teacherman's.

"Get out of my way," Culpepper says in a near hiss.

I wave at Thomas and Mateo to hurry, and then look back at Goldie. She's still on her side, her rib cage barely moving, but a faint whimper sounds in her throat. Maya whispers in her ear and kisses her on the side of the head. My stomach drops at the sight of them.

I look down to the boys as Mateo mouths to Thomas, *One. Two. Three.*

Mateo stands straight up, lifting his friend as high as he can. Thomas grabs on to the rope with both hands at the highest spot he can reach. He starts pulling himself up, his bad foot dangling around the rope as he swings his good foot here and there, trying to find the knots. But there's no use doing that with only one good foot. I guess it's just instinct. Mateo grabs the end of the rope, trying to hold it steady. At first Thomas does pretty well pulling himself up. He makes it about halfway before I see the strain getting the better of him. Beads of sweat break out across his forehead, and the muscles in his arms look stretched from here to high heaven.

"You murdered my child," I hear Teacherman say from somewhere in the field. "And your own wife. You brutalized hundreds of people you held here in captivity. You sold Retha Mae's husband and children right out from under her. You've fed on the souls of visitors and then turned them into this horrid shadow army. I will not let you harm these children too."

Before Thomas can make it all the way up, his arms begin to give out. His face is beet red and sweat pours from his brow. Thunder cracks the sky. The storm is reminding us that it still has a grip on Hollow Pines, and on us.

Maya leaves Goldie's side a moment and joins me. We huddle on our knees around the hole in the floor, shooting quick glances over our shoulders to make sure Goldie is still breathing. Thomas reaches out his hand, fingers all splayed wide, but he can't make it to the ledge.

Maya lies on her stomach and reaches down for him, but there's still a good foot or so between their outstretched hands.

"Come on, T," Maya shout-whispers. "You got this. Just a little farther."

Thomas strains to pull himself up more, but he doesn't even get another inch. His strength is completely gone.

"I can't do it," he says, breathless. "I can't go any higher."

My brain is working on overdrive. If Thomas falls, he could hurt himself even more and probably draw Culpepper right to us. And Mateo still has to come up.

I could yank Thomas up here real fast. But what if I do the same thing to him as I did to Goldie? I look back over my shoulder again at her. If it weren't for a faint whimper, you would think she was dead.

I rack my brain for another solution but come up empty. Thomas weighs more that Goldie does, so maybe it won't be as bad on him as it was on her, if weight has anything to do with it.

We don't have a choice. I have to take the chance and hope both Goldie and Thomas will recover. I reach down and extend my arm to him. So does Maya, but I'm able to ease down farther than she is without the worry of falling to the ground. Thomas eyes my approaching hand with a hint of fear. But he only pauses a moment before reaching back and swinging his right arm up to us, making one last desperate pull of the rope with his left. His agonizing groan is masked by an explosion of thunder just as our hands make contact.

–:–

SOMETHING HARDENED INSIDE Will. A hatred. He hated Ronnie. And he really hated Frankie. He hated the sound of their laughter. He hated the things they called him at school. He hated his father for hitting him and for the way he looked at Will with cold, angry eyes when he acted the wrong way, or talked the wrong way, or "ran like a girl," or "cried like a girl." He even hated his mother for leaving him.

Will's cheeks burned as the tears rushed forward. A sob choked him. He was suddenly dizzy and felt like he was falling, so he lay back on the roof, fighting to hold the sobs in. He didn't know why. There was no one there to see him cry. Nobody to make fun of him for it. His father wasn't there to slap him across the face and warn Will that he'd give him something to cry about if he didn't dry it up. But he didn't care anymore. His father would never accept him or his secret. He didn't think his mother would ever come back. Ronnie would never be his friend again. His grandma had died a month earlier. And Sarah would be going off to high school in the fall, making new friends and leaving Will to the bullies at Winyah Junior High.

Will had tried so hard for so long not to be what he was, who he was, but nothing worked. Not even praying and pleading with God to change him. And he couldn't fight it anymore. He was so tired, his head so heavy, his chest so tight. He finally let go. He let go of everything. And that was when it happened. When something deep inside him broke. He felt it just as sure as a bone break. It was like his spirit cracked right down the middle.

He slowly got to his feet, legs shaking. He didn't know why he chose to stand when he was so high up, given his fear of heights. The newly broken thing inside him made him do it. A sense of calm washed over him. It was surprising because he wasn't afraid of how high up he was anymore, even though he was standing straight up at the highest peak on top of the winnowing barn—the place where the field hands would free the rice from its husks, dropping the grain through the hole in the floor of the shed below, letting the wind blow all the bad stuff away. The chaff, it was called.

Will realized that he'd never be able to shed his husk and rid himself of his chaff.

He knew now that he couldn't be changed or fixed. There wasn't any prayer or magic spell or hole in the floor that could rid Will of his chaff—homo, sissy, queer. And in that moment, he decided.

He didn't want to be Will Perkins anymore.

# 22

THE MOMENT OUR skin touches, the white-hot sensation warms me from head to toe, but Thomas's eyes go wide as golf balls. Something clicks in my brain, like a light switch being flipped on. I yank Thomas up as fast as I can and let go of him as soon as he clears the hole in the floor. He lies on his side, not convulsing like Goldie did but shaking all over.

"Thomas," Maya says, alarm in her voice. "Are you okay?"

"Shock." Thomas sputters out the word, wrapping his arms around himself. "Like being struck by lightning or something."

Maya puts a hand on his chest. "Your heart is about to jump right out of you."

I sit dumbfounded. I've never had any living person describe what my touch feels like to them. Like a lightning strike, he said. No wonder it scared Goldie so much and caused her to have some kind of seizure. And startled Maya on the stairs when I just barely grazed her arm. I guess that's why ghosts don't go around touching the living, at least not the polite ghosts.

Maya rubs Thomas's arms, trying to calm him. I keep my distance.

"I'll be okay," he finally says, teeth chattering.

As soon as he's able to move, Thomas crawls over to Goldie. He leans over her, stroking her head.

He whispers in her ear. "It's okay, girl. I'm here. It's okay."

He puts his ear on her chest, then looks at us and nods. A good sign. Thomas keeps whispering into Goldie's ear, and the more he does, the more her breathing begins to steady, like his voice is the soothing balm she needed. After a couple of minutes, the dog lumbers up to all fours, the light coming back into her eyes. I breathe a huge sigh of relief.

Goldie walks around the shed a little unsteadily but getting her bearings. She stops in one corner, sniffing and scratching at something. But my eyes are mostly locked on Thomas. I hope he's going to be okay too. He looks up at me and gives me a look that I can't read.

"I saw," he finally says, his eyes boring into mine.

My stomach ties itself into knots as troubling memories of that day fifty years ago unbury themselves one by one.

"What did you see?" I say cautiously.

Now that I've asked the question, though, I'm not sure I really want to know what Thomas saw when he touched me. Before I can say anything, Mateo calls up from below.

"Guys!"

All three of us scramble over and peer down through the hole in the floor. Mateo is climbing up the rope like he does it every day.

"Somebody's coming," Mateo shout-whispers up to us. "I think it's the big scary dude. Culpepper."

I wonder what happened to Teacherman. And to Emma, Cornelius, Retha Mae, and Preacher, praying that they're okay.

Maya and Thomas reach down, each grabbing one of Mateo's hands. They pull him the rest of the way up.

"The rope," Mateo says, but his sister is already reeling it in.

Goldie whines again from the corner, digging in the rubble and wagging her tail. It seems like she's back to normal now. Thomas searches the floor around him and finds the square wood plank cover for the opening in the floor. He eases it into place, making as little sound as possible. But I don't know what good they think plain old wood or taking in the rope will do when it comes to keeping Jackson Culpepper the Third out of somewhere he wants to be. Our only hope is that perhaps Teacherman delayed Culpepper long enough that he didn't see or hear us come up here.

"Goldie," Thomas whispers. "Come here, girl."

Goldie trots over to him, just as smart and obedient as

she can be. She sits in front of Thomas and presents him with something in her mouth. We all take a closer look in the shadowy light, trying to make sense of the object. Mateo is the first to gasp and scoot away from the dog.

"What the . . . ," is all Maya gets out.

"Goldie," Thomas says. "Drop it."

She does as she's told, dropping the thing on the floor in front of her. We all stare at it, but no one says anything. I know I sure don't. Because we can all tell it's not just any old bone lying there.

It's a human bone.

# 23

I WAS ONLY five years old when President John F. Kennedy died on November 22, 1963. But I remember it just as plain as day because I was staying over at Grandma's house. She and I were watching one of her afternoon stories when all of a sudden, the show went away, and Mr. Walter Cronkite's voice sounded through the television speakers. We couldn't see him, though. It just said *CBS News Bulletin* on the screen instead of showing the man and woman we'd been watching on *As the World Turns*.

Mr. Cronkite told us that someone had fired three shots at the president's car in Dallas, Texas, and that Mr. Kennedy was hurt real bad. Then the man and woman from *As the World Turns* came back on the screen and went right back to talking and carrying on like nothing had happened, which as a five-year-old, I thought was kind of rude. The president had been shot, after all.

Well, Grandma started crying, and that made me cry. And then Mr. Cronkite came back on the TV screen a little later. This time, we could see him at his messy desk at CBS News, where he had three or four telephones sitting around. I remember wondering why Mr. Cronkite needed three or four telephones but figured it must have been because he was real important and lots of people wanted to talk to him.

Mr. Cronkite told us that the president had died. That made Grandma cry even more. And I cried some more. And Mr. Cronkite looked like he wanted to cry something fierce, but he held it in. I'll never forget how he kept taking his glasses off and then putting them right back on and taking them off again, like he didn't know what to do with them or himself. I always thought he was just messing with his glasses to distract himself from maybe crying right there in front of me and Grandma and the whole entire country.

Right now, I feel what I think Mr. Cronkite felt that day—overwhelming sorrow. Wanting to burst out into uncontrollable sobs, if that was possible anymore. If I wore glasses, I might have taken them off and put them back on and taken them off again right now too. I kind of wish Mr. Cronkite was here, because he always made me feel safe. And I don't feel very safe right now. I feel like the visitors see too much of me—at least Thomas does, because he saw something when we touched. And I know what it was, because I remember now. Seeing that bone lying on the floor in front of us brings it all back—a key unlocking the final, missing memory of how I died.

Thomas stands slowly and walks to the corner of the shed where Goldie found the bone. Maya follows him. Then Mateo. They all move stiffly and as quietly as possible, like they're walking through a graveyard. I guess they are, in a way. Goldie stays right by my side, watching them. She looks over at me and whines a little. I think she somehow understands what she found, and she's worried about me, which I think is awfully nice.

Thomas squats down, moving a bunch of debris out of the way. I brace myself for their reaction. I've tried so hard every day for fifty years to bury the memories of what I did that day. That's why I never came back to the winnowing barn after Frankie and Ronnie left me stranded on the roof. Deep down, I think I knew what I would find here. And I couldn't face it. Now the regret is as overwhelming as the sorrow.

The visitors don't scream or gasp or anything—probably because they already have a pretty good idea of what they'll find over in the corner. They stand there all quiet and prayerful-like as they stare down at the bones of Will Perkins. My bones.

Thomas turns and looks at me. "Do you need to see this?"

"No," I say, shaking my head.

Thomas walks back over and kneels in front of me, draping an arm around Goldie's neck. His eyes look as sad as I've seen them all day. I hope I'm not the cause of that, but I think I probably am. He doesn't even bother getting out the Tascam and recording.

"That day," he says calmly, "nobody pushed you."

He doesn't say it like a question, just says it flat-out. There's no use in lying to him now. I'm pretty sure he saw everything when we touched. So I shake my head again.

"And you didn't fall."

Another not-a-question. Another shake of my head.

Maya and Mateo stand behind Thomas. But I can't look up at them. I can barely look Thomas in the eye. I feel ashamed. Ashamed of what I did. I stare at the floor. I don't think I want to hear Thomas say the words I think he's about to say, though. So I say them myself.

"I jumped."

For a moment, there's complete silence in the shed. Only the clamor of the wind and rain outside disturb the uncomfortable silence. The visitors must think I'm a terrible person. I look up at them hesitantly. But they don't have judgmental looks on their faces or anything. They're all kind eyes and sad, but sympathetic smiles. Like friends would look when you tell them you did a bad thing, but they're your friends, so they don't make you feel worse about the bad thing you did.

"Were you just trying to get down?" Mateo asks, almost hopefully.

I could lie. I could say that's exactly what I was doing. Just trying to get down, and jumping seemed like the only way. But that's not what I was thinking when I did it. I didn't know for sure if jumping would kill me, but what

I do know is that I didn't care if it did. And I think that's nearly as bad.

"No," I say.

I don't look away from them this time. I can see the truth sinking deep into their eyes and weighing down their whole faces.

"Why?" Thomas asks softly.

I stare into his familiar eyes. "I didn't want to be here anymore," I say. "Or anywhere. I was so tired. And my head was so heavy. I just wanted it all to stop. The name-calling, the bullying, my daddy hitting me, wishing for my mama to come home but knowing she probably never would, my grandma dying, my best friend turning on me. I just wanted *everything* to stop."

Maya swallows hard, her eyes glassy. "You felt hopeless."

She hit the nail right on the head. Because that's exactly how I felt before I jumped—hopeless. I look at her and nod.

Maya sighs. "I felt pretty hopeless when I came out as trans. I was bullied too. And my parents didn't understand."

I don't really know what she's talking about, and I guess she can tell by the questioning look on my face.

Maya leans in, smiling at me. "I was assigned male at birth."

She pauses, I guess waiting for me to respond, but I still don't understand, and again, she can tell.

"Everyone said I was a boy," she says. "But that never

felt right to me. My parents named me Marco, and that name felt all wrong too. No matter what anyone said, I knew from the time I was little that I was a girl. I was Maya."

I'm trying to understand, but I'm having a hard time. So I stop trying to understand it myself, and just accept what Maya is saying—that she is Maya, always has been, and always will be. When I think about it like that, I kind of get it.

"I'm sorry I wasn't a better friend during that time," Thomas says quietly.

Maya's eyes go misty. "You were supportive. You were a fine friend."

Thomas sighs, looking away. "I felt like I was losing my best friend. I know that's dumb, and not right, but things *did* change between us. I'd never had a girl best friend. It was kind of . . . weird."

"Why didn't you tell me that's how you felt?" Maya asks. "All I knew is that you were pulling away from me."

"I'm sorry," Thomas says. "I'm an idiot."

"Yes," Maya says. "You are." She punches him on the shoulder. "Nothing has to change, T. You're still my best friend."

Thomas knocks a pesky tear out of his eye and nods at her.

"I wish there would have been someone you could've talked to, Will," Maya says to me. "To tell them all that you were going through. That's what I did when I felt hopeless—first my school guidance counselor, and then a therapist. And my brother, of course." She looks at Mateo and he gives a sheepish smile. "They all helped me a lot."

"I don't know how things are now," I say cautiously. "But back when I was part of the living world, I didn't think I could talk to anyone about how I felt."

Somehow, though, I feel safe telling the visitors now. So I do.

"I always liked boys the way my daddy said I should only like girls," I say. "I had crushes on boys instead of girls. And I thought I was in love with my best friend, Ronnie. I told him, because I thought I could trust him. But I was wrong."

Thunder grumbles overhead. Rain pounds down on the roof of the shed.

Thomas looks at me and sighs a little. "I'm sorry you felt so hopeless, Will. But none of it was your fault. There wasn't anything wrong with you. There *isn't* anything wrong with you."

I let Thomas's words sink in. I like the sound of what he's saying, but it's a little hard to believe after all these years of thinking *I* was the one with the problem.

"Boy."

The voice is a sinister hiss, like the voice of the devil himself. Mateo, Maya, and I freeze. Thomas strokes Goldie's back, silently urging her to be still and quiet.

"I know you're up there," Culpepper says, his voice sizzling in my ear.

"What are we going to do?" Mateo asks in a panicked whisper.

"I hear you up there, living child," Culpepper rasps above the wind with sandpapered syllables. "And I'll have your soul."

Mateo's eyes go wide, instantly welling with tears.

A crack of wood sounds outside and the shed shakes a little. Goldie barks at the floor. Another crack. Another shake. More barking from Goldie.

"What's he doing?" Thomas asks, steadying himself with one hand on the wall.

"He's chopping through one of the posts holding up the shed," I say, my voice rising over the noise of Culpepper's ax. "He could get in here if he wanted to. He's trying to scare you. That's the way he likes souls to be before he steals them—terrified."

Maya crouches, all her muscles tense. "Well, it's working."

I curl my fingers around the handle of the orange-and-black pistol tucked down in the waist of my jeans, even though I don't know how to shoot a gun. Daddy tried to teach me to shoot a shotgun once, but it didn't take.

An angry roar of thunder is followed by another crack of wood. The shed begins to sag a little at one corner. I don't think it can take another blow.

"Find something to hold on to," I call out.

Thomas braces himself in one corner, Goldie right beside him. Maya and Mateo give each other a quick twin-glance, but then they do the same, holding on to each other and crouching low.

The next wallop of Culpepper's ax to the post causes one side of the winnowing barn to dip lower. We hang there for a moment, suspended. Then it's like the whole world goes into slow motion, until finally the winnowing barn lunges for the ground.

# 24

**THE SHED BEARS** most of the burden of the fall.

The visitors end up in a pile in the corner—wood, Goldie, and my dusty bones scattered on top of them. Goldie wrestles herself upright, scrambling to get her footing on the now sharply slanted floor. Thomas, Maya, and Mateo begin to move around too. Thomas holds his bad ankle, his face creased with pain. Maya pushes debris off her legs and scrambles over to her brother. He's not breathing shallow or holding his chest like when he had those spells earlier, so I guess that's a good sign.

"I'm okay," Mateo says as Maya moves a board off his leg.

"T?" Maya asks.

Thomas nods. "Just my ankle. Other than that, I think I'm good."

"We need to get out of here before this thing collapses in on us," I say to them.

All three of them stare at me, dumbfounded looks on their faces. That's when I realize that I'm floating in mid-air, like I was the whole way down when the shed crashed.

"Oh, sorry," I say, easing myself down slowly.

The wood plank cover for the square hole in the floor came off in the crash. Maya and Mateo push Goldie up to the opening and she jumps through. I climb up the slanted floor, moving as humanlike as I possibly can, and spill out through the hole next.

The sun sits closer to the horizon now, storm clouds passing in front of it. It's probably late afternoon. The rain has eased up a bit and the wind has calmed a little. For the moment, the thunder is silent, and as welcome as the break in the storm is, it also feels a little eerie after the endless attack of wind, rain, thunder, and lightning all day. I glance around the wreckage and don't see Culpepper anywhere.

Mateo is the first of the visitors to climb out of the shed, then Maya. They both look around, making sure the coast is clear of Culpepper before helping Thomas out. Goldie pounces on him like she hasn't seen him in a year when he emerges.

"Good girl," he says, petting her head as the twins help him to the ground.

We all move away from what's left of the winnowing barn. It doesn't look all that threatening now. And it's hard to believe it ever did.

"Where did he go?" Maya asks, scanning the area again.

Mateo shivers. "It's cold."

I take a deep breath. I never did explain to the visitors why they felt those sudden chills in the manor house, and how it usually only ever means one thing. Culpepper walks around the corner of the overturned shed slowly, his footsteps heavy and *very* humanlike. The ax swings at his side and a snarl twists his barely skinned face.

The moment the visitors see him, they mask their fear as best as they can. They stand up straighter, square their jaws, and steady hard gazes on him. It's obvious they're tired of being afraid. Maya even balls her hands into fists like she's ready to fight Culpepper. But I know they're scared. Who wouldn't be? We're facing down a very dark spirit carrying a very real ax.

As if silently summoned by Culpepper, the shadow snakes move in, slithering through the tall grass from every direction. They surround us, boxing us in. We have nowhere to run. They don't advance on us, though. I'm sure they're awaiting Culpepper's command. I move to stand between Culpepper and the visitors, looking him straight in his empty eye sockets. I reach for the handle of the orange-and-black gun, but it's no longer tucked in the waist of my jeans. It must have come loose in the crash. I don't know if it could've hurt the demon anyway, but I would feel better having it. False security is better than none at all.

Culpepper takes a step closer to us, his raggedy

clothes flapping in the waning wind. Muted thunder rolls through the cloudy sky, the kind that always follows a passing storm.

"Move aside, boy," he says in a near growl.

The shadow snakes coil and writhe around us, their numbers growing steadily and their agitation sealed. Their dark, smoky bodies expand and contract in anticipation of their feast. Goldie crouches and growls at them, but the shadows don't seem too bothered by her.

"No," I say with as much resolve and bravery as I can muster. "You can't have their souls. They're leaving Hollow Pines. Today."

"They will never leave," Culpepper fires back. "At least not all of them."

Then, with a deafening roar, the demon rages past me, his ax raised high in the air as he charges straight for the visitors. They all scatter, giving him no easy target. It's one thing to not show Culpepper their fear; it's another thing to ignore the very real ax in his hand. Thomas and Goldie run one way, Mateo another, Maya in the opposite direction of her brother. But they can't go more than twenty feet or so in any direction because of the shadow snakes holding the line.

Mateo passes closest to him, and Culpepper swings the ax wildly at him. The blade misses Mateo's head by less than a foot. Goldie circles back, provoked by the strike at Mateo. The dog runs full speed in Culpepper's direction, her bark raw and vicious.

"Goldie, no!" Thomas yells.

But it's too late. Goldie springs into the air, launching herself at Culpepper. The demon is distracted by Goldie's charge, the dog sailing in his direction. Culpepper isn't used to being attacked because he's always the one doing the attacking. So he doesn't know what to think of Goldie. He quickly regains his composure, though, drawing the ax back. But before he can take a swing at the dog, Maya charges from behind Culpepper, snatching the weapon right out of his hand as she passes.

Culpepper spins around, surprised and disoriented. Goldie lands right in front of him, snarling like she's about to rip him to shreds, even though I know she can't. Still, her gutsy offense keeps Culpepper off guard. Something bright with color catches my eye in the grass a few feet away from Culpepper. My heart drums in my chest. It's the orange-and-black pistol. Even if the gun can't hurt Culpepper, maybe it will keep him distracted long enough for the visitors to get away. But he's standing too close to it for me to make a move.

Culpepper lets out an ear-numbing roar, almost like a war cry. The shadow snakes respond by advancing on us. Goldie forgets about Culpepper and sprints over to Thomas, planting herself between him and the army of shadows. They charge the visitors. Maya chops at the shadow snakes with Culpepper's ax. But all it does is break up the shadows momentarily before they slither off, re-form, and rejoin the attack.

I watch in horror as a lone, thick shadow snake projects itself at Thomas, easily looping around his ankle and yanking him to the ground. He struggles to free himself, but that just seems to make the shadow's grip on him even tighter.

"Guys!" he calls out. "Help!"

The twins run over to him, but the shadow snake is already pulling Thomas into the cover of the tall grass. Maya and Mateo each grab one of Thomas's hands, struggling to pull him back to the center of the circle. Goldie rushes over to Thomas, but before she can make it to him, a shadow snake strikes at her paws, tripping her up. The dog lands hard on her side with a sickening yelp.

I look back to Thomas. I can tell by his drawn features and sinking eyes that the shadow snake is already feeding on his soul. More of the creatures slither over to him, bullying their way into the feast. They coil around Thomas's legs, his waist, his chest, even his neck— literally choking the life out of him. Thomas's eyes go from bright and brown one second to lifeless and gray the next. His mouth hangs open and at an odd angle. He lets out a ghoulish moan. Mateo and Maya aren't making much progress getting Thomas away from the creatures as the army's numbers keep growing. I feel helpless.

I tear my gaze away from the horrifying scene and refocus on getting the gun. Even if a gunshot can't hurt Culpepper, maybe if directed at the shadow snakes, it will disturb them long enough for Maya and Mateo to pull Thomas loose. Culpepper stands right next to the orange-and-black pistol in the grass. He could easily reach down and grab it before I would ever be able to get to it myself. But the more the shadow snakes feed on Thomas, the more Culpepper seems spellbound. He stands with his arms stretched out like he's hanging on a cross, gazing up at the sky. Like Jesus, but not like Jesus at all. His shell of a body glows bright blue from within. He's growing more powerful by the second as the shadow snakes feed on Thomas's soul, as if it were his own hands tight around Thomas's neck, chest, waist, and ankles.

Culpepper rears his head back, letting the lingering rain fall into the gaping holes where his eyes, nose, and mouth should be. And that's when I find my moment. I make a run for it, lunging for the gun. As soon as I hit the ground and get my hands on it, I curl my finger around the trigger, roll over into a crouch, and aim at the shadows pulling Thomas into the tall grass. But I'm knocked off balance before I can shoot, and I land flat on my back.

Culpepper stands over me, one foot on my chest as if in triumph, the bright blue glow in his chest growing brighter. He's getting stronger with each passing second, and it sickens me to think he's gaining strength by feeding on Thomas's soul. There's not much time left before Thomas will be lost forever. And that's when it hits me. It's Culpepper's connection to the shadow snakes that keeps him alive—that keeps him strong. They consume, and he lives. They nourish him with their spoils. Without that connection to his captives, he is nothing. *They* need to be free of him just as much as we do.

I point the barrel of the gun up at the center of Culpepper's chest, at the bright blue glow. I squeeze the trigger, letting out a roar of anger and resolve as I do.

The motion of the gun firing is jarring, and I'm shocked to see a small ball of fire explode from the barrel. It soars right through the center of Culpepper's chest, where the eerie bright blue light glows, and keeps on going right through him. It shoots high up into the dim and stormy sky, momentarily illuminating the plantation with a bright red glow.

Culpepper stands there looking stunned, gazing down at his chest. The blue glow within is gone. He's empty inside and stumbling around like he can't keep his balance. He drops to his knees. For a fleeting moment, I breathe the slightest sigh of relief. But then I realize something that turns my stomach.

Thomas has gone completely silent.

# 25

IN A PANIC, I spin around and rush over to the visitors. Goldie is back on her feet, free of her attackers and pacing nervously around Thomas. I kneel beside Maya and Mateo, who are still clinging to Thomas's arms and making progress pulling him back toward them as the shadow snakes loosen their grip on his body and slither away into the tall grass.

Maya and Mateo roll Thomas over onto his back. Goldie gets as close to him as she can, licking his face and arms nonstop. His chest moves up and down, but his eyes are still, gray and lifeless.

"Did they steal his soul?" Mateo asks desperately.

I look over my shoulder. Culpepper lies facedown in the grass. His tattered clothes, dangling sheets of rotted skin, and what's left of his decayed body are disintegrating. There's not a single shadow snake to be seen now, much less the army that surrounded us before. Now that their connection has been broken, they've abandoned Culpepper. He's all alone, with no power to fight.

"They tried," I say, looking back at Mateo. "But I don't know."

"Look at his eyes," Maya says, excitement brimming in her voice.

And I see the reason for it. The gray in Thomas's eyes is slowly darkening. Those familiar brown eyes I spotted the first time I saw him are beginning to come alive again. Thomas's head sways from side to side, his shallow breathing deepening.

"T!" Mateo shouts.

"Thomas!" Maya adds.

Thomas rolls over on his side, and Maya pats his back. Goldie licks his face as the light in his eyes slowly continues to brighten. His face is regaining its color too. Or at least as much color as it had before. His eyes dart from one of us to the other.

"What happened?" he asks, his voice a little raspy.

Mateo smiles at him. "Will Perkins, like . . . saved your soul, dude."

Thomas stares at Mateo, blinking rapidly. Then he looks at Maya. She nods, her lips curling into a smile too. Finally, Thomas turns to me.

"What about Culpepper?" he asks.

I move out of his sight line and point to the small mound of ash and dust a few feet away.

Thomas stares at it but still doesn't look convinced. "But those shadow things, I could feel them crawling inside me. It was like they were sucking my insides out."

"They're gone," I say. "And finally free of Culpepper's hold on them."

"But how did you . . ." Thomas trails off, looking back at what's left of Culpepper, which isn't much.

"Just relax, T," Maya says. "We'll tell you all about it later."

She helps Thomas to his feet while Mateo searches around the rubble of the winnowing barn until he finds his red backpack, torn open and practically empty. He starts collecting its lost contents, which he finds scattered everywhere.

"Oh no!" he says, leaning down and picking something up.

We make our way over to him, Maya acting as Thomas's crutch.

"What is it?" I ask, tense again after only just letting down my guard.

Mateo turns to face us, holding up the very smashed and very shattered Tascam recorder.

For a moment, Thomas, Maya, and Mateo are silent, all staring down at the ruined remains of their podcast, their faces frozen. I feel terrible for them, because I know how hard they worked on it. But now that those recordings of me are gone, a wave of relief rolls over me.

Thomas lets out a defeated sigh. "Well, there goes journalism camp."

"And my A in social studies," Maya says.

Mateo shakes his head as he stares down at the destroyed recorder. "I wonder if the librarian was serious about that whole 'you break it, you buy it' thing."

"Nobody would have believed us anyway," Thomas says. "Our key witness being a ghost and all." He looks over at me. "Sorry, Will."

I hear him, but my eyes are glued to the ground, where one of my bones rests by Mateo's feet. He must see me staring at it, because he picks it up carefully and then pokes his head into the opening in the floor of the shed.

"Um," he starts timidly. "What should we do with—"

"Burn them," I say decisively. I look Mateo square in the eye. "Burn it all."

I can tell that remembering exactly what I did that day so long ago didn't help me move on from Hollow Pines. I don't feel any different. And I don't know if burning down my past will help me either, but I don't really care anymore. Maybe I'm stuck here forever. I guess I'm okay with that. I just don't want any reminders of what I gave up.

"You sure, Will?" Maya asks.

I look over at her and nod. I know the fire probably won't ever get hot enough to turn my bones to ashes, but burning them seems right, a sort of cleansing.

Goldie and Thomas sit in the damp grass as Mateo and Maya gather up the few stray bones scattered in the grass around the winnowing barn. Mateo hops back inside what's left of the shed as Maya passes my bones through to him. I walk over and peer inside. Mateo is building an impressive stack of dry debris and wood he's found in the small undemolished space inside the shed. Then he carefully places all the bones he can find lying around on top of the pile.

Mateo digs his matches out of the side pocket of his backpack. Maya stands silently behind me as Mateo strikes a match, holding it to the kindling he's placed all around the bottom of the pile. The small scraps of wood ignite after a few seconds. Mateo lights different spots around the bottom edges. He does it all with a reverent manner about him, like he's lighting candles at the altar of a church. Or like he's an usher or a pallbearer at a funeral, which I guess he kind of is right now.

Once he's satisfied that the larger pieces of wood and debris are catching fire, Mateo quietly gathers up his backpack and climbs out of the shed. He and Maya back away from the demolished remains of the winnowing barn, but I stand there for a minute, watching the flames grow inside, moving in and out, around, and over my bones, like a dance—a funeral dance. It's actually kind of beautiful. And peaceful.

It turns out this is the perfect place to start a fire, because the shed is mostly dry inside, but the outside and the grass around the downed winnowing barn are soaked. So I'm not worried about the fire getting out of control.

As I watch the flames, another wave of overwhelming regret consumes me. If I could do that day all over again, I bet I would do it differently. I know I would. All the things

I blamed myself for, none of it was my fault. But I was the one I punished.

I wonder if I'd made a different choice that day what would have become of me. I wonder if I would have grown up and found a boy to love who would love me back. Gone to the University of South Carolina and studied journalism, like I always wanted. Had kids I would have loved no matter who or what they were. Or one day even have taken over for Walter Cronkite on the *CBS Evening News*, like I always dreamed of doing. I'll bet I would have made a real good news anchor, if I'd had the chance. That day on top of the winnowing barn, all those years ago, I couldn't imagine any of that. I didn't think I had a choice. But I did.

I lean in a little closer and whisper to the boy in the fire. "I forgive you, Will Perkins."

Slowly, I back away from the shed as the flames envelop everything inside. The flames continue their funeral dance to a larger stage as the entire winnowing barn quickly becomes part of the performance.

I rejoin Thomas, Maya, Mateo, and Goldie. We all stand quietly, watching the show and paying our respects to the majesty and beauty of the fire and to the boy in the center of it all. I look up into the sky. The rain has stopped completely. There are no cracks or rumbles of thunder. The low-hanging sun breaks through gray clouds in the sky. And the storm winds have calmed to a warm and gentle breeze that softly caresses my face. And that's when I know.

I'm finally free.

# 26

I LEAD THE visitors through the muddy field and across the yard to Live Oak Lane. The Spanish moss welcomes us back, waving lazily from the tree branches above. I still can't get over the feel of the breeze on my face after all these years. I see it in the eyes of the visitors too—that drowsy look people get when a gust of warm, gentle wind brushes over their faces.

The late afternoon sun coats the sky with vibrant streaks of color—orange, yellow, purple, red—all mixed together like a massive painting in the sky. It's one of the most beautiful sunsets I've ever seen in all my years here at Hollow Pines.

The other lost souls—my friends—stand in the middle of Live Oak Lane. They let the visitors see them one at a time. Emma first. Then Teacherman. Retha Mae and Preacher. And finally, Cousin Cornelius.

Everyone except Miss Rebecca. They all wear easy smiles, something you don't see a lot around here. Cornelius walks up to me, holding his pipe in one hand and his straw hat in the other. His dark face, with its deep road-map wrinkles, gleams in the glow of the setting sun.

"Cousin," he says.

"Cousin," I say back, finding it hard to contain a smile. "I thought Culpepper had wiped you all out."

Cornelius kind of chuckles at that. "He tried for a long time."

"We held him off as long as we could for you," Emma says. "Looks like it all worked out. You're free now."

Teacherman steps forward. "So, you forgave yourself."

I nod.

"Good," Cornelius says. "Glad you finally figured it out."

I stare at the old man, trying to process his words.

"You knew?" I ask. "All this time, you knew how to move on?"

"We've had several theories over the years, but none of them worked," Teacherman adds. "A while back, we figured out that we all had one thing in common. All of us have something we haven't been able to forgive ourselves for."

I glance back at the visitors, standing just behind me, Mateo and Maya still serving as crutches to Thomas, and Goldie lying on the ground in front of them. They look just as dumbfounded as I feel. I can't believe in fifty years the other lost souls knew how to leave this place—or at least they had a pretty good idea—and they never shared it with me. I wonder if that's why Retha Mae and Emma told me things about their lives today that they never have before. Were they trying to give me a clue or something? About what I needed to do? And if they knew how to move on, then why are they still here?

"Why didn't anybody tell me?" I ask them, bewildered, a hint of irritation lacing my words.

"Well," Preacher says, crossing his arms over his broad chest. "You buried the memory of what even happened that day." He pauses to let the truth of that sink into my brain. And it does. "Besides, if we'd told you, you probably would've said the words just to get free of this place. Although that wouldn't have worked anyway. True forgiveness comes from the heart. Understand, boy?"

I think about that a second and realize that Preacher is right. Even though I was stuck here for fifty years, I was only ready to forgive myself today.

I nod to Preacher. "I do. I understand." I give him the most sincere smile I can muster. "And I'd be honored if you would call me by my name, Preacher. It's Will. Will Perkins."

A grin stretches across his face. And then he does a very preacher-y thing. He grabs my hand, grips it tight, and shakes it real hard, as preachers are known to do.

"It's a pleasure, Will," he says.

I glance back at the visitors, all of them glassy-eyed and quiet.

"They helped me figure it out," I say. "What happened

at the winnowing barn all those years ago. What I did. I wish I could change it."

"You can't change the past," Cornelius says, shaking his head. "None of us can. So it's best not to be ruled by it."

He says that last bit more to the other lost souls than to me, his gaze lingering on two faces in particular—Retha Mae's and Emma's.

I look over at Retha Mae, reading the inner struggle in her eyes. She's no doubt thinking about her husband and children that Culpepper sold off and she never could find. Something she's not yet been able to forgive herself for. I know Emma is thinking about her sister, Maisy, and how she wasn't able to save her from a terrible fate at the hands of Deacon Pope.

Retha Mae and Emma share a pained and knowing look. After several moments of wordless conversation between them, Retha Mae sighs heavily. She reaches out and takes Emma's hand, giving her a slight nod. Emma eventually nods back before resting her head on Preacher's shoulder. That's when it hits me—why they're all still here, and why Retha Mae and Emma opened up to me earlier about their stories after all this time. It wasn't for my sake. It wasn't about me at all. They were battling their own demons today, trying to make peace with the past. Trying to find a way forward.

"You've been waiting for Retha Mae and Emma to forgive themselves, haven't you," I say to Cornelius, Preacher, and Teacherman. "So you could all move on together."

Cornelius lifts his pipe to his lips and puffs on it a couple of times.

"We're family," he says, like that should explain everything. And I guess it does.

A few moments of silence pass before Mateo raises his hand like he's in school. "Excuse me, ghost people." His voice cracks a little. "I was just wondering about something."

The lost souls look up at him.

"What's that, son?" Teacherman is kind enough to say.

Mateo steps forward. "Who put Will's body up inside the winnowing barn?"

Teacherman looks over at Preacher, who looks over at Emma, who looks over at Retha Mae, and then they all look at Cousin Cornelius.

He nods solemnly, a confession. "I did."

"What in the world made you do that?" I ask.

Cornelius puts on his straw hat, tucking it high in the front and low in the back. He takes a slow drag on his pipe. "I seen what happened that day with them boys. Watched it all while sitting right over there on my front porch." He points to his cabin with his pipe. "Every bit of it." He looks down and shakes his head. "I just couldn't bear to leave you out there in the field, where buzzards and wild dogs and such could get at you. Thought you'd rest better up there. But when those other living folks came around searching the place, they looked near 'bout everywhere *but* up in the shed of the winnowing barn. So that's where you stayed."

I stare at Cousin Cornelius, speechless. That's just about the nicest thing anyone has ever done for me. But before I can say anything, or thank Cornelius for the kindness, he and the other lost souls make themselves invisible to the visitors. I'm not sure why.

Mateo scratches his head. "That is so—"

"Cool," Thomas says, a smile of wonder plastered on his face.

"Why did they leave?" Maya asks.

But that's the wrong question.

"They didn't," I say. "They're still here."

A rumble at the entry gates draws our attention, and now I understand why the lost souls made themselves invisible. A large car that sort of looks like a truck, with a rack of lights mounted on top, rolls past the stone columns, heading our way. I back up behind the visitors and quickly make myself invisible too.

"Will?" Maya asks, looking around.

"I'm here," I say behind them. "But it's probably best if I stay out of sight."

Thomas's eyes are glued to the approaching car. "Um, Will? There's one thing I didn't tell you."

"Huh?" I say, looking at him.

But he doesn't answer. He's so focused on the car, with a mile-wide grin stretching his face. Goldie barks a few times at the car, running alongside it until it comes to a stop in front of us. On the mud-splattered side of the car in big black letters, it reads,

# GEORGETOWN COUNTY
## SHERIFF

The door opens and an older white woman in a tan uniform with a brown tie gets out. Her hair is a mix of blond and gray, shoulder-length and wavy, and there's a holstered gun on her hip.

"Thomas!" she calls out, something like a mix of relief and joy washing over her face.

Thomas runs into the woman's open arms. "Grandma!"

I didn't know that Thomas's grandma was the sheriff. Now I wonder what else he didn't tell me.

Goldie jumps around the woman, excited to see her too. Thomas's grandma doesn't let go of him for a long time.

Maya and Mateo walk over to the car, too, so I follow them, staying a step or two behind.

"What are you kids doing way out here?" the woman says. "Your parents are worried sick. *I* was worried sick!"

She leans down and greets Goldie, scratching her under her chin until the dog about loses her mind. I don't know why, but when the woman smiles, something deep inside me sparks to life. I take a step closer to her, studying her face and especially her eyes.

"Here I am about to retire and you kids are trying to give me a heart attack before I can."

"We're really sorry, Sheriff," Maya says. "We didn't mean to cause a fuss."

"How did you find us?" Mateo asks.

I take another step closer to the woman. I'm immediately struck by her eyes. They're the brightest brown, just like Thomas's. And just as familiar.

"We got a call about a flare in the sky coming from this way. Y'all know you shouldn't be out here. This is private property. You're lucky I have four-wheel drive. That road is a near swamp." She eyes the way Thomas is moving while holding one foot up off the ground. "Darlin', what's wrong with your foot?"

"It's just a sprain, Grandma," Thomas says. "Our bike tires are flat, and we got stuck here in the storm. And—"

"What's burning over there?" the sheriff says, gazing out into the field. "Did you kids start that fire? I need to call it in."

She grabs a radio from her duty belt, pushes a button, and says something about the fire into it, but I can hardly concentrate on what she's saying. I take another step closer—close enough that I can read the name tag pinned under her sheriff's badge, and I freeze.

SARAH PERKINS-PADGETT

It's Sarah. My sister, Sarah. She's a whole lot older than I remember, but it's her. And she's a sheriff. And Thomas's grandma too.

She's so close now I could reach out and touch her. I don't know if it's because I'm free of this place now or what, but I suddenly remember how to cry. Tears stream down my cheeks as I reach a hand to Sarah's face, stopping only inches away from her cheek.

"Well, the fire department isn't too worried about it with everything being so soaked from the rain," she says. "But they'll send someone out later to be sure it's out. Wait, did you say all of you have flat tires? How in heaven did that happen?"

"Um...," Mateo says, looking from Thomas to Maya. "We . . . ran over some broken bottles in the sand," he finally gets out.

Sarah moves past me to open the rear door of the car. "Pile in and you can tell me about it on the way home." She looks over at Thomas. "We'll send your dad back with the truck to get your bikes. He and Sheila are worried sick, you know."

"Sheila's worried sick?" Thomas asks, his voice pitching higher on the words. Like he can't believe that's the case.

"Oh, don't be silly," Sarah says, patting him on the shoulder. "Of course she is."

I can't stop staring at her, mesmerized by her every movement. I'm still having trouble believing it's really Sarah. My mind floods with memories—swinging on the set in our backyard, tapping out Morse code messages to each other through the wall between our bedrooms, her holding me the night Grandma died, and comparing the notes Mama left us—they were exactly the same. My sister was always there for me. She was my one true friend.

Sarah leans down to help Goldie into the back seat, the dog licking her nonstop.

"Will?" Thomas whispers, out of earshot of Sarah. "Will?"

"I'm here," I say, moving closer to him.

"I'm sorry I didn't tell you," he says, obviously not sure where to look when speaking to an invisible person.

Sarah ushers the twins into the back seat with Goldie, chatting with them about how worried their parents are too.

"I kept meaning to tell you," Thomas whispers. "But I just didn't know what to say."

Sarah closes the back door and then rounds the car, passing right in front of me. I take a deep breath, drawing in the lingering scent of her shampoo—lavender and lilac—still her favorite, I guess.

"It's okay, Thomas," I say. "This was perfect." And it was.

He leans in. "We're family. You're, like, my great-uncle or something."

*Family.*

It's a word I never thought I would have much use for again. And it's comforting that I do now.

"Do you want her to know you're here?" Thomas asks as Maya does her best to keep Sarah distracted while we talk. "Do you want her to know your story?"

I ponder his question for a moment. But I don't think I want my sister to know what happened. It's a story best left buried in the ashes of the winnowing barn, and in the past. Besides, the last thing I want is for Sarah to blame herself in any way. After all this time, I figure she's made her peace with things. Why let her see me now and open all those old wounds when I can live in her thoughts the way she remembers me. Alive.

"No," I say quietly, the answer breaking my heart a little. "I don't think so."

Thomas nods like he understands.

"Just love her extra for me, okay?" I say softly in his ear. "For all the years I wasn't able to."

Thomas's eyes go misty on a dime. "I promise."

"Thomas," she calls to him. "Let's get this show on the road."

Thomas quickly wipes his eyes as Sarah approaches him. I instinctively take a step back.

"Come on, darlin'," she says. "Let me help you into the car. Careful with that foot now."

Sarah takes Thomas's arm so he can lean his weight into her as he hobbles around to the other side of the car. She opens the door for him, but before his head disappears into the front seat, he looks in my direction and mouths the words, *Goodbye, Will.*

I smile and whisper to myself, "Goodbye, Thomas."

The twins are pressed up against the window in the back seat, sending small waves in my direction. Or at least the direction where they think I am. And that's good enough for me. Even though they can't see me, I wave back at them. Sarah closes Thomas's door and comes back around to the driver's side, where I stand. I give her enough room to get by me, but I'm close enough to touch her if I dared. As she passes in front of me, I close my eyes and breathe in her scent one last time. One thing's for sure—lavender and lilac mixed with the jasmine and honeysuckle smells like heaven must.

*I love you, Sarah.*

I don't say it out loud, but she stops right in front of me before she gets into the car. Her wrinkled face creases in confusion. A strong breeze rustles through the spidery branches of the live oaks around us, blowing gentle waves through Sarah's gray-blond hair. She looks around, from the chapel down to the manor house, and over to the burning winnowing barn, as if searching for something. The puzzled look on her face deepens and I wonder if she knows I'm here. Maybe not me, exactly, but something. A presence. Or maybe she's just remembering that this is the last place her little brother, Will, was ever seen. But it's something, because I notice a single tear rolling down her cheek.

After another moment and another tear, she shakes her head a little, lets out a sigh, and brushes the stray tears away with the back of her hand. She eases down into the driver's seat and pulls the door closed. I back away from the car. Thomas, Maya, and Mateo are all *sort of* looking in my direction through the windows, as best as they can guess anyway. And they're smiling at me. Even Goldie pants and barks at me from the back seat—a happy, friendly bark that warms me from within. I wave again as the car pulls away, and I follow it down Live Oak

Lane, the taillights getting farther and farther away until they completely disappear down Hollow Pines Road.

Still invisible to the living, the lost souls are lined up on each side of the sandy drive, waving goodbye to the visitors as well. As I continue walking toward the stone columns at the end of Live Oak Lane, I first come upon Retha Mae standing alone. She gives me a warm smile and joins in right beside me. We walk a little way in a comfortable silence until we come upon Cornelius. He shuffles over and walks on my left, straw hat on his head and pipe dangling from his lips.

As we pass the chapel, Preacher and Emma walk over to us hand in hand, looking just as happy as they can be, like teenagers in love. They fall in beside Cornelius. Up ahead on the right, Teacherman waits patiently for us, his hands down in the pockets of his britches and his mustache freshly curled on each end. He steps in beside Retha Mae. We walk quietly toward the stone gates.

They've all forgiven themselves and can move on now, even Retha Mae and Emma. I can tell by the easy, unburdened smiles on their faces and the peaceful warmth in their eyes. I look back over my shoulder. I can barely make out her form in the distance, but I've seen her there so many times that I know it's Miss Rebecca standing in her bedroom window on the second floor.

I look over at Retha Mae. "What about Miss Rebecca?"

She sighs and looks down at me. "Either she can't forgive herself or she's afraid that her baby won't be waiting for her when she crosses over. At least here she has the nursery, and her memories."

I nod. It's sad to think of Miss Rebecca being stuck here forever. But maybe one day she will be able to forgive herself and move on. I look over my shoulder again and wave at her. I think I see her waving back, but I can't be sure.

We're getting close to the moss-covered stone columns that once stood as the entrance to one of the wealthiest rice plantations in South Carolina, where the most terrible things happened. But now the columns stand as our exit from this world and our entrance into the next. All I have ever known is Hollow Pines and the brief living time before—most all of it heartbreak and hopelessness. And the only thing I can think now is, *What comes next?*

We stop directly between the stone columns.

Cornelius looks down at me. "Ready, Cousin?"

I look up at him and smile. "Ready, Cousin."

He kind of chuckles at me. "Well, let's go, then."

I look straight ahead. I don't know what will happen when we move beyond this place, or if I'll ever see Cornelius, Retha Mae, Emma, Preacher, Teacherman, or Miss Rebecca again. But what I do know is that I have a family—some in the living world and some in the next. So, I'll never be forgotten and I'll never be alone.

I close my eyes, draw in one more deep breath of jasmine and honeysuckle, and take my first step into the unknown.

# AUTHOR'S NOTE

I was around twelve years old when I began viewing death as a solution to my problems.

I grew up in the Lowcountry of South Carolina in a strict religious home with an abusive stepmother. My mother died when I was just five, and as a mama's boy, I felt the loss deeply. In addition to the physical abuse perpetrated by my stepmother, my older brother and I were forced to call this stranger in our house *Mama*. And when she moved in, her first order of business was to purge our home of all traces of my mother. Most things belonging to Mama that could've been stored and saved for me and my brother to claim when we were older were given away. My brother was two years older and bullied me constantly. I was also keenly aware of my attraction to boys from my earliest memories of childhood, and the shame and guilt I intuitively felt about it consumed my thoughts on a daily basis.

Even as young as five, I felt an inherent stigma for liking boys *that way* as easily and as naturally as the attraction itself. In my case, I believe that stigma was born of several factors. One, the concept of same-sex attraction was never spoken of in my family, while in contrast, the inquiries about which girl I *liked* or if I had a girlfriend at school or church were relentless. The social order in school was another factor, where one's gender was recognized as either exclusively *boy* or *girl* and attraction to the opposite sex was exalted and reinforced daily as the only true manifestation of love possible.

Bullies often target LGBTQ kids, as well as the kids they suspect of being queer. However, being deeply closeted all the way through college, I was spared the misery of being harassed at school for being gay. The bullying I experienced came mainly from the pulpit, where the "sin" of homosexuality—often described as the *worst of all sins* back then—was a popular refrain in sermons. I was raised in a Pentecostal church, so at three services a week for eighteen years of my life, that's close to three thousand hours of mandatory, harmful programming. And that's not even counting revivals, camp meetings, and Sunday school. I'm not suggesting this was or is the case in all Pentecostal churches, of course, or that every minute of every sermon I sat through was antiqueer in some way, but you see my point.

When I was young, I never saw myself represented on television, in movies, in magazines, or in books. At times that made me feel like I was the only boy in the world who was attracted to other boys, and often it simply made me feel invisible and incredibly lonely. It's why I've made it my mission to write books I desperately needed as a queer kid growing up in the rural South. Kids like me are still out there. I know because they write to me and come up to me at book festivals and school visits and tell me their stories. They need to feel seen and have their experience, and their stories, validated. Just as important, young non-queer readers can learn empathy by reading stories about queer, othered, and marginalized kids.

As I consulted with child mental health professionals while writing this book, a common opinion was shared—*there is no one reason that leads a child to attempt or die by suicide.* It was a combination of all the things I've mentioned, the hopelessness I felt, and my undiagnosed and untreated depression that led to my own contemplations of suicide at such a young age.

According to data compiled by the Trevor Project (web.archive.org/web/20210608093914/thetrevorproject. org/resources/preventing-suicide/facts-about-suicide/):

* Suicide is the second leading cause of death among young people ages 10 to 24.
* LGBTQ youth seriously contemplate suicide at almost three times the rate of heterosexual youth.

* LGBTQ youth are almost five times as likely to have attempted suicide compared to heterosexual youth.
* LGBTQ youth who come from highly rejecting families are 8.4 times as likely to have attempted suicide as their LGBTQ peers who reported no or low levels of family rejection.
* Each episode of LGBTQ victimization, such as physical or verbal harassment or abuse, increases the likelihood of self-harming behavior by 2.5 times on average.

Currently I reside in Tennessee, and over the last several years I have been heartbroken by stories reported in our state and across the country of the rising rate of suicide among young teens who were bullied by people who knew they were or suspected them of being queer.

Channing Smith of Manchester, Tennessee, was 16.

Phillip Parker of Cookeville, Tennessee, was 14.

Jacob Rogers of Cheatham County, Tennessee, was 18.

Asher Brown of Houston, Texas, was 13.

Seth Walsh of Kern County, California, was 13.

Billy Lucas of Greensburg, Indiana, was 15.

Unfortunately, the list goes on and on. But the stories of these young boys were especially affecting and nudged me to tell a story that was raw and honest to the experience of queer adolescents who view suicide as a possible solution, as I did—even if it was deemed by some as an inappropriate topic for a middle-grade book. If Will's story saves even one young reader out there who feels hopeless, any possible pushback will have been worth it.

I recognize that as a *white* queer boy from a middle-income family, my challenges would have been even greater had I been a Black kid growing up in South Carolina only a decade after the Civil Rights Act was passed. My privilege also allowed me to easily swallow the whitewashed history of the South with which we were constantly bombarded. In elementary and junior high school, we were required to take classes in South Carolina history. As I grew older, I would learn through books, movies, television shows, and personal relationships just how inaccurate my education had been when it came to the subject of slavery in the antebellum South.

In a recent conversation with a young friend who had just graduated from high school in the South, he confirmed that his educational experience with this subject had not been all that different from the one I had decades ago. To say I was surprised and disheartened to hear this is an understatement. And this is not solely a Southern problem. In fact, as of this writing, more than a dozen states have recently proposed legislation limiting school instruction of how slavery, segregationist laws, and racial inequity have shaped the United States. Five states have passed such legislation. On the whole, it's still pretty easy for white kids to turn a blind eye to the real and ugly truths about slavery and issues of race. My hope is that this book will have some small part in changing that by sparking independent, critical thinking and encouraging meaningful conversations on the subject.

I have delved into antiracism work over the last few years—a journey I am still on—and the amount of unlearning I had to do was not insignificant. Deprogramming yourself from decades of systemic racism, especially as a son of the South, cannot be accomplished in a couple of years by reading a dozen or so books. But understanding the human cost of slavery and recognizing how it was and still is woven into the fabric of our society and our institutions was a necessary step I had to take to reconcile the Southern culture in which I was bred with reality.

When I was young, we lived not a mile down the road from a supposedly (definitely) haunted deserted rice plantation in Georgetown, South Carolina. It was very much as Hollow Pines is described in this story. My brother, our two neighbors, and I would sometimes ride our bikes down there, looking to explore the property. We had our share of scares there, some likely self-manufactured and others I'm not so sure about. I remember thinking that although creepy as all get-out, the place was beautiful back then, peaceful even. Had I truly understood or been taught about the atrocities that had been committed there, I'm sure I would have viewed it differently. I chose that plantation as the setting for this story out of a desire to engage young white readers with a part of our history that they simply don't have to face if they don't want to.

In that regard, I felt it was important not to pull any punches when it came to the subject of slavery in this book.

Also, it would have been an injustice to have the setting of a deserted rice plantation without acknowledging and paying respect to the countless Black people who would have suffered and died there. I've attempted to do that through the fictional enslaved characters of Cornelius, Retha Mae, Emma, and Preacher. Their stories were influenced by the enslaved experiences portrayed in the works of Toni Morrison (*Beloved*), Ta-Nehisi Coates (*The Water Dancer*), Ibram X. Kendi (*Stamped from the Beginning*), Colson Whitehead (*The Underground Railroad*), and others. Exposing young readers to these characters and sharing their heartrending stories and nonfictional stories like them is not only appropriate, but necessary to effect positive change in our society.

I have always believed that kids can handle hard truths when given the chance. In many cases, they are already living those hard truths. Shielding them from our history—warts and all—only temporarily delays their awareness anyway. And if there's one thing I am absolutely amazed by, it's this younger generation's ability to sniff out injustice when presented with the facts.

My hope for the future lies with them.

# RESOURCES

## The Trevor Project

*thetrevorproject.org*

According to their website, "Founded in 1998 by the creators of the Academy Award–winning short film *Trevor*, the Trevor Project is the leading national organization providing crisis intervention and suicide prevention services to lesbian, gay, bisexual, transgender, queer, and questioning (LGBTQ) young people. If you are thinking about suicide and need immediate support, please call the Trevor Lifeline at 1-866-488-7386 or text START to 678-678."

## National Suicide Prevention Lifeline

*suicidepreventionlifeline.org*

Free and confidential support for people in distress can be found at The Lifeline 24/7. Call 1-800-273-8255 for help.

## Gay, Lesbian and Straight Education Network (GLSEN)
*glsen.org*

Founded by a group of teachers in 1990, GLSEN diligently works to ensure that LGBTQ students are able to learn and grow in a school environment free from bullying and harassment regardless of sexual orientation, gender identity, or gender expression.

## Tyler Clementi Foundation
*tylerclementi.org*

As stated on their website, "In 2011, the Tyler Clementi Foundation was born out of the urgent need to address the bullying challenges facing vulnerable populations, especially LGBTQ communities and other victims of hostile social environments. The Tyler Clementi Foundation was founded by the Clementi family to prevent bullying through inclusion and the assertion of dignity and acceptance as a way to honor the memory of Tyler: a son, a brother, and a friend."

Turn the page for more from
GREG HOWARD!

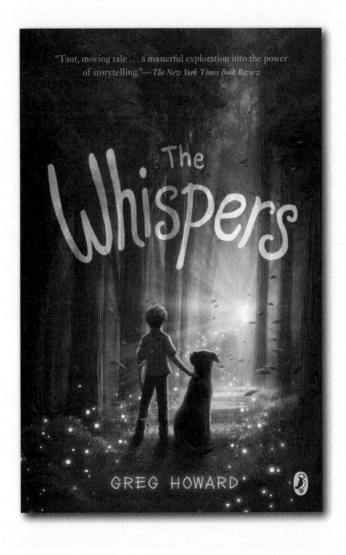

"Taut, moving tale . . . a masterful exploration into the power
of storytelling."—*The New York Times Book Review*

The Whispers

GREG HOWARD

There once was a boy who heard the Whispers.

He heard them late in the day as the lazy sun dipped below the treetops and the woods behind his house came alive with the magic of twilight. The voices came to him so gently he thought it might be the wind, or the first trickle of summer rain. But as time passed, the voices grew louder and the boy was sure they were calling his name. So he followed them.

The Whispers led the boy to a clearing deep in the woods where a rotted old tree stump sat in the center and fallen leaves covered the ground like crunchy brown carpet. The boy stood next to the stump, waited, and listened. He couldn't see the Whispers, but he knew they were there. Their wispy voices surrounded him, tickling the rims of his ears and filling every darkened shadow of the forest.

After waiting patiently for quite some time, the Whispers' garbled words finally began to make sense to the boy, and they told him things. The Whispers knew everything—all the secrets of the universe. They told the boy what color the moon was up close and how many miles of ocean covered the Earth. They even told him how long he would live—26,332 days. The boy was pleased, because that sounded like a good long time to him. But as they continued to whisper knowledge into his ear, they never showed themselves to the boy. He only caught glimpses from the corner of his eye of their faint bluish glow fading in and out around him. He so badly wanted to see them, to know what kind of creatures they were. How big were they? Or how tiny? Were they thin, or fat, or hairy? Were they made of skin and bones like him, or of tree bark, or leaves, or dirt? Or something else entirely?

The Whispers told the boy that if he brought them tributes, they would give him his heart's desires. The boy wasn't sure what a tribute was and he didn't want very much anyway. He could hardly call them heart's desires. Maybe a new pair of sneakers so the kids at school wouldn't tease him about his raggedy old ones. Maybe a better job for his father so he wouldn't worry so much about money. And he would love to see his mother smile again, something she rarely did anymore. But he guessed what he really wanted was to see the Whispers with his very own eyes.

One day, as the boy's mother made a batch of her special blackberry jam, he asked her what a *tribute* was. She thought about it a moment and finally told him that a tribute was like a gift to show respect. The boy eyed his mother's handiwork spread over the kitchen table. Everyone loved her jam. When she took it to the local farmers market, she always sold out. And her blackberry jam was his personal favorite. He was sure it would make an excellent tribute for the Whispers. When his mother left the room, the boy took one of the jars from the table and hid it under his bed.

The following afternoon, as the sun was setting, he went back to the clearing in the woods with the jam tucked under his arm. He left it sitting on the rotted old tree stump for the Whispers. Satisfied with his tribute, the boy spoke his heart's desires aloud and then hurried home as not to scare the Whispers away.

When the boy's father got home from work that evening, his mood was lighter than usual and the lines of worry had completely vanished from his face. He told the family that he'd received a promotion at work and tomorrow the boy's mother should take him shopping to buy him new clothes and shoes for school. This news made his mother smile. The boy was amazed that he'd received three of his heart's desires with only one jar of jam. Surely the Whispers would reveal themselves to him if he took them a tribute even better than a jar of his mother's blackberry jam. And he knew just the thing.

The next day, when the boy returned from shopping with his mother, he snuck out of the house right before sunset and took his new sneakers to the clearing in the woods. He kept them in the box, neatly wrapped in tissue paper so they wouldn't get scuffed or dirty. They were the nicest shoes he'd ever owned, and surely this tribute would persuade the Whispers to show themselves.

When he approached the rotted old tree stump, he saw that the blackberry jam was gone. The boy wasn't surprised. He was sure the Whispers enjoyed his mother's jam just as much as everyone else did. He put the box with his sneakers on top of the rotted old tree stump, stood back, and waited. And waited. And waited. He waited so long, he wasn't sure the Whispers were pleased enough with his tribute.

Finally something tickled the back of his neck with the lightest flutter of breath grazing his skin. It spoke his name and asked him what he wished. The boy froze. The Whispers had never come that close before. They must be pleased with his tribute after all. He was excited, but afraid if he moved it would scare them away, so he closed his eyes and remained perfectly still.

"I wish to see you," the boy said in barely a whisper of his own. "I want to know what you look like. It's my heart's desire."

At first there was no clear answer, only a garble of Whispers conversation that he couldn't understand. Then the words slowly pieced themselves together like a puzzle in his ear.

"If we reveal ourselves, you can never leave us," the Whispers said, their velvety voices caressing his ear through the warm summer breeze. "You must stay here in the woods with us forever, for you will know everything, and that is a burden too great to bear in your world."

The boy swallowed hard. He closed his eyes even tighter and stood very still as sweat trailed down his neck, the Whispers' words chilling him from head to toe.

"Are you sure this is what you wish?" the Whispers asked. "To see us? To stay with us and become a whisper in the wind?"

The boy began to worry. He thought about all the things he would miss if he stayed in the woods with the Whispers forever. He would never get to ride his bike again, or go swimming in the pond with his friends. And he would never see his mother and father again. It seemed like an awfully high price to pay just to see what the Whispers looked like. Besides, he'd already offered them his brand-new sneakers, and they were the nicest things he owned. Wasn't that enough?

"No," the Whispers said, reading his thoughts. "It is not enough. If you see us, you must become one of us. And then you will know everything there is to know. You will hear everything. See everything. But the only tribute we can accept for that is your soul."

The boy stood there with his eyes closed tight, scared he might accidentally see one of the Whispers and then the choice would be made for him. He needed a moment to think. The boy wondered what else there was to know. Because of the Whispers he knew the color of the moon up close, how many miles of ocean covered the Earth, and how long he would live—26,332 days. He knew he had a home to which he could return. He knew his parents loved him and his father worked hard to take care of their family. And the kids at school would tease him a little less now that he had brand-new sneakers.

The boy knew it would be dark soon and if he waited too long he might never find his way out of the woods. Then what would the Whispers do with him? He felt around until he found the box with his sneakers on the tree stump. He grabbed it, turned, and ran as fast as he could. He held the box close to his chest and didn't dare open his eyes. He tripped and fell. Got back up and ran into one tree after another. Branches whacked him across the face and chest, but he kept running blindly through the woods.

Only after he'd gone a good long ways and the tiny voices had faded behind him did the boy dare open his eyes. Even then he was careful not to look around. He stared straight ahead until he got to the tree line and ran the whole way home, never looking back, not even when he reached his house.

After that the boy never heard the Whispers again, but he didn't mind. He already had his heart's desires. He had his mother. And his father. And his friends. And his brand-new sneakers. Plus he knew what color the moon was up close, how many miles of ocean covered the Earth, and how long he would live—26,332 days. He didn't know *all* the secrets of the universe and maybe he never would, but he knew plenty.

*This was Mama's favorite story. She told me the story every night until the day she disappeared. Then I started hearing the Whispers.*
*And I followed them.*

# 1

## THE WORLD'S WORST POLICE DETECTIVE

Fat Bald Detective thinks I had something to do with it. He doesn't come right out and say it, but the way he repeats the same questions over and over—like if he keeps on asking them, I might crack under the pressure—well, it's pretty clear that I'm suspect number one. I don't know why he thinks I'm guilty, other than the fact that he's not very smart. He's not nearly as good at this as the cops on TV, and they're only actors. He just sits there smiling at me, waiting for me to say something more. But I don't know what he wants from me. I mean, sure I have secrets. Big ones. The kind of secrets you take to your grave. But I would never hurt anyone on purpose. Especially not Mama.

I push my hair out of my eyes and look up at the clock on the wall. It shouldn't be too much longer. Maybe I can just wait him out. I look at the desk in the corner of the cramped office. It's cluttered with books, stacks of file folders, and a darkened computer screen decorated with a rainbow of Post-it notes because Fat Bald Detective can't remember anything. There isn't one inch of clear space anywhere to be seen on his desk. It's very unprofessional.

That was one of our words from the calendar—I think from last January. It's still on my wall.

*Unprofessional* is when someone or something doesn't look or act right in the workplace.

*Good, Button. Now use it in a sentence,* Mama would say if she were here.

Then I would say something like, *Fat Bald Detective's office is very unprofessional because there's crap everywhere and it smells like Fritos.*

That would have made Mama laugh. I could always make her laugh when we played the word-of-the-day game. Mama says it's okay if you don't always remember the exact dictionary definition of a word as long as you can describe the meaning in your own words and you can use it in a sentence. Now that I think of it, there should be a picture of Fat Bald Detective's office beside the word *unprofessional* in the dictionary.

His office is nothing like the ones in the police stations on TV. There aren't any bright fluorescent lights in here, or cool floor-to-ceiling walls of glass so he can see the whole department and wave someone in at a moment's notice just to yell at them. There's only one small window with a view of the parking lot, and Fat Bald Detective seems to prefer table lamps to fluorescent lighting. And although you can't smell the offices of the police stations on TV, I always imagined they'd smell like leftover pizza and cigarette smoke—not Fritos. I guess it's better than doing this in one of their interrogation rooms. At least in here there's a couch for me to sit on before they lock me up and throw away the keys. Then it hits me. It's the couch. The couch smells like Fritos.

"And what happened after that, Riley?" Fat Bald Detective says—*again.*

Fat Bald Detective has a name. It's Frank. He said I could call him Frank the first time he brought me in for questioning. Mama doesn't normally approve of us calling adults by their first name, but Frank told me to and he's the law. I figure I should probably cooperate as much as possible so he doesn't get any more suspicious than he already is.

Frank actually has three names. They're all printed on his door and on the triangle nameplate on his desk. Grandma says that people who use three names are *puttin' on airs*, but I don't think Frank has any airs to put on. He's short, and bald, and round, and looks like Mr. Potato Head without the tiny black hat, so I think *Fat Bald Detective* every time I look at him.

"I don't remember," I say.

He keeps asking me what happened that day and I keep telling him I don't remember. We've played this little game for almost four months now. I was ten when we started. I'm a whole different age now. I've had a birthday and a summer break since then. I even moved up a grade in school. Detective Chase Cooper on *Criminal Investigative*

*Division: Chicago* can solve a case in an hour. Forty-four minutes if you fast-forward through the commercials. But Frank will never be as smart as Detective Chase Cooper. Or as handsome. Frank's really not a bad guy, though. He means well. But I don't think he's ever going to crack this case, at least not before I turn twelve. He's running out of time. So is Mama.

Frank and his officers should be out there trying to find the perp—following up on leads, canvassing the neighborhood. That's the way they do it on TV, and they *always* catch the guy. They don't sit in poorly lit rooms that smell like Fritos questioning the eleven-year-old son of the missing person over and over. But maybe this is just the way cops do things out here in the country. Maybe they don't watch much TV.

"Tell me again what you do remember," Frank says in that smiley-calm voice of his that I hate. Like I'm ten or something and if he talks real soft and slow, I'll spill my guts.

I sigh as loudly as I can, just so my irritation is clear. "Like I already said, Mama was taking a nap on the sofa in the living room."

It *was* strange because we only use the living room for special occasions, like on Christmas morning to open presents, or when the preacher from North Creek Church of God used to visit. Somehow the couch in the living room is called a *sofa* and the one in the den is just a *couch*. The living room furniture is not very comfortable, but Mama says it's not supposed to be. Like that makes any sense—furniture that's meant to be uncomfortable. I've told Frank all that before, so I don't repeat it. I've learned only to repeat the important stuff. Otherwise Frank finds new questions to ask. I don't like new questions.

Frank laces his fingers together on top of his basketball of a belly and smiles again. I don't like his smile. It looks like a plastic piece of Mr. Potato Head's face that he can pop on and off anytime he wants.

"And where were you while your mother was lying down in the living room?"

I roll my eyes at him. Daddy wouldn't like that.

*Be respectful of authority,* he would say. *Frank is just trying to help.*

But I've answered this same question so many times. If he can't remember, then why doesn't he write it down on one of his five thousand rainbow Post-it notes, or turn on a tape recorder like they do on TV. I wonder where he went to detective school. Probably one of those online courses, but poor Frank got ripped off. If Mama were here, she'd add a *bless his heart.* It sounds nice, but I don't think it's meant to be.

"I was outside playing with my friends," I say.

Frank raises a bushy eyebrow at me. "And . . ."

"And when I came back inside, Mama was lying on the sofa in the living room. Like I just said."

"And then what did you do?" the world's worst police detective asks.

"I touched her hand to see if she was asleep." I say it like I'm quoting a Bible verse I've been forced to memorize and recite on command.

Frank looks down his snap-on nose at me. "And how did it feel, touching her hand?"

This is a new one. What the heck does he mean, how did it feel? It felt like skin and Jergens hand lotion, that's how. And how is this going to help them find Mama? Why doesn't Frank ask me more about the suspicious car that was parked in front of the house that day? I told him about it the first time they hauled me down here for questioning, but he hasn't asked about it since. Instead he's wasting time asking about me touching Mama's hand. *World's. Worst. Police. Detective. Ever.*

"She felt a little chilled, so I pulled the cover up over her hands. I didn't want to wake her, so I went back outside to play."

Frank scrunches his face like that wasn't the answer he was looking for. He thinks I'm hiding something. Like *I'm* a suspect, which is crazy because I want them to find her. I promise I do.

"And that's the last thing you remember?" he says. "Touching your mother's hand while she was lying down on the sofa? Nothing else?"

He knows it is. Unless he somehow found out about Kenny from Kentucky. Or the ring.

*Stick to your story,* I tell myself. That's what people on TV who are accused of a crime always say—*stick to your story and everything will be fine.* No one has actually accused me of anything yet. But they might as well, the way they all look at me—like they know I'm hiding something.

"Yes, sir," I say, being respectful of authority. Even Frank's authority. "That's the last thing I remember."

Frank squints his eyes at me. Yep. He thinks I'm lying. Or crazy. Or both. But technically I'm not lying. Kenny from Kentucky is long gone and they've never asked me about the ring, so I've never told them. Besides, Daddy will blister my hide if he finds out I have it. I wonder if the ring is considered evidence. Can they put me in jail for withholding evidence? I think there was an episode of *CID: Chicago* about that. I can't remember what happened, but I'm sure Detective Chase Cooper solved the case in forty-four minutes.

Frank's talking now, but I can't understand what he's saying. His voice sounds like that teacher from *The Peanuts Movie*, which Mama and I watched together.

*. . . wah waah wah wah, waah wah waah . . .*

I nod my head every now and then to be polite and respectful. Frank has some real wacky theories about what might have happened to Mama that day, so whenever he starts speculating like this, I turn on my internal Charlie Brown teacher translator.

*Speculating* is like when poorly educated police detectives make dumb guesses about a case without having any evidence.

*Use it in a sentence, Button,* I imagine Mama saying.

*Frank needs to get off his big round behind, stop speculating about what happened that day, and go find Mama before it's too late.*

Frank glances over at the clock and lets out one of his *this isn't getting us anywhere* sighs because he knows I'm not listening anymore.

"Your father's probably waiting for you outside," he says. "You know, Riley, it's been nearly four months now. I'd much rather you tell me what happened on your own, but if you can't—or won't—I can help you fill in some of the blanks if you'll let me."

Oh crap. I know what Frank's talking about from the cop shows on TV. It's when they start telling the perp what *they* think happened. They make their accusations over and over, louder and louder, until the perp finally confesses.

"How's the case going?" I ask, changing the subject. "Any new leads? New information? Have you found their car yet?"

Frank inhales slowly, then releases a long stream of sour-smelling air through puckered lips. "There's no new information, Riley. You know that." He stands and waves me toward the door. "If you remember anything before I see you again, have your dad call me, okay? It's very important."

I get up and walk out, shaking my head so Frank knows what a disappointment he is to me. What are we paying these people for with Daddy's hard-earned tax dollars if they can't even find my mama?

# 2

## TWENTY-EIGHT WORDS
## IN THREE DAYS

We eat supper early that night—just the three of us at the kitchen table. We haven't eaten in the dining room since Mama disappeared. We used to eat dinner in there every night. Now it sits dark and empty like a tomb or a shrine. I don't think we'll use it again until Mama comes home safe and we can all sit in there as a family again. We can eat, and talk, and laugh like we used to. Daddy will tell lame jokes, Mama will ask us about our day at school, and my brother won't be mean to me anymore. But for now it's just a dark room collecting dust on our memories of her.

We sit in silence, Danny wolfing down his mashed potatoes like it's his last meal ever, and Daddy staring at his plate like he's reading tea leaves. Every couple of minutes, he moves some food around with his fork, but that's about it. He hasn't always been like this, just since Mama was taken. I don't think he knows how to *be*, without her here holding us all together. That was her department, not his.

Before Mama disappeared, Daddy laughed a lot. And he always loved scaring Danny and me, or pinning us down on the floor and tickling us until we almost peed ourselves. He'd do the same thing to Mama sometimes until she would scream and laugh and holler like a crazy person. Now when I look over at Daddy, all I can see is the bald spot on top of his head. I don't think he likes to look at us anymore, least of all me. I know it's because I can't remember what happened that day. And because I look the most like her. And because Mama and I share a name and a birthday. But also because of *my condition.*

Or maybe he blames me and that's why he can't look at me. Maybe he thinks I could have done something to save her. Called out for help. Gotten the license plate number of the fancy car that was sitting in front of the house that day. Locked the front door after I went outside. But Mama was in the house, so why would I lock the door? And how did I know something bad was going to happen to her? She just disappeared without a trace, right out of our front living room. That's another reason we don't go in there anymore. It's like a crime scene that no one wants to disturb in case there's still some undiscovered shred of evidence hidden in there. Fibers in the carpet or something. I'm surprised Frank hasn't put bright yellow police tape across the door. Maybe he should. Who am I to say? Detective Chase Cooper would know what to do.

Since no one is talking or looking up, I glance around the kitchen as I pretend to eat. I see Mama in every nook and cranny. Like the dish towels hanging on the oven door handle with the words *As for me and my house, we will serve the*

*Lord* embroidered on them in red frilly letters. I was with her when she found those at the Big Lots in Upton. She loved them so much she bought two sets. But that's not a lot of money at the Big Lots. Probably like three dollars or something. And the Precious Moments cookie jar on the counter—she found that at the Salvation Army store. It has a picture on the front of a boy and a girl with really big heads and droopy eyes sitting back to back on a tree stump.

*Love one another.*

Mama likes things with nice sayings printed on them.

She says, *It can't hurt to be reminded to love each other every time you reach for a cookie, right, Button?*

Mama loves baking cookies. She makes them for me to take to school for my teachers and to sell at Mr. Killen's Market to raise money for the church. She even made a big batch last Christmas for the prisoners at the work camp outside of Upton. She's real good at cookies, but one time she tried making me blackberry jam like in the story of the Whispers and it was terrible. It was so bad that we laughed and laughed while we ate some of it on toast that I burnt. Another time she tried to teach me how to make biscuits and gravy, but I burned my hand on the stove, so that was the end of my cooking lessons.

All I'm allowed to make now are frozen fish sticks and Tater Tots in the oven. Frozen fish sticks are gross but we've eaten them a lot the last four months. I don't mind the Tater Tots. But Grandma supplied tonight's meal even though Daddy tells her she doesn't have to do that anymore.

Grandma hates the idea of us eating fish sticks and Tater Tots so much. I wonder what Mama's eating right now. Or if she's been eating at all. What if whoever took her doesn't give her enough food to stay alive until the police can find her?

"Frank said there aren't any new leads in the case," I say, breaking the unbearable silence. My words hang in the air like lint.

Daddy looks up from his plate and stares like he doesn't even recognize me. Danny stops eating and glares at me from across the table. He never wants to talk about Mama's case. Even Tucker lets out an anxious groan under the table, like he knows I should have kept my big mouth shut. He misses Mama too. He hasn't been the same since she disappeared, but the vet can't figure out what's wrong with him. I think he's just depressed.

"Finish your peas and take Tucker outside," Daddy says, looking back down at his plate.

I think that makes a total of two dozen words Daddy's said to me in three days, so I hit the jackpot this evening. I eat my peas one at a time and with my fingers. I know it annoys him. If Mama were here, she'd give me the Mama side-eye. But she's not. And Daddy doesn't even look up to scold me. He just plows circles in his mashed potatoes with his fork. If Danny or I did that, he would yell at us and tell us to stop playing with our food.

Daddy used to like me. He even took me on my very first roller coaster ride, and he wanted it to be the same one he took his first ride on—the Swamp Fox at Family Kingdom Amusement Park in Myrtle Beach. It's one of those old-timey wooden coasters that make that loud *clack, clack, clack* noise when they go up the first climb. The newer coasters don't make that sound anymore and Daddy says it's not the same without it. I was so scared and screamed my butt off the entire ride, but Daddy didn't mind. He just laughed and laughed like a crazy person with his hands raised high in the air the whole time.

When I was six, we were on vacation in Florida and Daddy took us to an alligator farm. He picked me up so I could get a better look at the big, slimy creatures. Then he thought it would be real funny to pretend like he was going to throw me over the fence like gator bait. A fat one spotted us and slowly came crawling our way while Daddy kept up his act for *way* too long, swinging me back and forth and back and forth.

*One, two . . .*

On *three,* I almost crapped my pants. But he never got to three, so I'm pretty sure Daddy wasn't trying to feed me to the alligators. I screamed bloody murder anyway. But Daddy didn't mind. He just laughed and laughed like a crazy person. To this day I can't even look at an alligator on TV. But I have to admit, it was fun. Daddy was fun. Not anymore.

Danny's phone vibrates on the table, which gets him a hard look from Daddy. His phone is supposed to be off during dinner. Danny grabs it and tucks it into his lap. It's probably some girl from school calling. Danny likes girls now. *Ugh.*

"Sorry," he says to Daddy without looking him in the eye.

Daddy stares at him a moment, and finally his face softens. Just a tad. He doesn't yell at Danny. He would have yelled at me, but Danny's a daddy's boy just as much as I'm a mama's boy. And I don't have a phone yet. It's okay. I wouldn't want any girls calling me anyway.

Daddy gets up and goes to the window over the sink. He mumbles as he lifts it open, "It's stifling in here."

Wow. Twenty-eight words in three days. But those last four I have to share with Danny.

"What does that mean, Daddy?" I say, although I have a pretty good idea. I just want him to notice me.

"What does what mean?" he kind of grunts back.

"*Stifling.*"

He looks over his shoulder at me and gives me a flat look. "It means it's hot and stuffy."

I push my luck, trying to lighten the mood. "Use it in a sentence, Daddy."

He squints at me like he can't remember my name or why I'm here. "What?"

"Use the word *stifling* in a sentence," I say, feeling hopeful.

"I just did." He looks out the window, dismissing me with a slight shake of his head.

Danny stuffs his mouth and grunts his agreement with Daddy. Danny eats like a pig and always sides with Daddy.

Actually Danny does *everything* Daddy does, so now that Daddy doesn't like me, Danny doesn't either. He used to play with me before Mama disappeared. Now he just acts like I don't exist. He barely even talks to me. Stays in his room with the door closed doing Lord knows what, and hangs out with his new high school friends in Upton. He's only three years older than me, but he treats me like a baby.

Tucker must have sensed the tension in the room, because he lets out a long, flappy fart that sounds like a balloon deflating under the table. Danny looks at me and his lips curl up, exposing teeth caked with mashed potatoes and gravy. Danny never smiles at me anymore, but he thinks farts are hilarious. Especially dog farts. Even I can't help but smirk, just a little. But we both freeze, waiting to see how Daddy will respond. It could go either way. The seconds tick by long and slow like they did during the sermons at North Creek Church of God when we used to be churchgoing people.

I dare to look over at Daddy standing at the sink. His shoulders are shaking a little. Laughing or crying, I can't tell. He turns to face us and I see that it's both. He's laughing softly, but at the same time his eyes are moist. I'm surprised because I don't think I've seen Daddy crack even a polite smile to anyone in the last four months. His laughter sparks life into the room and we know it's okay now. We have permission to join him, and we do. Hard. It's the first time since Mama disappeared that there's been any laughter in this house. It sounds amazing, echoing around the kitchen and then drifting out the window. Tucker scrambles from under the table, barking excitedly and joining in our rare moment of happiness. Daddy's laughter eventually dies down, though. His smile doesn't totally disappear, but it fades a little. His eyes are still misty.

A strong honeysuckle-scented breeze rolls in through the open window and brushes my cheeks. I close my eyes and breathe it in deep. It's almost like she's here, like she heard us laughing and rushed into the kitchen to see what all the fuss was about. Mama loves the smell of honeysuckle. She always yells at Daddy for cutting back the bushes in the yard. It grows like crazy around our house. Mama taught me how to pinch off the bottom of the blooms, slide the stem out, and lick the nectar off. She calls it nature's candy. Now whenever I catch a whiff of honeysuckle, I think of her and I wonder if I'll ever see her again. Right now, it's like she's reaching out to me from wherever she's being held captive—calling to me to come find her. To rescue her. The police are useless, so I may be her only hope.

"Take that gassy mutt outside, Riley," Daddy says, his smile completely fading.

Wow. He said my name. And he wasn't yelling or cross sounding or anything. Just said it like normal. Like he would say Danny's name. I hop out of my chair with a small jolt of satisfaction, or pride, or something pumping in my veins and guide Tucker to the kitchen door.

Looking back over my shoulder, I smile at him. "Okay, Daddy."

But he doesn't see me. He's already turned his back on us again. He stands at the sink, his shoulders shaking. I'm not sure if he's laughing again or if he's gone back to crying. I don't think I really want to know for sure, so I grab Tucker by the collar and hurry out the door.

# 1

# THE OFFICE

**I sit behind** the huge oak desk in my office at the world headquarters of Anything, Incorporated, organizing my homework like I do every Sunday afternoon. I spend a lot of weekends in the office. If I didn't, I'd never get anything done. I think CEOs of big-time companies like mine shouldn't be required to attend middle school. It seriously gets in the way of doing important business stuff.

I've created an Excel spreadsheet on my laptop and sorted my assignments into three columns:

```
Teacher Will Check
Teacher Won't Check
Teacher Will Collect but Won't Check
```

Normally I'd have my assistant handle this kind of thing, but she quit last week. It's okay, though, because she was a climber. More interested in having a fancy title than doing a good job for the company. She started as an intern about a month ago, recommended by one of our board members. She was terrible even back then. I could never find a stapler when I needed one, and my printer was always out of paper. I thought if I gave her a real title and some responsibility by promoting her to assistant to the president, she'd step up her game. But she didn't. All she wanted to do was criticize me. Her boss! That's not how it works in the corporate world.

I open my "Brilliant Business Tips" Excel spreadsheet, scroll down to the next empty cell, and type:

**Michael Pruitt Business Tip #347: There's only one way to the top. Keep your head down, apply yourself, and do your time.**

It sure would be nice to have someone handle all this busywork now that my assistant bailed on me. I'd much rather be spending my time doing real boss stuff, like planning my next exciting business venture. Retail wasn't the right fit for me. Neither was professional sports instruction. But I have a million other ideas. Those are just two recent ones that didn't work out.

Pap Pruitt always says, *If at first you don't succeed, try, try again.*

I've had my share of failures, but I never give up. I know I'll have a successful business empire one day just like my hero, Pap Pruitt. Technically Pap is my grandfather. He taught me everything I know about business.

My desk first belonged to Pap when he started his real

estate business at seventeen years old. When Pap moved into the nursing home, Dad didn't need it for his landscaping business, so he lets me use it. It's a real boss-looking desk and I always feel real important sitting at it. I also feel close to Pap when I'm at my desk. He's been in the nursing home for a while now, and I don't get to see him as much. Plus he's sick a lot, so Dad doesn't always let me go with him to visit Pap. He didn't let me go today, which I guess is why Pap's been on my mind.

Pap was a super-crazy-successful entrepreneur when he was younger. He started his own general store, a dry cleaning business, two fast-food franchises, a hotel called the Old Pruitt Place, a pet-grooming business, a landscaping business, *three* automatic car washes, a boiled-peanut roadside stand, and a whole lot more. I asked him once how he became so successful. I remember the sparkle in his eye when he grinned a little and said, *All it takes is a dream and a prayer.*

I've got lots of dreams. And even though I'm not the best at prayers, the Almighty is pretty used to hearing from me when it comes to a new business idea. Pap started his business empire in his garage with only a hundred dollars, a dream, and a prayer. Pap's blind now because of the diabetes, but he's still a wicked-cool guy. I really want to make him proud, but he didn't have to build his business empire *and* go to middle school at the same time. I guess Pap was a late bloomer.

It's a little embarrassing, having to do homework at your real job. I'll bet Malcolm Forbes never had to do that and he was, like, one of the most successful business guys ever. Luckily my office is pretty private, but that doesn't always keep the riffraff out. Sometimes it can get so noisy in here, especially when the dryer's on its last cycle like it is now. It sounds like a space shuttle getting ready to launch. And there must be a shoe in there, because something bangs against the side every few seconds, distracting me from my work. I lean back in my executive, fake-leather desk chair and stare at Dad's tools hanging on the wall, waiting for the banging to stop.

The annoyingly long honk of the buzzer sounds and the pounding inside the machine finally fades away. I hit the Talk button on the intercom on my desk.

"Mom," I say, pretty loud so she can hear me from anywhere inside the house. And because I'm annoyed that there's a washer and dryer in my office.

No response.

I hit the button again. "Mom!"

A few seconds later, her voice crackles through the intercom speaker. "Yes, Mikey, what is it?"

I sigh and press the Talk button. "Mom, I asked you not to call me that when I'm at work."

"Oh, sorry, honey. *Michael*, what is it? Is the dryer done?"

We've talked about *honey*, too, but I'm too busy to get into that right now.

"Yes, ma'am," I say.

"Okay," she says. "I'll be right there."

Dad found the old-timey intercom system at a garage sale

and hooked it up for me. It's lime green and nearly the size of a shoe box, but at least it works. Dad thought it'd be a perfect addition to my office and an easy way for Mom to call me in for dinner. Dad gets it.

Mom comes through the carport door—*without knocking*—carrying a laundry basket.

"Mom, the sign's out," I say. "You're supposed to knock when the sign's out."

"It's getting late, honey. I thought you'd be closing up shop by now."

She's wearing light blue mom shorts and one of Dad's old white button-down shirts.

"I'm rebranding," I say. "It takes a lot of thinking time."

Wait a minute. That would be a cool business idea. I could be an expert at helping businesses rebrand. Like I could go down to the Burger King on Palmetto Street and pitch them the idea of updating their brand to make it more modern and hip. The first thing they need to do is change their name to something more welcoming of all people instead of just men. Something like Burger Person or Burger Human Being would be a good choice. I open up my spiral-bound *Amazing Business Ideas* notebook and write that million-dollar idea down before I forget.

Anything Modern and Hip Rebranding
A division of Anything, Inc.
Michael Pruitt—President, Founder, CEO, and Brand Expert

"So how come the putt-putt lessons didn't work out?"

"*Croquet* lessons, Mom," I say. "Not putt-putt."

"Oh, right," she says. "We used to play croquet all the time when I was a kid."

"I know," I say.

Grandma Sharon gave me their old set of clubs and balls and taught me how to play last summer. None of the kids in the neighborhood had ever heard of croquet, which was perfect because it made me the local expert. I might have added a few new rules to the game to make it more interesting, but my students never knew the difference.

Mom rests the basket of towels on her hip. A shoe sits on top. I wonder why she only washed one. It's a perplexing mystery.

I write down another incredible idea in my *Amazing Business Ideas* notebook:

Anything Perplexing Mystery-Solving Detective Agency
A division of Anything, Inc.
Michael Pruitt—President, Founder, CEO, and Head Snoop

I put a star beside that one because that's a super-crazy-good idea.

"Well, how many kids signed up for croquet lessons?" Mom asks.

Before I can answer, my little sister, Lyla, appears in the doorway cradling her fat gray cat in her arms. The cat's name is Pooty. Lyla named him that because he farts a lot. I hate that cat.

"He had four students show up for the first lesson," she says with all the innocence of a demon-possessed doll in a horror movie. "They each paid him a dollar, if you can believe that. But no one showed up for the second lesson. He made four dollars, but he gave them each a whole bottle of water, so he probably lost money."

"I haven't run the final numbers yet," I say, looking back at my spreadsheet, trying to ignore Lyla and her gassy cat.

"And kids around here don't know what croquet is anyway," she adds like she's some kind of marketing expert. She's nine.

"That was the beauty of it," I snap back. "Nobody knew if I was teaching it wrong or not."

"It was a dumb idea, if you ask me," she says.

"You were a dumb idea," I mumble under my breath.

"Mikey! That's enough," Mom says.

"She started it," I say in a pouty voice that makes me sound like a little kid.

Mom shifts the laundry basket to her other hip. "She's only nine. Be a better example."

That's Mom's excuse for everything Lyla does. *She's only seven. She's only eight. She's only nine.* You see where this is heading, right? It's never going to end.

"Sorry," I say, even though secretly I'm not.

Lyla smiles at me like she won or something.

*There are no trophies for being possessed by the devil, Lyla!*

7

"I'll give a full report on the Sports Instruction division of the company at the next board meeting," I say to Mom.

She kisses me on top of the head. "Sounds good, honey."

I sigh. I don't think she's ever going to get the *honey* thing. And don't even get me started on the kiss.

Mom leaves, but Lyla still stands in the doorway. Both she and Pooty glare at me. The cat hates me as much as I hate him. He always stares at me like he's planning to murder me. That's why I lock my bedroom door every night before I go to bed. You just never know with cats.

"So what's your next big idea, Mikey?" Lyla says, stroking Pooty's head like an old movie villain who's trying to take over the world. I wouldn't put it past her, even though *she's only nine*.

"It's Michael when I'm in the office," I say. "You know that."

She looks around the cramped, unfinished space with tools hanging on the walls like they're standing guard. "You mean our carport-storage-and-laundry room?"

I turn my back to her, attacking the keys of my laptop like I'm typing a really important email. "You didn't mind it when you worked here."

I hear the door close behind me.

Thank God. She left.

# 2

# THE WALK-IN

"My talent was being wasted."

*Or maybe not.*

Lyla sits in the metal folding chair beside my desk; it used to be her work area. I asked for a cubicle wall to put between us for privacy, but the board denied the request. They said it wasn't in the budget.

"You were my assistant, but you wanted me to make you junior vice president of the company." I shake my head at her. "Not going to happen. You're too young and you don't have enough business experience."

She swings her legs. "Your loss."

Pooty settles into a ball on her lap, staring at me like he's going to eat me. I shake my head again and look back at the spreadsheet. My sister is three years younger than me, but she acts like we're the same age. Or like she's my *older* sister. She's always been weird that way. Mom calls her precocious. I call her a pain in the butt.

A three-rap knock sounds at the door.

"Come in, Dad," I call. Dad never forgets to knock when the sign is out.

He hurries in and over to his wall of tools. "Sorry to bother you, Michael. Just need to grab the spatula. I'm grilling burgers."

Forbes, my cocker spaniel, follows Dad in, but Pooty hisses at Forbes and he retreats with a whine. Pooty's a bully and Forbes is his favorite target. Poor Forbes. Pooty would fit right in with Tommy Jenrette and his jerk friends at school.

Lyla looks up at Dad and plasters on the big baby smile she's way too old to still be using. "Dad, did you know that Mikey's latest business idea was a humongous flop?"

Dad looks over at me. "Oh no. Is that right, Michael?"

I look away, mumbling back, "You'll get a full report at the next board meeting."

"Oh, okay, then," he says, and I can hear the support in his voice.

Like I said, Dad gets it. He built A to Z Landscaping from nothing to one of the busiest in southeastern North Charleston, in spite of the lame name. *Time to rebrand, Dad!* He even advertises in the *PennySaver* and the online Yellow Pages. Pap Pruitt taught him well.

"How was Pap today?" I ask, my voice tightening around the words.

Dad's face sags. Not a good sign.

"Not great," he says, fake-smiling. "But he's hanging in

there. He asked about you. Maybe he'll be well enough for you to visit him next Sunday."

A lump swells in my throat and I swallow it back. I just nod and fake-smile back at him.

"I want to go see Pap, too, Daddy," Lyla whines.

Dad musses her hair. "Like I said, honey. We'll see."

After the shadow of sadness fades from Dad's face, he grabs the big metal spatula off the wall over my desk. "Dinner in twenty, okay?"

"Okay, Daddy," Lyla says, baby-smile wattage at one hundred.

"And don't worry, son," he says. "I bet your next idea will be the one. Pap is so proud of you. I am, too."

I don't say anything because I'm afraid my voice will fail me now. I know Pap and Dad are already proud of me. But we all know that Pap won't be around too much longer. I just want him to see my first big success.

Pooty yawns very disrespectfully as Dad closes the door behind him. I fake-type some more, hoping Lyla will get the hint and go, too. My eyes are itching and no little sister wants to see her big brother cry. Not even Lyla. But she doesn't get the hint. She just sits there swinging her legs and stroking Pooty's back.

"Don't you have homework?"

"Already finished," she says. "What are you working on?"

"None of your business," I say. "You didn't want to work here anymore, remember?"

She cocks her head. "I never said I didn't want to work here. I just wanted a better job than being your dumb assistant."

Before I can respond, there's another knock on the door. Maybe Mom remembered this time.

"Come in," I call out. I can't get anything done today with all these interruptions. I bet Pap Pruitt never had to put up with this.

The door creaks open behind me, but Lyla doesn't say anything, so I spin around in my chair. Standing in the doorway is a kid I kind of recognize from school, but I don't remember his name. I think he's in the eighth grade and I don't hang out with any eighth graders. I only recognize him at all because he's the *wrong* kind of popular at North Charleston Middle School. And I've got enough problems at school without hanging out with kids who are the wrong kind of popular.

Lyla and I just stare at him, which I know is super-crazy rude and unprofessional, but I can't help it. He's wearing sandals, neatly pressed jeans, and a white tank top with You Better Werk! printed on the front. He's taller than me and thick all over. Especially in the stomach area. After an awkward silence, the boy finally speaks up.

"Is this Anything, Incorporated?" he says, glancing around the room with stank face, like my office is the inside of a garbage dumpster. But I can't even be mad at him for that because—*OMG!*—he knows the name of my company. How wicked cool is that?

He glances over at the washer and dryer and then back to me. "I mean the sign on the door says so, but—"

"Yes!" I say a little too excitedly.

I snap out of my surprise at having someone who was actually looking for my office who's not a member of my family and who didn't think this was a laundromat or a hardware store or anything. I've never had a walk-in before.

I stand, extending my hand to him and clearing my throat. "I'm Michael Pruitt, president, founder, and chief executive officer of Anything, Inc."

The boy steps inside from our carport, closing the door behind him. He takes my hand and shakes it. His grip is loose and kind of clammy but he has a bright smile and sparkly eyes framed with—*is that glitter?*

"Yeah, I know," he says, letting go of my hand, still looking around my office, but without the stank face now. "We go to the same school."

"Mikey doesn't have any friends at school," Lyla says, looking down at Pooty, scratching his head. "They all think he's a weirdo loser and that all his business ideas are lame because none of them have ever worked."

*And OMG!*

I glare at her, my face heating from the inside out. Why did I ever trust her with sensitive company secrets? The boy looks like he doesn't know how to respond to that. Who would?

I clear my throat, plastering on my fake smile again. "Of

course I have friends, Lyla. You remember Trey and Dinesh. We've been friends since first grade."

Lyla smirks and shakes her head. "Nope. Never heard of them."

I grit my teeth through the fake smile. "Don't you have somewhere to be, Lyla? Somewhere that's not here. Like your room? Or China?"

The boy coughs into his elbow. Pooty poots. I wave the air around with my hand like I'm trying to swat a fly so my walk-in doesn't smell it.

"I bought a candy bar at your general store one time," he says, like he didn't notice Murder Kitty's gas attack. "I thought that store was a pretty cool idea. It was in a good location and had plenty of candy bars and other snacks that kids like. I got the chocolate one with peanut butter and nuts."

Pride curls my whole face into a grin. "That was one of my bestsellers. Could hardly keep them in stock."

"You sold three," Lyla pipes up matter-of-factly. "I was in charge of inventory, remember?" She looks over at the boy and sighs, like being a pain in the butt is so exhausting for her. "The Anything General Store got blown away by a baby tornado three days after the grand opening."

*I swear to God.*

The boy gives me a sympathetic look. "Oh. Sorry. I wondered why it was gone so fast. I came back the next week for another candy bar."

My face flushes hot again. "My dad built the store out

of big sheets of cardboard, so, you know—lesson learned."

Dad did a great job on the store. He built it in the front yard close to the foot traffic of the sidewalk. He said that's called *location, location, location*. The store had a wooden frame of two-by-fours, a flip-up sales counter/window, and a real door in back. Well, a real cardboard door. But the store was no match for a baby tornado. Lost all my inventory, too. Our next-door neighbor, Mrs. Brown, thought her bunny rabbit, Hedwig, started pooping magic pellets. I didn't have the heart to tell her they were just Skittles.

The boy nods and smiles at me like he understands. I think it's kind of nice of him.

I point at Lyla, trying to be professional. "This is my *former* associate, Lyla Pruitt, and her gassy and very unfriendly cat, Pooty. They were just leaving."

"Hey," the boy says, waving at Lyla with a big, wide smile.

She stands, but doesn't say anything. She doesn't even smile back. Instead, she hefts Pooty up to her chest, giving my walk-in that creepy-kid stare of hers as she takes her sweet time leaving. It's extremely unprofessional.

**Michael Pruitt Business Tip #348: Human-demon dolls make terrible receptionists.**

I learned that one the hard way.

# THE VISITORS

-:-

## ACKNOWLEDGMENTS

Any author worth their weight will gladly confess that writing a book is a team effort. My team is an embarrassment of riches and includes the most brilliant, capable, loving, encouraging, honest, funny, and fiercely loyal people on the planet. This was the most challenging story I've ever written, and there were times when I honestly didn't know if I would be able to see it through. But the following saints and sinners pulled me, sometimes kicking and screaming, successfully and graciously over the finish line. I am forever grateful to them all.

STACEY BARNEY, my astoundingly gifted editor. What can I say? You never cease to amaze me with your ability to cobble together a great book out of the nonsense I send you. For your skill, insight, discerning eye, intellect, and of course your patience, or some such. Thank you.

**Bri Johnson (B-Jo!),** my rock-star agent. I've said it once and I'll say it again—you changed my life when you took a chance and rescued me out of your slush pile. I can't imagine this journey without you in my corner. Thank you.

**G. P. Putnam's Sons Books for Young Readers/ Penguin,** my otherworldly publishing team—Jen Klonsky, Caitlin Tutterow, Cindy Howle, Lizzie Goodell, Carmela Iaria, Venessa Carson, Trevor Ingerson, Summer Ogata, and the entire school and library, marketing, and sales teams. Thank you.

**Manuel Šumberac,** illustrator *(manuelsumberac.com);* **Kristin Boyle,** art director; and **Suki Boynton** and **Maria Fazio,** designers, for the most amazing cover and book design in history. Thank you.

**Writers House**—Amy Berkower, Cecilia de la Campa, Allie Levick, and team—for five wonderful years you've had my back in every way possible. Thank you.

**Mary Pender/UTA,** my queen of film and TV, for bestowing your golden touch on me. Thank you.

**Audra Boltion/The Boltion Group Public Relations,** for opening doors, finding and creating opportunities, tooting my horn, and taking this ride with me. Thank you.

RUTHIE SHAW, ANDIE EYSSEN, CAMDEN THOMAS-BUSH, and VIOLET THOMAS-BUSH, for your wisdom and counsel on all things younger than me. Thank you.

For professional guidance, data, and perspective:

SCOTT RIDGWAY, M.S., Executive Director, Child Advocacy Center, 15th Judicial District, Wilson County, Tennessee *(cac15.org)*

DAN DUMONT, LMSW, Program Counselor, Just Us at Oasis Center, Nashville, Tennessee *(justusoasis.org)*

CHILD MIND INSTITUTE *(childmind.org)*, for information and sources. Thank you.

INDEPENDENT BOOKSTORES, especially those who have graciously hosted me and promoted my books in your sacred space: Parnassus Books, Nashville, Tennessee; Malaprop's Bookstore/Café, Asheville, North Carolina; Union Ave Books, Knoxville, Tennessee; Star Line Books, Chattanooga, Tennessee; Anderson's Bookshop, Naperville, Illinois; Park Road Books, Charlotte, North Carolina; Joseph-Beth Booksellers, Lexington, Kentucky; Books of Wonder, New York, New York; Litchfield Books, Pawleys Island, South Carolina; and Little Shop of Stories, Decatur, Georgia. Thank you.

To find an independent bookstore in your area, please visit indiebound.org. To order books online while benefiting local bookstores, please visit bookshop.org. To order audiobooks while benefiting local bookstores, please visit libro.fm.

CHUCK LONG/OUT AND ABOUT TODAY *(outandabouttoday. com)*, for your endless energy, enthusiasm, professionalism, and support from the very beginning. Thank you.

JAMES GRADY/OUTVOICES NASHVILLE *(nashville.out-voices.us)*, for your consistent and generous coverage. Thank you.

LIBRARIANS AND TEACHERS, for your heart, perseverance, and bravery. Never doubt that you are changing (and saving) lives every day. Thank you.

MICHELLE, HAL, and TOM, my BFFs. For thirty-plus years of unconditional love, pee-inducing laughter, and unwavering support. Thank you.

TRAVIS, my person. For all the things. Thank you.